Wish Me Home

ALSO BY KAY BRATT

Wish Me Home

A Novel

KAY BRATT

Published by Lake Union Publishing, Seattle

www.apub.com

Amazon, the Amazon logo, and Lake Union Publishing are trademarks of Amazon.com, Inc., or its affiliates.

ISBN-13: 9781477819944
ISBN-10: 1477819940

Cover design by Ginger Design

Printed in the United States of America

For Cory, the best CASA there ever was.

Chapter One

Don't turn around and look again, she told herself. *Think of something else. Do not show any acknowledgment and it will go away. Do not let the sight of it limping make you crumble.* At almost thirty years old, Cara wished she could forget the past but the smallest thing conjured up random recollections. Not that she'd call the dog behind her small— but from first glance, it had made her remember things better left unremembered.

Now it just needed to go away.

She kept walking, picking up her pace. Even over the sound of traffic she could hear light panting and his pads hitting the asphalt. She could widen the gap between them, but there was nothing she could do about the memories the dog invoked. They had a will of their own, coming and going even when unwanted and resented, reminding her of her dismal beginnings and the emotional baggage she still carried.

When she and her sister, Hana, were seven, their mother died and because their father was out of the picture and no family stepped up to take them, they were placed in a foster home, where they were paraded around like trophies. First the neighborhood, then family events, and even church as the foster mom bragged about doing her Christian duty to foster the "poor, defenseless twins." But at home, away from the curious looks, they were treated differently than the woman's biological children. There wasn't any physical abuse, and unlike some later homes they'd float in and out of, they were given plenty to eat. Still, it wasn't a good placement. Kids knew when they weren't really wanted. Or at least she and Hana did. And over time they learned that unless fostering was something done from the heart, with no thought of reward or recognition, it seldom worked out.

But . . . that family had a dog.

Cara had loved Reno, probably too much. Bigger than them at the time, the golden retriever was the first pet they'd had close contact with. She and Hana had pretended it was theirs, and with all the attention and affection they gave it, Reno's loyalty soon turned to them rather than the other children in the house. At night, Reno crawled in between her and Hana, making them feel protected. The other kids—who didn't give the dog any attention, much less wanted him in their beds—began to complain.

That hadn't sat well with the foster mother.

At first, she simply got an attitude when Cara or Hana showed too much affection toward the dog. But soon she refused to let Reno interact with them at all. When he'd try, he'd be yelled at, kicked, or sent to stay outside—a punishment that made him howl with sorrow and made Cara and Hana sick with guilt.

They talked it over and decided they had to break their bond with the dog to prevent it from being isolated from its own family. It hurt, but they began to pretend they weren't interested in Reno any longer, ignoring him when he came into the room and refusing to allow him on their bed. She winced, remembering turning her back on Reno when he'd come to her for a pat or kind word—the same simple things she and Hana longed for and never found either—and how the dog looked so confused and hurt at the sudden coldness. But they were convincing and Reno soon regained his family rights.

He went back to a quieter existence, but at least he was allowed to be a part of the family and not left outside to wonder why he'd been parted from his pack.

And once the appeal of showing off twin foster children faded, they were soon transferred to another home anyway. No one even said goodbye as they were herded out that door, their meager belongings packed in garbage bags they clutched to their chests.

Reno was the only one sorry to see them go, and Cara had never forgotten him.

She felt tears and blinked them back. Reno—and her stint as a foster child—was long gone. Suck it up and get over it, her sister would say. And she had a long road ahead of her and needed to get her head in the game. Figure out where she was going. Try to come up with a plan. Do something. Anything.

But that was hard to do when a dog—one that reminded her of Reno—was still following her. She pretended not to notice and, for a moment, increased her pace before feeling like a complete monster and slowing down again to accommodate his limp. She sighed in frustration and did the math at the mile marker.

Five miles until the next exit.

And she couldn't take care of a stray dog.

Didn't dogs need leashes? And food? And water, of course. She couldn't even carry enough water for herself—how was she supposed to carry around enough for the dog? She was homeless and could barely fend for herself. How was she supposed to be responsible for another creature?

From the looks of its skinny body, it probably didn't eat much.

No. She wouldn't make up reasons to justify keeping him just to curb her loneliness.

And why was a dog walking on the interstate anyway? The limp made her wonder if someone had thrown him out. How could people be so cruel? Discarding dogs and children as though they meant nothing? Or, maybe he belonged to some redneck who let him ride in the back of a pickup truck, no harness to keep him from jumping out. That was it—he must've leapt from the truck, a flight of freedom from human stupidity that resulted in injury.

She told herself to stop thinking about the dog and walked on, focusing on other things, like the fact that she was in plain sight—out in the open where anyone could spot her. And the reality that her money was running so low that she might have to eventually stop and ask for work. She didn't need much, but humans did require food. And the occasional shower.

So far she'd been lucky enough that most of the people running the truck stops had allowed her to pay for a shower. But at five bucks a pop, she didn't splurge often. To that end, she was becoming quite proficient at taking sponge baths in public bathrooms.

She didn't want to pull her money out and count it while she was still walking alongside the interstate, but if she remembered right, she was down to just over three hundred dollars.

Her life was just one vicious cycle of screw-ups.

Turning down the offer of a college education was one of their bigger mistakes. If Cara only had a degree—in anything at all— things could've been much different. It was so long ago, but she still remembered their eighteenth birthday and how monumental it was. The day represented their first opportunity to decide their next course in life.

They could either remain under the state's watchful eye while taking advantage of a few free years of college or become completely emancipated.

Back then, it was an easy decision, but in hindsight, it had been a careless one. She could easily blame Hana, who had convinced her they needed to cut all ties with the system, but the truth is that Cara had also wanted that freedom.

So that's what they'd done. Walking away, Hana had used her fast finger and given their case manager a final good-bye. But once on their own Cara realized they could've used that education, no matter how minimal it was, because without a college degree, their employment options were slim and kept them below the poverty level.

Just like many other teens, they started out flipping burgers, but it didn't take long before they were the oldest on the shifts. It was humiliating knowing that most people used fast-food jobs only as a stepping-stone, but that because of their circumstances, they would probably be in the rut forever.

Hana was the first to realize it one day and threw her hands up and quit, taking Cara with her.

Yes, her sister was always dragging Cara into something. Or out of something. Just look at her now. Because of Hana, she'd burned out of town with only a few hundred bucks. Now Cara was on foot—destination unknown. Her circumstances couldn't get any worse.

Hopefully.

She stole a sideways peek and saw the dog was still behind her, slowly making his way around high bundles of grass and debris, stepping gingerly on his front right foot in his attempt to keep up. She kept walking.

After the fast-food debacle, Cara had scored them jobs cleaning rooms at the No Tell Motel. It was just as humiliating, but it paid their apartment rent—at least until the day a random customer caught Hana in a room alone and tried to assault her. Cara had come in just in time and her screams had saved her sister.

That time.

She stopped and bent over, taking a long breath and pulling it all the way down to her lungs. She felt nauseated for a moment. She needed to think of something else.

Anything but her sister.

The car.

She started moving again. Cara felt her cheeks redden with shame that she'd taken the car that they shared, and she wished she could talk to Hana and tell her that it had ended up being a lemon anyway.

Right now it was sitting more than fifty miles behind her at the place it had drawn its last breath—a Burger King parking lot.

If her sister were there right now, she'd probably get mad at first, but then tell Cara that the car was no big deal because obviously karma had other plans for them. That's the way her sister was, always talking about fate, karma, and the cosmic forces at play. But why couldn't Hana see that here they were on thirty's doorstep, and no closer to something good happening in their lives than they'd been on twenty's doorstep? Karma had obviously skipped by them, moving to the next humans on the list.

Hana would've loved the fact that Cara was heading out without a destination in mind—letting the wind take her wherever it may, as long as it was far from Sandy Springs, Georgia. But Cara wasn't like Hana. Traveling around like a gypsy without a plan was too unsettling. She needed to decide where to go that would put her far from her past and soothe her troubled soul. She needed a destination.

Key West.

She stopped. A van went by and blew its horn at her. The thirteenth horn blow of the day. But more important, where had that thought come from? She'd never considered going to Key West. It hadn't even crossed her mind once. All she knew about Key West was that it was located on the southernmost tip of the continental United States, part of Florida, and that Ernest Hemingway had owned a home there. But she'd never been out of Georgia, much less ventured toward what would probably feel like the ends of the earth.

But why not? Maybe having a destination, instead of just running aimlessly, would help her to focus on moving faster. And while she was there, she could see where Hemingway wrote a few of his most famous stories.

Turning to check on the dog, she noticed his tail begin to wag when he caught her glance. She stopped, pausing to get his input. "What do you think about Key West, Dog?"

The tail wagged some more and the dog picked up the pace to bridge the distance between them, until it stopped in front of her and sat down, heaving a sigh as if to say, "Finally. Can we take a break now?"

Cara knelt down and patted his head, causing him to wag his tail so hard she thought it would break. "So you like that idea, do you?"

He stared up at her as though she held the answer to some long-lost secret and he was hanging on her every word until she spilled the beans.

Cara studied him, trying to determine his breed. The best she could describe his color was a creamy off-white—though most of that was probably dirt. While he looked similar to a Labrador, his ears were a bit too floppy and his fur too soft. He could've had shepherd in him, though she wasn't sure if shepherd dogs were known to have white hair. She finally decided he was a mix—what she'd heard called a Heinz 57 dog.

"Oh, don't worry, I don't have a pedigree either. If I were a dog, you'd find me in the discounted mutt aisle."

She didn't know why she suddenly felt a lump in her throat. She wasn't the rash one—the one who didn't think before making a move. She'd always been the practical twin—the sensible one who made the right decisions. And her reputed common sense told her that a drifter without a home couldn't provide for another living creature. But the nonpractical side of her brain reminded her of how lonely the open road was.

"Okay, new deal. You can go with me to Key West."

More tail wagging.

"We'll see Hemingway's house and then I'll find a nice shelter to take you in and they'll help you find your family."

The tail stopped.

"Don't argue. Second part of the deal is that you need a name. I can't think of you as just Dog. I know if you're ever reunited with your old family, they'll go back to your real name but for now, please, just choose something."

She waited.

He waited.

"Fine. Right now there's only one thing on my mind. So I formally dub you Hemingway. I'll call you Hemi for short." The name had come out of her mouth before she'd realized how close it sounded to Hana. Maybe in some way she was trying to keep her sister with her. She wouldn't focus on that, though. "Are you okay with the nickname?"

The tail started back up again, making Cara laugh. Suddenly without warning, the dog got up and darted off the side of the road, down the embankment, and into the line of trees.

"Where're you going?" she called out, as though he'd answer.

She watched him go, debating whether she should follow. She really shouldn't get involved. She knew that. She should just take the opportunity while he wasn't looking to separate herself from him. From the responsibility of another living thing.

Yet her heart wouldn't let her walk away.

Sighing, she went after him.

When she stepped into the grove, she had to wait a few seconds to let her eyes adjust. Finally, she saw him. When she approached, a wide pink tongue protruded and he began to pant. The weather was cool for a spring day, so Cara could only guess that he was in distress. She could see two dark, marble-like eyes and they were staring back at her, practically burrowing right down to her very soul. The depth of the almost-human gaze told her the dog wasn't dangerous, but he did look afraid.

She wondered what had changed. He'd been anxious for her to show him attention, but now he wouldn't come out.

A memory came flashing back. She and her sister, side by side in the back of a small dark closet with their arms encircling their knees, chanting what they'd thought for years were the magical words that would take them out of whatever sterile, cold house they'd been remanded to and back into the arms of their mother. Cara could imagine that had someone opened the closet door, they'd have looked just like the dog, a bit of hope mixed with fear.

For them it had never happened. The magic declined to visit two small girls from the poor side of town. And no one ever opened the closet door because no one cared. Out of sight was out of mind. And the safest place to be back then. But they usually emerged when their hungry bellies urged them to.

Right on cue, hers gave a low rumble.

But it could wait. She needed to deal with the dog. Maybe she could find a tag somewhere on him. A phone number. Or something? She couldn't imagine he didn't have someone somewhere missing him and wondering where he'd wandered off to.

She sat down where she was. It wasn't like she was expected anywhere. There was at least six hours until dark when she'd have to find cover. That would give her plenty of time to see if the dog wanted to come out.

She waited.

He didn't move. Instead he watched her, a look of wary resignation on his face. He was tired, too.

Cara pulled her backpack off her arm and put it in front of her, unzipping it. She didn't have much food to share, but whatever she could find, she'd at least offer it. She dug past rolled up socks, the extra set of clothes, her dog-eared paperback, and her Family Dollar shampoo until her fingers found the few cans of tuna in the bottom. Funds were low—getting lower every day—and tuna and crackers was something she'd found that gave her energy and didn't cost much. She pulled out a can, and setting the bag aside, she opened the flip-top of the can.

Gently, she set the can on the ground and used her foot to push it closer to the dog. He watched her warily but didn't move. She moved a hand toward her backpack, in a reflex to find her phone, then remembered she'd left it in the car. She'd seen enough episodes of *Dateline* to know people could be tracked by the pings their phones make on cell towers.

She probably wouldn't have used it anyway. She couldn't call home. There were no friends to worry about her being out of contact. And to be honest, the phone had never been more than a nuisance to her. Text messages made it possible for people to say mean things to someone that they'd never say in person. She wasn't proud to admit it, but she and Hana had waged war through texting many times. Not only that, but the ease of pecking out a few words made it harder for anyone to have any privacy, because someone was always just a ping away, asking, "Where are you? What are you doing? When are you coming home?"

She was glad to be rid of it.

That left her no one to talk to but the dog.

"Did you know that Ernest Hemingway went to war for our country and when he was stationed in Italy, he drove an ambulance? That's where he met Agnes, his first love. She was the American nurse who tended to him when he was hit by a mortar shell and landed in the hospital."

The dog looked unimpressed.

"He was only nineteen and Agnes was twenty-six, but he insisted he wanted to marry her when they both returned to the states."

The dog blinked and Cara took that as a cue to tell him more.

"Agnes shattered that dream when she wrote to tell him she'd accepted the proposal of another man. They say Hemingway pined after Agnes for years."

Cara talked on for some time, her voice getting lighter and lighter until she realized how tired she really was. Up at first light, she'd walked fifteen miles already that day and had planned at least fifteen more. Her calves ached and the sounds of the cars going by barely made it through the dense trees. The low humming was like a lullaby, and Cara was tired of waiting for the dog to respond to the food or her cajoling.

She noticed the dip in the ground and the bed of leaves that rested there. She thought of Hemingway's words that graced one of his many memorials. "He loved the fall, the leaves yellow on the cottonwoods . . ."

Even though she'd never been to Idaho and had only seen it in photos, the memorial and the beautiful words were branded in Cara's mind. She could understand his love for the outdoors. The peacefulness within the trees welcomed her, inviting her to stay a while. She paused, considering her next thought. Yes, a short nap before she tackled any more miles was exactly what she needed.

Releasing her small blanket from the Velcro straps at the bottom of her bag, she moved slowly, unrolling it, then spreading it over her shoulders before lying back. With the bag under her head and the softer sounds of nature around her, she closed her eyes. As she drifted off to sleep, a small voice inside her head whispered that she hoped the dog was still there when she woke up.

❧

It was raining. And cold. Cara curled up tighter, bringing her knees closer to her chin and ignoring the stab of pain as her hip grated against the hard ground. The leaves that had looked so inviting suddenly felt nonexistent, and her body screamed out in silent reproach. To make it worse, the drop of rain that rolled onto her nose refused to drop off, even with a shake of her head. She reached up to brush it off, but her hand made a connection with something foreign.

She opened her eyes to find the dog staring down at her, its tongue making another turn up and around her nostrils. There wasn't any rain, unless she counted dog slobber as precipitation. Above her the sky was dim, barely visible through the tall trees that swayed in the slight wind, stern and stoic, reminding her of soldiers guarding a fallen brother.

But she wasn't fallen.

Sitting abruptly, she held her hands up in defense against the sudden invasion of her personal space. Just as quickly, she dropped them, feeling at first silly, then ashamed when the dog backed up a few feet and flinched.

It obviously didn't have a mean bone in its matted body.

She looked over at the can and found it empty, satisfied he finally trusted her enough to come forward and eat. But she was surprised.

"What kind of dog likes tuna?" Cara muttered under her breath.

Its ears perked up and it tilted its head in confusion.

"Or like me, are you just hungry enough not to be choosy?"

The head tilted the other way, this time one ear flopping over.

"Never mind." She felt another pang of hunger and remembered the other can of tuna. Looking back at his soulful eyes, she knew she'd have to share again. No one, much less herself, could possibly turn down the hopeful expression the dog had suddenly adopted.

Judging by where she could see the sun going down, it was close enough to suppertime. Tonight she'd be walking in the dark to find shelter. But first, she dug in her bag and got out the other can of tuna and the sleeve of crackers. While she worked to open both, the dog sat down, watching her every move.

She pulled her one lone plastic spoon from the bag, spread a tiny bit of tuna on the first cracker, and laid it down in front of the dog.

This time he only waited a few seconds, then looked up at her.

"Go ahead," Cara said, nodding at him.

He seemed to understand, because he rose and limped over to the cracker, picked it up and swallowed it whole in one fell swoop.

"What's wrong with your paw?" She remembered he'd been limping and felt a rush of pity when she looked down at the paw he held off the ground and saw it matted with dirt and dried blood. She'd have to see what she could do with it, but first she needed to get something in her stomach. She'd never been one to be able to deal with blood or anything visually uncomfortable. It was she who'd always hid her eyes during the worst parts of scary movies as Hana narrated them from beside her.

Her sister again.

She wished she could stop bringing Hana into every single moment of her life. It was hard to move on when her sister's presence kept stepping in, refusing to be ignored.

Still, it would be easier to deal with a bloody paw if she wasn't already light-headed from hunger.

The tuna was going quickly. But she had to give the dog credit, he sat patiently waiting for his turn, somehow knowing and agreeing that every other cracker belonged to her. Naturally, when it came to the last bit of tuna, Cara couldn't keep the cracker for herself but instead broke it in half.

The grateful wag of the dog's tail was her reward for sharing.

Once done, Cara turned to the dog and crossed her arms, looking down at him. She hadn't found any evidence of a collar, which meant no identification tags, either. Like her, he was obviously traveling incognito. She knelt down in front of him. Gently—ever so gently—she picked up his paw and turned it over.

He whimpered and she dropped it.

"You scared me. Stop whining so I can see what's going on here." She picked the paw up again, this time with a firmer grasp. She turned it over, and to her horror, through the dirt and blood she saw a long sliver of glass embedded in the dark pink pad of his paw.

She looked up at him, noticing that he kept his eyes off his paw and trained on her face.

He trusted her.

No one else had ever trusted her. Except for Hana. But did Hana really count? A sister she'd shared a womb with—and just about every waking moment since—as they'd entered the world screaming and kicking. Trusting your twin was instinctual, wasn't it?

At least that's how Cara felt. Now that she'd spent some time with the dog—feeding it and discovering it was injured—she realized that she just couldn't take on the responsibility of his care.

She was tired of shouldering responsibility. Look where it had gotten her so far in life. Nowhere.

It wasn't going to be easy, but she was going to retract her promise. "Okay, Hemi. This is probably going to hurt. But I'll do the best I can to put you out of your misery. And no, that's not a euphemism for putting you down. I'll pull the glass out and then sorry, buddy, but you'll be on your merry little way and I'll be on mine."

She put his paw down and went back to her backpack. She carried two bottles of water with her at all times but she was running really low. She was washing out the plastic bottles and filling them with water from rest areas and public bathrooms, then using them until they were too flimsy to go on. Then she found more and the cycle continued.

She pulled the half-empty bottle from the side loop, unscrewed the top and poured a tiny bit of the water into the empty tuna can, then set it in front of the dog. He lapped it up quickly while she took a few sips herself.

For water straight out of a gas station faucet, it tasted so good.

She grabbed a roll of her socks and unraveled them, then took one sock and the remaining water back over to the dog.

"Now I know I'm being too emotional, because here I am donating one of my last socks to your hurt paw."

She set the water and sock down, then once again lifted the paw. Quickly, before the dog could squirm, she grabbed the edge of the sliver of glass and pulled it out, causing a fresh spurt of blood from the wound. She fought a wave of dizziness at the bright red blood, instead focusing on pouring the rest of the water over the wound, washing out as much dirt and blood as she could.

"You sure have done a lot of walking, bud. Your pads are a mess."

He began to wiggle backwards and Cara held tightly.

"Oh no, you don't. You aren't putting that paw back onto this dirty ground without my sock over it." She worked fast to use the sock as a bandage, wrapping it round the paw and then tying the two ends together tightly. When she finished and let the dog go, he fell back from the sudden release, then immediately sat back up on his haunches and wagged his tail at her. He flashed his gratitude with a lopsided grin.

"You're welcome."

She put her single sock back in her bag. Who knew when she'd need another one-off? Then using her small spade she'd bought for just this reason, she dug a hole in the ground, then tucked both cans, the broken piece of beer bottle from the dog's paw, and the cracker sleeve into it and covered it back up.

She might not hold much worth to most, but at least she didn't litter.

Rolling the blanket up she scanned to make sure she'd left nothing else behind. She reattached it to the bottom of her backpack, sealing the worn-out Velcro as best as she could before tossing the bag back over her arm. Looking around to be sure she'd not left any evidence of her being there, her eyes alighted back on the dog.

He still sat watching her. Cara raised an eyebrow at him, impressed that he hadn't tried to gnaw at the sock. He obviously knew what was good for him. She hoped by the time he got bored enough to chew it off, the wound would be closed and no longer susceptible to infection. She couldn't help but notice that in addition to his paw issue, his matted white fur was a mess.

But he *was* adorable.

She couldn't do it. There was no way she was purposely leaving him behind. And she wouldn't force him to go.

So she'd let him decide. If he followed her, so be it.

Turning away from him, she walked out of the grove, climbed the embankment, and was back on the shoulder of the highway, the cars zooming by once again.

She waited a few seconds, then looked behind her.

Hemi was standing right there looking at her and waiting on her next move.

She now had a destination.

And a travel partner.

She hoped leading the dog out of state wouldn't make it harder to find his family, but stopping now was out of the question, as she had to get some distance between herself and the situation she'd left behind. And she was going on the hope that Hemi had one of those chips implanted somewhere in his scruffy neck—that his information was stored in a database and he simply needed to be scanned, then voilà, his family could be found.

It felt good that she planned to help the dog. With those decisions made, she felt more grounded. More like herself. And having a sense of purpose again was like taking a huge breath of fresh air. She waved the dog on.

"Come on, Hemi. I see the Golden Arches sign a few miles ahead and if we're in luck, they'll have the Dollar Menu."

Chapter Two

As they walked, she talked, and Cara noticed that Hemi was getting better at keeping up. Her sock was either doing a good job cushioning his wound from the earth, or the dog was simply happy that she was no longer ignoring him. She had to admit, having him with her made her feel that it wasn't the end of the world—he was such a friendly dog that one couldn't help but feel better around him.

She wished Hana could meet him.

"Hemingway had a six-toed cat."

Of course, the dog didn't answer and Cara told him more. A parade of cars zoomed by them, then a highway patrolman turned on his car's blue light and disappeared around the curve. Cara felt bad for the driver who was about to have a really bad day.

Another string of cars passed and someone blew the horn, then someone tossed an empty soda bottle out of a window, narrowly missing her with it. It scared her and she jumped, but Cara refrained from reacting, knowing the driver could turn around and come back. She had to keep in mind that she was all but defenseless by herself.

"It's okay, Hemi. They're just assholes," she said.

She breathed through the flush of anger, then when her pulse slowed again, she continued with her story.

"You see, Hemingway loved the ocean and took a lot of excursions to fish or just be out there, taking in the salty air. A sea captain friend of his gave him a pure white cat with six toes."

Up ahead she saw the exit and heaved a sigh of relief. She was starving.

"He named him Snowball and he loved that cat. Kept it at his home in Key West. They say there are dozens of descendants of the cat still on the property, most of them with six toes."

Hemi looked up at her briefly, then turned his attention back to the road. Cara sensed he thought she was talking nonsense.

"Well, you'll get to see for yourself if you don't believe me. They call them the Hemingway Cats, and they're real."

As they walked, Cara considered what Hana had always called her "infatuation" with all things Hemingway. But she couldn't help it. Ever since she'd done a report on him in the fifth grade and found out that his family was cursed with the tendency to commit suicide, his legacy held a grip on her. Maybe it had something to do with what her mother had done, but she found it fascinating that so many of Hemingway's relatives resorted to giving themselves what he called "the gift of death."

His father, sister, and brother had all killed themselves. And a granddaughter. She could've told Hemi all that, but it was just too morbid to speak aloud. Not to mention just plain sad that such a gifted man had chosen to end his life.

Hemingway had money, achievements, and family. In his novel, *For Whom the Bell Tolls*, he'd even said, "The world is a fine place and worth the fighting for and I hate very much to leave it." Those very words he had penned, so if he thought the world a fine place, what was his life lacking?

Cara thought of her mother, a woman who held no wealth and didn't have the courage to continue on in the world. Her act of cowardice that resulted in her death had catapulted Cara and Hana into the challenging and unfair foster-care system where they'd floundered for the rest of their childhood. Despite that, Cara didn't hate her mother. She only felt pity—and in her darkest moments, longing, for what she'd lost.

She felt her good mood slipping away and put her attention back on pacing herself. Now that they were close to food, though, she felt like running. Her stomach needed filling and her bladder needed emptying.

Sighing, she looked at Hemi's paw and saw the sock was starting to look baggy. She needed to fix it up as soon as she could. Up ahead, the highway patrol car came into view again. He had a white Honda pulled over and appeared to be at the driver's window, writing a ticket. Cara considered walking right on by him, tempted by the sudden growl from her belly.

But she knew better than to take that chance. Quickly, she stepped off the shoulder of the road. Cara kept her steps quiet in the hopes that the officer wouldn't notice them. The brim of his hat hid his face as he kept his attention on his clipboard. They were just about to the tree line when he looked up.

"Come up here!" he yelled out briskly, then lifted a hand and beckoned her closer before looking back down at his papers.

How three little words could hold so much authority, Cara didn't know, but she'd always been a rule follower and his command froze her in place.

Hemi looked up at her, questioning the interruption in their pace. Or maybe he sensed the terror that flooded her from her nose to her toes. Was her short journey going to be over? Would she have to go back and be held accountable? Hemi wiggled, bringing her back to the present.

She sighed, then slowly began walking until she was behind the patrol car. She led Hemi to a grassy spot farther from the vehicles zooming by on the road. She looked down at him. He seemed to raise his eyebrows at her. She owed him an apology. He was going to have to find his family on his own now.

Should she scare him off? Stomp at him to get him to make a run for it?

He waited, looking up at her with such trusting eyes.

But perhaps the officer was a dog lover and would make sure Hemi got to where he needed to go—would keep him safe and not just drop him at a shelter.

"Sit," she told him, her decision made.

To her astonishment, he did.

"Good dog."

They waited and finally, the officer ripped a paper from his pad, handed it to the driver of the Honda, and gave him permission to take off. Cara noticed the patrolman was a nice-looking man, maybe in his early thirties. Thin as a rail, but he still held himself proudly and with confidence. He was the kind of man who would turn her sister's head far too quickly. Hana always said she loved a man in uniform.

"Have a nice day," he said, walking away from the white car and straight over to where Cara and Hemi waited on the grass.

"Do you really think they're going to have a nice day now that you wrote them a big fat ticket?" Cara asked. She was shocked at her forwardness, feeling like the inner Hana in her had suddenly emerged. She wished she could stuff the words back into her mouth.

He frowned at her, then looked off over her shoulder. "Let's put it this way. Just last month we pulled a woman from a car after she hit a tree doing seventy-one miles per hour. She was wearing her seat belt and every air bag around her went off, but she still died instantly. The saddest part is, she left behind three small children, who thankfully weren't in the car with her that day. That person I just ticketed was doing over eighty miles per hour. Don't you realize how reckless a person's driving turns when they get into that range of speed?"

Cara shook her head. How could she? Her car had only gotten up to fifty on a good day, and that was with the pedal to the floor going downhill.

"Where's your car?" he asked, looking behind Cara.

"I'm walking." Cara didn't bother to tell him that she'd had a car, but it'd died in a huff and a cloud of black smoke three days before. She looked at him, letting what she knew would happen just happen.

The expected pause.

Next, the appraisal.

And hopefully, the dismissal.

It didn't matter if she was standing on the edge of a long highway, or serving someone from the other side of the counter at one of her many low-paying jobs, or simply daring to walk among the perfumed, fancied-up people who lingered at the makeup counters in the mall stores. Because she looked poor, people assumed she was stupid. And because they assumed she was stupid, they barely acknowledged her existence. And if they acknowledged her existence, it was for only a brief moment of pity. To one of the chosen few, like this patrolman, Cara and her sister had always been mostly invisible.

"Okay, no car. But what are you doing walking along the interstate? That's against the law."

She thought fast, trying to come up with something smart to say that could potentially keep her out of trouble, but unlike Hana, who could always twist a tale to her benefit, Cara had nothing. So she stuck with the truth.

"I just got on the interstate a day ago, but until then I'd been taking highways and back roads."

He looked at her backpack, then her worn-out shoes. Finally, he glanced down at Hemi, who sat watching the exchange, a quizzical expression on his face. "Where you two headed on this adventure?"

She shrugged. If she were Hana, she'd have smarted off with something like "adventure is more than a destination, it's a state of mind," but she wasn't Hana and didn't have her knack for smooth sarcasm, so she simply didn't answer.

He nodded as though she'd answered verbally. "I see. It's not illegal to walk in this country, but you can't be on the interstate. And if you do slip back onto it, can you at least walk facing the traffic? That'll make it easier for you to see what's coming at you."

Cara was stunned. Was he just going to give her advice and let her go? Her biggest fear was that he'd ask for her license, or her name, then run it. She didn't know if something would show up, but she didn't want to take the chance, either.

"Are you one of those walk-across-America people?"

Hmmmm. That was a good cover, though she wasn't sure what it actually meant. She nodded. "Yes, that's what I'm doing. I thought I'd shave a few miles off by hitting the interstate, but I promise not to do it anymore, officer."

He stared at her for a moment and she held her breath, waiting for whatever came next. His expression was doubtful. "You aren't outfitted too well for a walk across anything."

Cara kicked at a rock. "Well, I was. But then half my stuff got taken from me when I crossed paths with someone who wasn't such a gentleman."

Another half truth. She had run into someone who'd stolen from her, but it was only her walking stick and an umbrella.

"Where you planning on sleeping tonight?"

She felt a rush of irritation. He sure was nosy.

"I haven't quite planned it out yet."

"Have you eaten today?" he asked.

Cara looked anywhere but at him. She hated the pity that was in his voice. She could take anything except that.

"Look, are you going to arrest me or something? Because I need to go. My dog is hungry and I promised him a cheeseburger." She glanced behind her, then pointed at the Golden Arches of the McDonald's ahead.

So close.

Yet so far.

He frowned. "A cheeseburger? You need to give that dog something healthier than that. My dogs get Alpo. From the can."

Well, good for you, Mr. Big Spender, Cara thought, but kept her mouth shut.

"Hop in and I'll give you a ride. If you want a place to stay tonight, I know of a shelter that'll take you and your dog about fifteen miles from here. You can rewrap that paw when you get there."

She ignored the passive-aggressive jab that she wasn't taking care of her dog sufficiently because a bed—or a cot, most likely—would be welcome for a change. For the most part, Cara planned to avoid shelters unless she could find one that was women only. But most towns didn't have the luxury to segregate women and men, and she felt safer finding a place outside, where she could be alone. But her back hurt from walking. So did her knees, feet, and ankles.

Okay, so everything is hurting.

She looked down at Hemi and he was giving her that hopeful look again. He was tired. And his paw hurt. Maybe a night with a roof over his head would make him feel better. And they'd hopefully have a place where she could wash his cut really well. She ignored the warning bells going off in her head and nodded. So far he had thought she was just one of the many nomads her age who wanted an escape from the grind and tried to find it by wandering from place to place.

She decided to take a chance. Not for herself, but for Hemi. "Fine. We'll go. But first take us by McDonald's so we can eat."

The officer reached up and tipped his wide-brimmed hat. "I'll make sure you get to eat. Oh, by the way, I'm Officer Sanders and I'm glad you decided to trust me." He motioned toward his car.

Not trust—desperation, Cara thought as she headed that way and Hemi followed. It wouldn't be her first time riding in a cop car, although the other trips had usually been when she and Hana were being rescued from one unsafe environment and transferred to yet another one. Most of their transfers were done by their caseworker, but it wasn't unusual for local authorities to get involved.

He beat her to the car and opened the back door. She realized he hadn't asked her name and felt a rush of relief. Still, his gesture pricked at her.

"You want me to ride in the back?" *Like a criminal,* she almost added.

"Sorry, regulations say no civilians in the front."

She sighed, then took her backpack off and threw it onto the seat and climbed in. Hemi hopped in after her, not waiting to be invited.

"Buckle up," the officer said, then shut the door and went around to his side and climbed in. The first thing he did was fasten his seat belt, then he used his controls to open Hemi's window.

"Dogs love the rush of fresh air," he said.

Hemi proved him right when he immediately went to the window, stuck his snout out, and inhaled deeply, his tail wagging furiously.

The officer pulled back onto the interstate and Cara said a silent prayer that he wasn't taking them directly to the local precinct to be investigated further or arrested for loitering—or worse, that he knew exactly who he had in the back of his car.

Yeah, so I have trust issues.

But they were well earned.

Chapter Three

Much to Cara's steadily building suspicion, the officer drove up the ramp and onto the road, then right past the combo McDonald's and gas station. He didn't consult her either. He cruised on by as though she weren't sitting in the seat behind him wishing she'd have stepped into the tree line right when she'd first spotted him.

Looking at the back of his head from the backseat, she felt like a kid again. There was a day once when one of the nicer foster fathers took her and Hana to McDonald's. He'd swooped in just as their foster mother was working up to one of her out-of-control tantrums and he'd ushered them out the door and into the car.

When they were in the dining room, being visually assaulted by the garishly colorful mascot Ronald and his friends pasted around the room, Willie—that was their foster father's name at the time, and Cara was surprised that she even remembered it—set two Happy Meals on the table. He'd urged them to eat up, as he talked to them about his wife's shaky childhood and inability to truly love anything, including herself. Hana had bumped Cara's knee more than once, a silent urge to stay quiet and let him spill his guts as long as they could enjoy the rare treat. Cara had barely been able to eat, her mind filled with questions about why every adult in their lives thought they were old enough to understand—without apology—why they'd decided that they weren't the family for her and Hana. For with each chicken nugget she'd picked up, she'd known she was one bite closer to their current placement being disrupted.

"I feel you glaring holes into the back of my head," the patrolman said, jerking her back to the present.

"You passed McDonald's." *And I really need to pee*, she added silently.

Hemi didn't notice anything. In his glee to put his snout into the wind, he'd stepped up on the armrest and was oblivious to anything going on inside the car. His ears flapped back and forth and his face stretched in the wind, making him look like a cartoon dog.

"I thought you could use a better meal than McDonald's can provide. Maybe some meat that's recognizable? Or at least something without enough salt and carbohydrates to kill a person."

"They have salads." Cara spoke softly and carefully. She'd heard of policemen—highway patrol officers—using their authority to gain sexual favors and she was starting to feel like maybe she should try to talk her way out of there before they arrived at whatever sleazy destination he had in mind for his little fantasies.

"My mother runs a diner. It's nothing fancy, but she has a room in the back and I know she'll let you use it to clean yourself and the big guy up a bit. You can even shower if you want."

She didn't believe anything he said. Now he was talking about her in the shower. What a creeper. She wished she hadn't been trained from early in life to fear authority. She hated the way she was suddenly hunkered down, her body curling into itself with fear.

It was almost as though he could see into her head and know that just the morning before, she'd been rudely kicked out of a public bathroom at a small gas station for trying to wash up in the sink. Taking a shower was probably the only bait she'd almost fall for. But she'd been around enough to know that kindness didn't come free.

"Why are you doing this?" she finally said.

He took a hard turn, and she had to hold the handle over the window to keep from falling over on Hemi. When he spoke, his words sounded sarcastic. "Doing what? Being hospitable? What—do you think all officers of the law are hard-asses?"

She let that one float, choosing not to answer.

He looked in the rearview mirror, meeting her gaze for a second before turning his eyes back on the road. "Sorry. I don't usually cuss but you must not be from around here. In the South, people help people. I'm not trying to con you. And I'm not trying to woo you."

"Woo me?" She hadn't heard that term since she'd watched an old Judy Garland movie with Hana a few years back.

He lifted his left hand from the steering wheel and waved it in the air. "Yeah, woo you. You can get that out of your head right now. I'm married."

"Since when has a ring stopped a man from cheating?" she said under her breath.

He heard her. "Since I said my vows. And anyway, we have children."

They went a few more miles, easing into what looked like the downtown of a small community. She saw a few people strolling on the sidewalks, some window-shopping and some moving faster. It looked like the set of a sitcom featuring one of those quaint Southern towns. When they drove by a bearded, gruff-looking man sitting on a bench, a guitar on his knee and a cup at his feet, his voice carried out and into the car window.

"That's Leroy. He sings for his supper. And everything else. We call him the Waycross crooner."

"Oh, so this is Waycross." Cara didn't know what else to say except she wished she had the chops to sing for *her* supper.

"No. Waycross is another thirty miles or so from here, but that's where Leroy is from so the name stuck. This is Nahunta, the official county seat of Brantley County with a population of just over one thousand people."

He sounded proud of his proclamation.

Cara raised her eyebrows at the back of his head but said nothing.

"After you clean up and eat, if you want to be taken straight to the town shelter, I'll come back for you. Our church even has an outreach program, if you want me to call my pastor."

"No, that's okay." Cara cringed. Not church. Anything but church. She'd been through so many flocks and coverings of prayer for her and her sister's salvation, she couldn't even count. All she and Hana had ever wanted was to go back to their mother, or be part of a real family. But it didn't matter because from where she'd been standing, it appeared that nothing ever came from the prayers pointed their way.

He pulled into the parking lot of a small brick building. The sign over the top read Chicken and a Biscuit and boasted a painted chicken running after a biscuit with legs.

"This is a restaurant?"

He pulled into a spot and cut the engine, then turned and smiled at her.

"The best in town—and probably the whole state of Georgia. On that I give you my word." He opened the door and climbed out, taking the time to remove his hat and lay it on the seat before turning to open her door.

"What about Hemi?" She glanced over at the dog and he was finally out of the window, watching them while his tail wagged.

"Bring him. Mama loves dogs," he said, turning around and leaving Cara to follow.

"Well, come on, then," she said to Hemi, exasperated at their new predicament.

At the entrance, the officer hesitated. He waited until she approached, then he stuck his hand out. "Now that we're here, you can call me Greg."

She looked at his hand, pausing before putting her own out. When he grasped it, his fingers closed around hers in a tight, warm grip. Hemi stood below them, watching them impatiently.

"And your name?" he asked, not letting go.

"Um . . . I'm . . . Hana." She didn't know why she uttered her sister's name; she only knew it was safer than using her own. She could only imagine the amusement that Hana would've gotten out of the situation, especially considering that all their lives people had been confusing their names.

"Hi Hana. And Hemi. Now that we've been introduced, let's go get your bellies full."

He opened the door and the brash sounds of bells clanging made her jump, then the aroma of fresh fried chicken hit Cara slapdab in the face, making her brain go all haywire. She hadn't eaten a real meal in many days, and the close proximity to food made her weak with hunger.

The huge room was clean and cozy, decorated in red with accents and various Coca-Cola signs on the walls. All the checkered tablecloths added to the country flair, and Cara could see herself and Hana becoming regulars, if this place had been located back home.

Several tables were full, and when she stepped through the door with Greg—it felt so weird thinking of him having an actual name other than Officer—everyone turned to stare.

Cara felt the heat climb up her neck and into her cheeks until she thought she'd burst from internal combustion. She wanted to melt into the floor, disappear into thin air—whatever it took for them not to dissect her ragged clothes and poor hygiene.

"Greg!" an old man called out, lifting his hand in a greeting. Beside him an older lady sat, waving and smiling.

"Mr. Harding, Mrs. Harding. Nice to see you."

The wife pointed behind the long glass front counter. "Your mother is in the kitchen helping Maisy pull the meat for tomorrow. It's pulled-pork day and you know what that means—a big lunch crowd."

Greg nodded. "That's fine. We'll go on back."

He led the way, beckoning for Cara to follow. She complied, eager to get out of view of the others in the dining area. Hemi tagged along quietly, never getting more than a few steps behind her. She couldn't help but be constantly surprised at his willingness to stay with her, even without being leashed.

They went around the counter and Cara got a view of an old-fashioned buffet-style spread of food. Her mouth watered as they passed, taking in the smells and colors all on display. She saw green beans with crumbled bacon, then mashed potatoes—a favorite staple for both her and Hana—before her eyes settled on the mounds of golden-brown fried chicken.

But Greg led her the other way, and when they turned the corner into the small kitchen, two women looked up from their places at a long, stainless-steel counter. Plump as can be, the both of them, and they were a colorful pair.

They'd stopped talking midsentence, and it was obvious which woman was which. "Greg, I didn't know you were coming by," the plumpest one said, then put her hands on her hips. "And I told you not to come back around here unless you've got my grandbabies with you."

"They're at soccer practice, Mama," he replied, but with a respectful tone laced with affection.

"Oh Lawd, child. You've grown another few inches since you were here last week," said the woman Cara guessed to be Maisy. She was the more vibrant of the two, with her colorful scarf and soft, dark skin.

They both looked Cara up and down, but their gazes weren't what she was used to. They were missing the usual judgment and pity.

Greg put a hand on her shoulder. "This is Hana."

"Hello, Hana." Then his mother put her hands on her hips and shot Greg a disapproving glance. "Now you know dogs aren't allowed back here."

Greg turned and saw Hemi waiting just behind Cara's legs. "Whoops. I thought he'd stay in the front."

"Oh, I'm so sorry," Cara blushed, realizing her mistake.

"Well then . . ." Greg said, laughing slightly. "Let me also introduce her dog, Hemi. Hana needs to clean up a bit and they can both use a good meal. Hana, this is my Mama and her right hand, Maisy. They'll fix you right up."

His mother moved quickly to the sink, rinsing her hands off and drying them on her red-checkered apron before crossing over to Cara. Before she could react, she found herself enveloped in warm, pillowy arms, immersing Cara in the aroma of baby powder.

"You darn right we'll fix you up," his mother said, finally allowing her to squirm free. Cara looked up at her, noticing the woman was completely made up, long eyelashes and rosy lipstick, too. She looked like Cara's idea of what a real grandmother should look like. She let out a pleasant laugh. "And you can call me Miss Kim. Everyone does."

She'd said it all in one seemingly long, fast sentence, not giving Cara a chance to respond. She went back to where she'd been working and grabbed a handful of shredded meat, then bent down and whistled.

Hemi waltzed over there effortlessly as though Cara had not just pulled a long sliver of glass from his paw a few hours before. His tail about wagged off while he greedily, but somewhat politely, ate the meat from her outstretched hand.

"Oh Lawdie, I hope you're taking that dog with you when you go, girl. We don't need no more critters round here," Maisy said. "You hear me, Miss Kim? Don't even think on it."

"Oh yes, Hemi stays with me," Cara said, the words slipping out and surprising her. How quickly she'd come to think of the dog as hers. But he wasn't—and she'd make sure he understood that when they made it to Key West.

But until then, he might as well be called *hers*.

His mother let out an exasperated sound. "Oh Maisy, I doubt she's thinking of leaving her dog behind. Without him with her out there on that open road, she'd be as lonely as a pine tree in a parking lot."

Cara looked at Greg and he rolled his eyes and shrugged his shoulders.

"Mama, I'm on the clock, I have to run. But I'll be back," he said, easing backward toward the door.

His mother stood up and chased him down, hugged him, then stepped back and pointed her finger in his face. "Now, son, you be careful out there. Don't be pulling anyone over in a remote area that you can't be seen. I'll be praying for you."

Cara felt panicked. He was really leaving her? With them?

"But—I—" she stuttered, not knowing how to ask him to stay. She'd never been around such openly affectionate women and she didn't know what to say. Or how to act.

He came over and leaned his head to whisper, "I promise their kindness won't kill you. Try not to look so terrified." Then he smiled and waved on his way out. "Mama, I'll be back later. You know what to do."

Then just like that, he was gone. And so was her ride.

His mother rubbed her hands together as she looked at Cara. "So. You want to eat first, or wash that hair?"

"Miss Kim!" Maisy shrieked. "Stop being bossy. Maybe she don't wanna wash that beautiful hair! She's pretty just like she is."

Cara reached up and touched her hair, embarrassed at how greasy it was. Long and mousy brown, it was far from beautiful, and Maisy was generous.

She felt her bladder about to burst and found her words. "It's fine. I know I look a sight. Do you have a public restroom?"

Greg's mother crossed the room to her and took her hand. "Of course we do, honey. But you ain't no stranger now, seeing how my son brought you in and dropped you right in my lap. That kind of makes you like family, doesn't it?"

Family—a word that always made Cara cringe. And tongue-tied. It wasn't just that her family was so screwed up. It was that plus the fact that she'd been diagnosed with a problem in her ovaries when she was nineteen and the doctor had told her she'd never bear children. Ironically, Hana, who always claimed she knew she'd never want to be a mother, didn't share that problem.

"So that settles it. You'll use the guest bathroom. Come on over here, Hana."

Miss Kim led her and Hemi through a door on the far side of the kitchen, into what appeared to be half storeroom and half bedroom. There was another door off of it.

"This is where we put overnighters sometimes," she said, pointing to the room, then a small door on the other side. "And over there is the bathroom. You'll find fresh towels, shampoo, and even some of that smell-good stuff you can use for soap. My Clyde bought it for me last year for Christmas and it makes me itch. But you're welcome to all of it, Hana."

Cara didn't know what to say. "Thank you" didn't seem sufficient. And she still felt a bit unnerved by it all.

Hemi whined and Miss Kim bent down to him. "And you, handsome fella. I got a big, deep sink with your name on it, but don't you worry, after we're through we'll fill that belly up to the top."

Whatever magical words Hemi thought he heard, he obviously understood the food part because he easily followed the woman out of the room. The last thing Cara heard of them as she went into the bathroom and shut the door was the woman telling Hemi his sink was in another building—and that she had to get him out of her kitchen.

Cara hoped she hadn't just seen the last of Hemi, but her concerns immediately evaporated when her attention was captivated by the huge claw-footed tub that took over her vision, beckoning like a lost friend.

Chapter Four

For most of their lives Cara and her sister's height and weight were almost identical. But there was one time that Cara weighed ten pounds less than her sister. It was when they were eleven and had spent the entire year being bounced around from home to home even more than usual. Food was scarce—at least at some of the houses. When it came to slim portions, and almost nonexistent ones, she always gave her share to Hana and pretended she wasn't hungry.

She'd been born three minutes before Hana and that's what big sisters did. They took care of their little sisters.

But right now, in this moment, no living soul could pry the chicken from her hands or the potatoes off her plate. To say it was like manna from heaven was putting it much too mildly. To top it off, she was puckery clean from her long soak and her hair smelled like peaches. Real life, true-to-God peaches. And the tea—good Lord, it was the best sweet tea she'd ever had in her life.

Silently she thanked Patrolman Sanders for doing his Christian duty.

On the floor beside her feet, Hemi was curled up asleep but he looked—and smelled—like a different dog. It was amazing what a bath and haircut could do. His coloring was now almost white and he smelled delicious.

Miss Kim had even rewrapped his paw with a real bandage. Cara had noticed it right away and felt embarrassed at her homemade sock job.

Hemi was being treated like a first-class show dog.

Miss Kim said she'd fed him until he couldn't take anymore. She told Cara he could get up in the booth with her, but Cara declined. Somehow that didn't seem right to let a dog sit at the table others had to eat at later. Not that she'd mind herself, but she was afraid someone would say something, seeing how there were still a few straggling customers coming in for takeout.

Miss Kim sat across from her, hands wrapped around a thick mug of coffee. So far the woman had kept a respectable distance, surprising Cara with her lack of questioning. When Cara had climbed out of the tub and gotten dressed, she'd considered slipping out the back door to avoid what she thought was a sure interrogation waiting for her. But the draw of the fried chicken and mashed potatoes, and of Hemi out there being held hostage by Miss Happy Homemaker, had made her face the music.

And it wasn't half bad.

Literally. The music playing from an iPod was a soothing blend of old Elvis, mixed with some bluesy tunes that she didn't recognize but knew she liked anyway. Cara listened as she finished her second piece of chicken, scraped the last spoonful of potatoes off her plate, and leaned back in her seat. She resisted the urge to let out a long, drawn-out burp, an act that would've been mortifying.

"You got room for a small piece of my peach cobbler, don't you?" Miss Kim asked. "I've got just enough left from today to make a good dessert and I threatened my husband, Clyde, that if he took it, I'd skin him alive."

Cara shook her head slowly. "I sure don't, Miss Kim. I'm so sorry. I can't possibly eat another bite. Can I get it to go?"

"You sure can, honey."

The silence settled between them, then Miss Kim looked up again. "You know, I met a man in here one day a few years ago who was also walking his way across a few states."

"Really?" Cara feigned interest. She doubted his story was similar. Her journey wasn't for fun or any sort of self-discovery.

Miss Kim nodded emphatically. "Really. And he had a lot of equipment, too. Even carried a tent to sleep in when he couldn't find shelter."

"Well, I can't carry a lot of equipment." Cara thought about the blisters on her shoulders, put there from the weight of her backpack. But she really wished she had a tent.

"Oh no, he didn't carry it. He pushed a small cart that held everything. Said it kept the pressure off his knees and legs. Claimed it was a lifesaver."

"A cart would be handy, but I'm sure they're expensive," Cara said. She used her finger to draw circles on the table, thinking of her small budget. She'd taken the time to count out her money after getting dressed, and it was lower than she'd thought. Only two hundred eighty-eight dollars left.

The woman nodded knowingly. "It's getting late. Do you want me to call Greg? He'll swing by and pick you up, take you wherever you need to go."

Cara looked down at the table. She really wasn't ready to hit the road just yet. She was warm. Fed. Clean. And most important, comfortable. All the things most people took for granted but that she hadn't felt in a while.

"Or . . ." Miss Kim trailed off until Cara met her eyes again. "You could stay back there in my guest suite and get you a full night's rest before returning to your adventure."

She let the offer hang in the air, giving Cara time to consider. Underneath the table Hemi let out a long yawn, rearranging his body to face the other direction before he closed his eyes again.

Cara stared out the window, straining to see through the dark. She still remembered the day in court when she and Hana were in the back room waiting for their social worker and the woman popped in with a stranger in tow and introduced them to her.

"As of today, you girls have your own assigned CASA," she'd said.

Hana had been the first to start pelting out questions.

"What do you mean a *casa*?" she'd asked, straightening in her chair to the full height her ten-year-old body would allow.

"The judge has decided that what you two need is an advocate," the woman had said, then gestured to the one she'd called the *casa*. "It's capital *C*, capital *A*, and so forth. And now you have your own Court Appointed Special Advocate. That's what we call a CASA for short. Her name is Melinda Barnwell, but you can call her Ms. Melinda."

Melinda had pulled up a chair and was sitting quietly, watching the conversation take place. Cara had looked at her and when their eyes met, she'd looked away, uninterested in one more person from the courts.

Hana had felt the same way. But much more vocally.

"But I thought *you* were our advocate," she'd said to the tenth or so children's services caseworker to be given their case. It sounded funny to hear the word *advocate* coming from her, but it was a term they were both familiar with after all the dealings they'd had with social services.

"Well, I am your advocate, but I'm not doing this for free. The state pays me and I have to cover many children in addition to you, which is why sometimes you feel you aren't getting the attention you need. This woman," she said, gesturing to Melinda, "she works for free, with just a few cases, and her goal is to speak on your behalf."

Melinda finally reached across the table to shake hands. Cara hadn't wanted to; she didn't trust her any more than she'd trusted the countless others who floated in and out of their lives.

At ten, Cara had had enough of the system, and she felt much older than her actual age. Little had she known then that Melinda would end up being their biggest ally and the one constant in their lives for the next eight years. It was true—Melinda had used every trick in her book to try to get them a good placement, with families who would keep them. But despite her passion they'd never made it to somewhere they could call home.

But she had been there for other things.

It was Melinda who she and Hana had called when they'd both started their periods in the same week and were afraid to tell their latest foster mother.

Melinda had dropped everything to come with an explanation and supplies. And it was Melinda who had bought both of them their first prom dresses, bringing at least a dozen or so over from a secondhand shop for them to choose between.

But annoyingly, it was also Melinda whom Hana had talked to the first time she got her heart broken. Since it was by Cara's boyfriend, obviously Hana wouldn't have talked to her own sister about it. Melinda had first worked to comfort Hana, then brought the two of them together and helped them sort out their first big spat.

She'd also made them promise each other never again to fight over a boy, telling them that boyfriends come and go, but sisters are forever. She'd been the one to come to them weeks before Christmas and ask her and Hana if there were one wish she could grant, what would it be.

Hana had answered immediately, speaking for them both.

"Wish me home," she'd said.

Melinda's eyes had filled with tears and she'd claimed that if she only had that power, she'd honor the wish in a heartbeat.

After that, those little three words became their litany before bed each night, chanted just like Dorothy in *The Wizard of Oz*, as she tapped her heels. Instead of "amen" at the end of their prayers they said, "Wish me home."

Now with just a welcome bath and a meal, and the offer of a warm bed for the night, she thought of Melinda.

Melinda would be older now. A lot older. And she'd given up her volunteer work because she had trouble with her legs, but still, she'd told them she'd always be just a phone call away if she was needed.

Cara replayed the events of the past month and wished suddenly that they had taken her up on her offer, accepted her kindness, even asked for help. Maybe if they had, Cara wouldn't now be a road warrior, sitting in some strange diner about to sleep in an even stranger utility room doing duty as a guest room.

"What do you think, Hana?" Miss Kim said, reminding Cara that she was being deceptive to someone who'd been nothing but kind to her. Still, she couldn't take the chance that anyone was looking for a girl named Cara walking the highways.

It felt like paranoia. But whatever it was, she had to keep it up.

"I think I'll accept your offer," she said, surprising herself with her answer. She was changing. The old Cara would've run away at the first sign of someone offering her something for free. Because she knew from experience, rarely anything ever came free.

❧

Cara burrowed deeper under the old-fashioned quilt, bringing the lace-trimmed sheet close to her face and inhaling the comforting smell of fabric softener—a luxury she and Hana couldn't afford. The delicious clean aroma from the bedding and the sight of the silly granny gown that Miss Kim had loaned her were dizzying.

Hemi lay curled against her legs, the small baby blanket Miss Kim insisted on giving him arranged over his back.

Once she'd agreed to stay a night to rest up, Miss Kim had fluttered around like a mother hen, turning down the bed and showing her how to shut off the lights. She'd offered her a book to read and Cara had told her she had her own, which prompted a whole new conversation about her favorite authors. Cara hadn't admitted anything about Hemingway to the woman, not wanting to leave her any kind of clue about her destination. So she'd named other books she'd enjoyed, some by Jane Austen and Louisa May Alcott, an admission that had made the woman so pleased she rubbed her hands together with glee.

Miss Kim had gone into a diatribe about how these days, young people were far too into ridiculous reality television, with their noses buried in smartphones.

After an hour or so of conversation about the shape of the current generation and their lack of self-motivated creativity, Miss Kim promised her a big breakfast and skirted out the door. Cara was relieved because for a moment there, she'd thought it was going to turn into a *Little House on the Prairie* moment, complete with a tucking into bed and a kiss on the head.

Now she lay restless, exhausted but unable to sleep. It was close to midnight, and she needed to get as many hours of shut-eye as she could, but her mind refused to shut down. Thoughts, fears, and memories swirled together like a hurricane in her head.

Cara was glad to at least have Hemi with her, because it was at night that she missed her sister the most.

She and Hana had slept together through most of their childhood, usually for necessity but admittedly also by choice. They were thirteen the first time they were put into a home that offered them separate bedrooms. They'd immediately declined and the foster father had taken apart one of the twin beds and put it back together in the room with the other, pushing them together to make one big bed. The mother had been disappointed that only one of the two rooms she'd spent so much time fixing up in anticipation of them coming would be used, but Hana had adamantly refused to be separated.

Once they'd gotten over the initial awkwardness, that home hadn't been too bad. The foster mother didn't have any drinking problems or rage issues, and the foster father was quiet but nice. She'd almost started to hope with that one. Even imagined the couple would want to adopt them so their nightmare would be over. But Hana had squashed that dream when she'd caught wind of it, reminding Cara to be loyal to their mother's memory.

Hana had been right. Not eight months into that placement the foster mother got pregnant. At first it wasn't a big deal. They even helped her redecorate the empty room, transforming it into a nursery that most kids could only imagine. By the third trimester of her pregnancy, the couple decided three children were more than they were ready for and, alas, fostering wasn't for them.

Turning over and facing the other way, trying to get comfortable, Cara took a deep breath and pushed that bittersweet memory back down before a sneaky little tear showed up.

Suck it up, Hana would tell her if she were here. *Never let them see you cry.*

There was another time they weren't even given a bedroom to sleep in. That was probably the nastiest place they'd ever been sent to. A double-wide trailer in the country with five state kids already there. She and Hana were told to find a spot wherever they could to sleep. That first night, even the couch was claimed, so they'd curled up together in sleeping bags that smelled like dog urine. The most shocking thing was that two days in, the electricity in the house was shut off. The parents brought in kerosene heaters and the smell had made Cara's head hurt, and Hana had thrown up.

Their CASA, Melinda, had finally made her monthly visit and was outraged at the squalor. She and the foster mother had gone head-to-head, but ultimately there was nothing Melinda could do because a family didn't have to provide electricity or even plumbing to keep their kids. As long as they had food, access to water, and a way to heat the home—in this case by kerosene heaters—then they were in compliance. It didn't matter that it was a stinking hellhole that would make a grown man shudder; the state deemed it appropriate.

Oh how she hated that word—*appropriate.*

She and Hana had gotten a nasty case of head lice there and one night, they swiped a jar of mayonnaise from the pantry, coating each other's hair with it, then covering it with grocery bags. The foster mother had woken up, stumbled into the kitchen, and screamed at them so loudly her rolls of fat moved in waves with every word. Hana had been brave enough to point out the fat-waving phenomenon, almost causing the woman to have an aneurysm.

The state finally determined that that woman had more foster kids than she could handle and removed half of them, including her and Hana.

Cara let out a muffled laugh, making Hemi lift his head and look her way.

"Sorry, Hemi," she said.

The moonlight shone in through the back window and Cara could've sworn that Hemi's eyes looked sad. Suddenly she wondered if, like her, he had been through a lot of homes, never feeling settled or secure.

As though he knew she was thinking of him, Hemi moved up closer to her chest. She reached a hand out and buried it in his fur, and he flipped over on his back, an obvious plea for a belly rub. Cara complied, rubbing little circles on his stomach. She thought it was doing something nice for him, but as she moved her fingers round and round, she realized the soft touch of her hand on his warm, trusting body was helping her to relax. She sighed thankfully as her eyes began to droop, until finally, everything stopped.

Chapter Five

If the banging of pots and pans hadn't woken her, the wafting of fresh bacon frying would have been sure to get her butt moving and out of the bed. Cara sat up, then her feet hit the floor and her eyes reluctantly opened to find Hemi already up and staring intently at her, as though willing her to wake up.

"Okay, okay," she mumbled, rubbing her eyes.

She looked at her watch, then blinked and looked again. Yep, it said just after four in the morning. Were they all crazy?

Another clanging of metal on metal spurred her into the small bathroom, where she'd left her clothes. She rushed over and did her business at the throne, thinking of the many times when she and Hana were little and always seemed to have to go at the same time. They'd run to the bathroom together and both squeeze onto the toilet seat, competing to be the first to finish as they wiggled and giggled, their feet dangling and an arm wrapped around each other.

She pushed the amusing memory from her mind and went to the sink and washed up, noting the dark circles under her eyes. Maisy might not think she was so pretty now.

When she pulled the nightgown over her head, she almost lost her balance when she reached for where she'd left her jeans draped over the towel rack and found them gone. Looking around, she saw that along with everything else she'd had on the day before, the jeans were folded up neatly. A tiny lavender-colored sachet, made of some sort of silk and tied with a drawstring, rested on top of the pile.

Emotion at that act of kindness filled her up. Miss Kim had snuck in—when, Cara couldn't fathom, since she'd been awake until midnight—and taken the clothes and washed them.

Cara picked up the pile and held it to her nose, inhaling the intoxicating lavender scent. Then she quickly dressed, ran a comb through her hair, and brushed her teeth. Finally, she exited the bathroom to find Hemi waiting outside the door. He saw her and whined.

"Oh sorry, I forgot you have a bladder, too," she told him, then led the way to the back door. She opened it and he pranced down the stairs, picked a nearby bush, then proceeded to water it. When he finished, he trotted back up the stairs, his next objective most likely filling his belly.

Once again Cara contemplated making a run for it, especially since she was already outside. But she needed her backpack and, anyway, the aromas were an undeniable pull, slowly reeling her in.

Hemi moved past her and led the way to the kitchen, his posture all business. Cara had no choice but to follow. She opened the door to witness a flurry of flour as Maisy dumped a generous heap out onto the counter. Beside it, Cara could see she'd already been hard at work rolling out dough and cutting out biscuits.

Miss Kim was at the stove, stirring a huge pot. She noticed Cara immediately.

"Well, good morning, sleepy angel," she called out. "How about putting on an apron and helping us get the biscuits onto the pan and into the oven? I'm working on the sausage gravy. The first wave of hungry fellas ought to be here shortly."

Cara lifted her eyebrows. Where all the hungry fellas came from so early was what she wanted to know.

"The aprons are on the hook behind the door," Maisy added, flashing a wide smile. "You'd better hurry. You wouldn't believe how fast Miss Kim goes from sugar to spice if we fall behind schedule."

Cara's feet finally moved. She went to the door and grabbed a yellow flowery apron and tied it on around her clean clothes, then she crossed the room and joined Maisy at the counter.

"You know how to make biscuits, or do you want to stack and cook 'em?" she asked.

"Whatever you want me to do," Cara answered.

Maisy's hands stopped the kneading and she turned and looked at Cara, giving her a stern look. "You mean you know how to make up some biscuits?"

"I do."

Her words earned her a stern look.

Maisy leaned over and whispered. "Child, if I let your hands into my biscuit bowl and you don't know what you're doing, we'll have us a revolt in the dining room in about two hours. So tell me, you know how to make biscuits or not?"

Cara felt a rare moment of pride. She'd made a lot of biscuits over the years, depending on the simple ingredients when nothing else was available in some of the sparse pantries of their placements. She'd made her first batch when she was ten or so, but she'd only gotten better at it over the years. She decided to take a chance and let Maisy know she wasn't the average drifter.

"Move over," she said.

From the other side of the kitchen she caught Miss Kim's glance and saw the wink aimed directly at her. At least one of them had some faith. But there was no time to worry about what Maisy thought. She needed to get busy. She planned on earning that bath and dinner.

And hopefully, breakfast, too.

Cara reached up and felt the colorful bandanna tied around her hair. Maisy had given it to her—pulled it out of her pocket and told her to get it secured over her head before putting her hands in her dough.

Cara couldn't believe how much she'd enjoyed the morning and how fast six hours had gone by. It was just after ten and working together, they'd served nearly a hundred customers, most of them working men stopping by on their way to a blue-collar job. She saw crews from an electric company, mechanics, and all other sorts of uniforms walk through the door, most of them friendly but respectful. But whoa—what a lot of work it was to serve up a hearty Southern breakfast to so many hungry mouths.

Cara didn't see how the two women did it alone every day, as all three of them had worked as hard and quickly as possible to keep everyone happy.

"Sit down, Hana," Miss Kim called out from the corner table.

Maisy waved at her, telling her to hurry before they had to start preparing for the lunch crowd.

Lunch? They'd just finished with breakfast and already they were talking about lunch? She had no idea how they'd accomplish such a big switch. The kitchen looked like a cyclone had hit it. But she headed over to them, grateful to see three heaping plates full of the goodies they'd been serving all morning.

Cara had nibbled here and there, just to keep her stomach's growling to a minimum, but a full serving of everything was exactly what she needed. She sat down across from the two women and picked up her fork. From the other corner of the room, Hemi rose from his designated spot on a folded blanket Miss Kim had laid down, and he came over and curled up under Cara's feet.

"Do you mind if I say the blessing?" Miss Kim asked.

Cara laid her fork back down and bowed her head. She didn't care what they said as long as they hurried. She wasn't sure what kind of religion they followed, but she hoped it was one that prayed fast.

Miss Kim said her prayer in a breathy voice, so low that Cara could barely hear her. But she did catch mentions of keeping her safe on her journey and the speedy healing of Hemi's paw. When she said, "amen," they all dug in at the same time.

As she ate, Cara watched Maisy's plate. One of the biscuits that lay on top of it was less than perfectly shaped and obviously Cara's own handiwork. She said her own small prayer that the old woman would think her skills worthy of the confidence she'd shown by letting Cara take her place. None of the customers had complained, but the real test was in Maisy. First, though, she nibbled at the bacon. Then she ate a few spoonfuls of the buttery grits. Finally, when Cara thought she couldn't take it anymore, Maisy picked up a biscuit and bit into it.

She chewed slowly, a funny look on her face. Then Maisy leaned her head back and let out a long, loud trail of laughter. "I just don't believe it! This here biscuit's good, I tell you. It's good! And from a young'un, no less! You've got to tell me your secret."

Cara laughed at the incredulous look on Maisy's face. She could find herself becoming real attached to a personality like that. The relief that flooded through her was immense, though she had no idea why. She'd say good-bye to these people today, and why should she care what they thought?

But she did.

She smiled at Maisy. "No big secrets. I take care not to touch them too much—just barely mixing it before I roll it out."

Maisy bobbed her head up and down. "Making biscuits is just like being in a relationship. It's never good to be too kneady."

Cara laughed. "And I was glad to see you use White Lily flour. It's really the only flour that I've found makes good biscuits."

"I know that's right." Maisy bobbed her head up and down some more. "Some of these fancy chefs say the type of flour *don't matter*. Don't matter to who? That's what I should ask. Those fools are all over the cooking shows, and now they're making up recipes for low-fat yogurt biscuits. Now you tell me—who in their right mind is gonna want to eat a low-fat yogurt biscuit? That sounds God awful to me."

Cara laughed. "I agree. I want my biscuits dripping with calories. Bring on all the fat I can—every gram tickles another taste bud."

"I knew you could do it," Miss Kim said softly, daintily adding a generous smattering of butter to her own biscuit. She took a bite, chewing with a smug look on her face.

"One more thing. You always want to lay your biscuits on a pan with the sides touching. They're like good friends. They help each other rise up," Maisy said, then smiled at Miss Kim.

Cara didn't reply to that one. She'd never actually had a good friend other than Hana, and she sure wasn't going to start a conversation about her sister.

They all dug into eating, aware that the clock was ticking. Cara began wondering how to bring up that she needed to hit the road soon. Daylight was wasting and though it had been fun, she couldn't stay to help with lunch.

Maisy got up, taking her empty plate with her. "I'll go check on the BBQ. Today's gonna be easy. I love pulled pork and slaw menu days. I can almost do my work with my eyes closed."

"Thanks, Maisy. I'll be in there shortly," Miss Kim said, putting her fork down and wiping her mouth.

Cara picked up her biscuit, sopping up the last bit of gravy before she popped it in her mouth. She had to admit, it was the best sausage gravy she'd ever had. She could feel Miss Kim's eyes on her and felt a lecture was coming. Sure enough, when Cara swallowed the last bite and washed it down with her orange juice, Miss Kim made her move.

"If you'd like, you can stay on here for a while. Get yourself back on your feet. I'll give you room and board, and throw in a few bucks an hour. You keep whatever tips you earn."

Cara swallowed. She sure didn't want to hurt the woman's feelings. And truthfully, she could see herself staying on, if only to bask in the sweet Southern hospitality the restaurant seemed to be steeped in. But she couldn't. Staying wouldn't be right after they'd been so kind to her. She'd bring them nothing but trouble and she couldn't have that on her conscience.

She had to go.

"Miss Kim, I can't tell you how grateful I am. For everything. The bath, the bed, breakfast—and you even washed my clothes! Thank you for it all. But I can't stay."

She nodded solemnly. "I could tell by the look in your eyes when I first saw you that you'd be moving on fast, but I wanted to at least offer."

"Again, thank you so much. We—me and Hemi—we're so grateful." Cara looked down at Hemi, as though expecting him to chime in. But he was napping. His full belly had put him into a food coma.

Miss Kim stood. "Well, then, since you are insisting on continuing this road trip, I have a gift for you. Actually, it's from me and Clyde."

"I can't accept anything else from you, really—"

Miss Kim held her hand up. "Yes, you can. And you will. I know you didn't get a chance to meet my Clyde yet, but I told him about you. And I told him about this thing you're doing—traveling with your dog. You thought I was the one who gave him a bath, haircut, and wrapped his foot, but it wasn't me. It was Clyde. He's a big man with an even bigger heart of gold. He stayed up half the night working on something for you and I think he's ready for you to see it."

Cara didn't know what to say. She was astonished. Were these people for real? Why were they doing all this? For her?

"Come on, follow me," Miss Kim said, leading her out the front door.

Hemi got up and followed them out. They went around the side of the building and over to a garage. It was full of tools and all the things that reminded Cara of the car she'd left behind in need of repairs.

"Clyde?" Miss Kim called out.

From around the corner of a rusty old truck, an older man with a gray beard appeared, pushing a bicycle with some sort of trailer attached. He came all the way to them before he stopped. He nodded at Hemi first.

"Hey, buddy," he said.

Hemi's tail wagged and Clyde pushed the kickstand down with his foot, then knelt in front of the dog. "So you ain't mad at me no more for cleaning that paw?"

More tail wagging.

"Yeah, that's what I thought. And I know why, too." He stood and reached in his shirt pocket, pulling out a long piece of jerky. He tore an inch or so off and gave it to Hemi, who scarfed it down in one bite. "Deer jerky. The dogs love it."

"Come on, Clyde. Tell her what you got there. This girl is itching to get back on the road and your own dogs need feeding. I'm sure they can smell that jerky all the way from behind the house, and pretty soon they'll be trying to dig out from under those blasted kennels."

Cara was confused. Why was he pushing a bike?

Clyde looked at Cara and his face reddened. Cara could tell immediately that he was the quiet part of the couple—that words didn't come easily to him like they did his wife. There'd been other men in her life like him, some of them foster fathers. Even some really good ones. Just none that had ever stuck.

"This here bike and trailer is for you," he said. "I mean—you do know how to ride a bike, don't ya?"

Miss Kim laughed. "Of course she can ride a bike, Clyde. Do you know anyone her age who can't?"

Cara didn't say anything at first because she and Hana hadn't learned how to ride a bike until much later than other kids. They'd just never had anyone in their lives who cared enough to teach them. Finally, when they'd gotten hold of an abandoned bike left at the school basketball court, they'd taught each other. After multiple circles around the paved court, taking turns running behind as they supported each other, they'd returned to the house they were staying at bruised, bloody, but triumphant that they no longer had to feel ashamed they couldn't ride. But she set that memory aside, since it wouldn't help her figure out what was happening here, at this moment.

"I'm sorry, I don't understand," she finally said.

"What's not to understand, Hana? Greg abandoned the bike here years ago when he moved on to the next hobby. It's old, but it's made of good stuff. Clyde here worked late last night putting new tires on it and fixing up that homemade trailer for your equipment," Miss Kim said.

"And for the dog," Clyde said, his gaze on Hemi.

"The dog?" Cara still felt confused. Were they going to ask her to buy the bike? She was almost broke and what she did have left needed to go for food.

"Right," Clyde said. He pointed at the wooden base under the canopy. There was a small pillow there, some sort of pad that looked like it had come from a dog bed. "I made the trailer with a low center of gravity, and a wide wheelbase to make it stronger and keep the wheels from snagging on obstacles. The pad here is for Hemi. You can pull it out and let him lay on it when you camp, but missy, you be careful where you decide to lay that head."

His voice went from scolding back to helpful in two seconds flat.

"I put a canopy over everything so if it rains, he don't get wet. But there's still adequate ventilation and if you want, you can peel it back further and attach it with that little hook. You need to let that dog walk some every day, but not overdo it until that paw is healed completely. And don't forget, hot sidewalks and highways burn the bottoms of dog's feet just like they do ours. Keep him to the grass if you can."

He paused for a moment, then went to saddlebags at the back of the bike. Cara still wasn't over the cool canopy he'd made, a trick that reminded her of covered wagons back in pioneer days. He pointed at the bags. "These here are a bit ragged but should hold everything you've got in that heavy backpack of yours eventually. For now they're filled with food—Miss Kim couldn't resist."

Cara couldn't believe the thought the man had put into everything. And Miss Kim, she had so many little sneaky tricks. Cara had never met people like him and his wife before. Surely they couldn't be *giving* her the bike and trailer. She reached into her pocket, pulling out her money pouch.

"I only have a few hundred and I need some for food," she began, unzipping the pouch. "But you can take the rest—"

"You put that money back in your pocket, little miss," Clyde said gruffly, finally looking her in the eye. "This here stuff is a gift. We don't aim to take anything for it."

Miss Kim clapped her hands together and began to gleefully tell her all the things she'd put in the bags. "Peanut butter and crackers. Pop-Tarts, dried fruit, trail mix, some dog food for Hemi—oh, and Clyde, tell Hana about the tent!"

Clyde pointed to the back of the trailer at a small blue bundle. "It's the tent that Greg used in Boy Scouts. It might have a hole or two, but it's yours. I also put an atlas underneath it. Can't get anywhere if you don't know where you're going, and as far as I know, you probably don't have one. If you want a piece of advice, stay off the interstates and keep to the four lanes and small roads. Highway One is only a few miles from here. I suggest you take this here bike around the lot once or twice before you load the dog up. Make sure you can handle it all right."

Cara couldn't help it. The dam she'd spent years building against all the hurts and resentments—the emotional barricade that both she and Hana had constructed—it threatened to fall. She swallowed once. Then again.

Finally when she felt she had it under control, she looked up.

"Thank you," she said softly. "Thank you so much. And I'm sorry I lied. My name isn't Hana—it's Cara."

Miss Kim came close and hugged her.

"Oh, honey. Don't you know that it isn't your name that makes you so precious? It's that sweet spirit of yours that is shining right out of those hazel eyes. We can call you George if it makes you feel any better. We just want you to know there are people out there who care." Over the woman's shoulder she saw Clyde and the first inkling of a smile peeking up over the top of his bushy beard.

He nodded once, then turned and rambled back into his shop.

Chapter Six

Cara lifted her chin, breathing deeply to inhale the suddenly salty breeze. Georgia was finally behind her and despite the soreness from using muscles she'd never even known she had, they'd made it. Not to their final destination, but to something almost as good—a place on her bucket list.

All her life she'd lived in a state that boasted a coastline, yet it was an embarrassment that at her age, she'd never seen the ocean. She and Hana had always been placed hundreds of miles away from the beach, and most of the foster families that they'd lived with could barely afford groceries, much less vacations. The few who could didn't offer to take them. When she was a child, the beach and the rolling sea were up there with the Tooth Fairy or Santa Claus, something you hoped was real but were resigned to probably never seeing.

When she and Hana were seniors in high school, they'd talked about sneaking off to join some of their classmates on spring break at this beach or that one, but they never had any money to pay their way or to outfit themselves in cute summer shorts or swimsuits like the other girls did. So time went on, and for a long time they forgot about seeing the ocean. Then one day the subject came up and they made a pact. They'd save money and go together once they were out of state care.

When they did finally become emancipated and moved into their first apartment, they set up a money jar, planning for the moment they would take their first vacation. Each of them added to it when they could, a dollar here and there, letting it accumulate in the hopes that one day their beach trip would be more than a dream. But the jar always seemed to be emptied for other things—small emergencies that their paltry paychecks couldn't cover.

But finally, for Cara, the long-awaited day had come. Unfortunately, Hana wasn't there to share it. She turned her head to the side so that Hemi could hear her. "Have you ever seen the ocean, Hemi?"

His silence was an answer she took as no, and she smiled at the realization that at least they would see it for the first time together. If it couldn't be Hana, she was glad to at least have Hemi beside her.

She was so close now that she could smell the salty ocean spray, feel the crispness against her face.

They'd left Miss Kim and Clyde behind in Georgia when they'd crossed into Florida. She'd thought briefly about the implications of crossing that state line, but she'd pushed the thought away and, as she moved farther south, she felt closer to Hemingway with every mile.

The first day on the bike had been a bit shaky but Hemi had believed in her, his proud posture showing full confidence that she wouldn't turn them both over. She took it really slow that day, stopping after only three hours. When she'd realized how many more miles she could cover on the bike than on foot, she'd felt a sense of exhilaration that helped her push through her fatigue and made her move faster the next morning.

She smiled at the muscles she could feel building throughout her legs and arms. She was a cycling machine!

But even Wonder Woman had to stop sometimes.

Getting to Key West was her overall focus now, but for the time being, the beach was calling her name and a slight detour would be well worth the effort.

Amelia Island was a place she'd heard of and though it was now gaining a reputation as a resort island, she also knew it boasted many Victorian mansions. She hoped she'd be able to ride by them without any issues, just to look. Most of them had been converted into bed-and-breakfasts, and Cara wished she had the funds to stay in one for just a night. To sleep in a historical room, probably in a huge Victorian bed, now *that* would be something to remember. However, she was glad just to get a chance to finally see the beach. According to the atlas, there were thirteen miles of beach in Amelia Island, so hopefully she'd find an out-of-the-way place to pitch her tent for the night.

At the top of the bridge to the island, she pedaled harder, finding a new reserve of strength as she tackled it. She'd learned that giving it her all to get up an incline always meant that she could relax going down.

Once off the bridge, Cara passed a wooden sign: Welcome to Amelia Island, Home of Historic Fernandina Beach.

She felt a sense of satisfaction as she slowed to an easy pace, taking in the scenery. She especially noticed the towering live oaks that lined the road, their gigantic limbs stretched wide and dripping with moss, as though they stood there ready to welcome her in.

To her left she saw a marina, the waters and parking lot around it lined with boats of all shapes and sizes, their masts and sails waving in the wind as they waited to be crewed onto the ocean waters. Around the marina was a tall metal fence, complete with gates—a hint that she wouldn't be able to get to the water from there.

She continued on and turned down a side street, then another, before spotting a patch of blue in the distance. First it appeared to be the sky, but after she stared a moment while pedaling, Cara realized it was water.

She pedaled harder.

A half mile later, she saw a sign that read Main Beach Park. "I see it, Hemi," she called out, pedaling faster.

A few more turns and she was as close as she could get with the bike and trailer. She found a small lane, bicycles parked on either side, and maneuvered hers into a long space in front of the overgrown beach-access path.

Hemi jumped down before she'd even given him the command, and she shot him a scolding look.

"You're as excited as me, I know, so I'll cut you some slack this time."

She grabbed her bag and headed up the path, trying to see over the tall tufts of dune grass that separated the beach from the road. She stepped onto the wooden boardwalk and Hemi followed, his nose twitching at the smell of the sea.

When finally she was over the hill, she stopped at the edge of the boardwalk and relished the warm and surprisingly strong breeze that caressed her face. As far as Cara could see there was water and sand. It was the most beautiful, peaceful thing she'd ever laid eyes on. She felt a wave of sadness that Hana wasn't there to experience it with her, but Hemi snapped her out of it when he let out a joyous bark and took off toward the water.

Now she followed him, eager to feel the sand under her feet. When she stepped onto the beach, Cara dropped her bag, then sat to peel off her shoes and socks. She rolled her jeans up, then took off after Hemi.

She found herself laughing as they played, finding a simple joy in Hemi's attempt to bite at each incoming wave, then jump back when it didn't retreat. The water was cool, tickling at her feet as she moved. Cara couldn't believe it had taken her so long to experience such an amazing feat of nature.

When she tired, she went back to her backpack and sat down, her arms wrapped around her knees as she stared out over the ocean. Hemi finally wore down and joined her, sighing his happiness before curling up and closing his eyes.

Cara stared for a few more minutes, her mind wandering as she took in the irony of her situation. Most of her life she'd been monitored, the state knowing everything about her: where she lived, what her health was, even how she did in school. After that, she and Hana were still connected at the hip, one never making a move without the other.

But now she was sitting there staring out at the huge sea, letting the sounds of the surf lull her senses, and not a single soul in the entire world knew where she was.

It felt freeing.

And it also felt lonely.

She looked down at Hemi and was thankful that she at least had him. For a while, anyway. Sighing, not sure suddenly if she was happy or sad, she laid back, using her bag as a pillow. She'd just close her eyes for a minute, though the comforting caress of the ocean breeze on her skin easily lulled her to sleep.

When she awoke a half hour later to the sound of Hemi growling and a jolt from under her head, she was disoriented.

She sat up and looked straight into the wild eyes of a shirtless and shoeless man pulling on her bag. With one glance she could tell he was homeless, his scraggly hair standing on end and his jeans soiled, ragged at the bottoms. But he was strong, she'd give him that. He almost had her bag out from under her head.

"Hey! Stop it!" she shouted, grabbing the handle and holding on.

Hemi growled again and snapped, coming dangerously close to the man's hand. Cara put an arm out to hold Hemi back and yanked her bag free.

The man laughed, throwing his hands in the air before he sauntered away.

Cara watched him go but she was shaking. She looked around and saw the beach was nearly deserted. The experience could've been much worse, and once again she was glad for Hemi's protection.

Then she realized if they were going to get to their next destination before dark, they had to roll. The state park was eight miles away, and that was where she planned to spend the night before jumping back on the A1A to finish her trek to the Keys.

⁓❧⁓

Despite hurrying, they'd barely made it to the state park before dark.

Once there, it had taken only minutes for her to find a place to park her bike, and she'd chosen one of the last sites anyone else would've wanted. No picnic table, no electric hookups, just a small hollowed-out area between a trio of trees. She'd been drawn to it because though there were plenty of other campers with trucks, tents, and even small mobile trailers, the small indention she'd chosen was easily overlooked. That meant it was also her best bet for leaving her bike while she trotted to the bathhouse. Her stomach growled angrily, reminding her that she was starving, but Cara couldn't even think about digging into her meager staples until she was clean.

But she did work quickly to set up the small tent, so that when she returned, she wouldn't just get dirty again trying to get her site sleep ready. It hadn't taken long—she'd become a pro at getting the ancient thing to prop up just right. When it was set, the bedding laid out, and she'd moved most of her food inside—as meager and unappealing as it had become with the delicious smell of dinner being grilled all around her—she looked around once more. It felt safe enough, so they headed to the bathhouse.

"Hemi, you stay right here." She tied him to a post outside the ladies' side of the big green building. She'd found the rope coiled up on the sand just before she'd left the beach and snatched it up, thinking it would be a good leash if she was in a bind. Now, she was thankfully going to get her first shower in a few days, but she hoped he would be fine out there without her.

He whined and she gave him one last look before slipping through the door.

Only one shower stall out of the six was in use and she slid into the one closest to the door, wanting to stay as near to Hemi as possible. She'd not left him tied alone since they'd met and she wasn't exactly sure how he'd take it.

She set her backpack on the bench that was conveniently located at the far side of the shower and turned to the faucet. It wouldn't be a long, luxurious soak, but as she turned the water on to test the temperature before undressing, she looked forward to washing the road out of her hair.

The pipes let out a loud sound, causing Cara to jump before she realized it wasn't the pipes. She turned the water off, thankful that she hadn't yet gotten undressed, and she stepped out of the stall. As soon as she turned the corner and was back outside, Hemi stopped midhowl and his tail took off like a rocket in a wagging frenzy.

"Hemi, you can't be howling," she said, bending down in front of him. She looked around and saw a family eating their dinner at their campsite, the kids watching her every move. Embarrassed, she gave them a little wave, then hissed at Hemi. "I'm just going to take a shower and dogs aren't allowed in there."

She stood and started backing up toward the door, watching him. But as she slipped around the concrete wall, out of sight, he howled again. It was an awful, anguished kind of howl, too. The kind that would bring on too much attention for Cara's taste.

"Fine." She went back to him, untied the rope, and led him into the bathhouse. What were they going to do? Throw them out? If so, she'd at least get a shower first.

Hemi was happy and she took him to the stall where she'd left her bag. Thankfully, it was still there. She pointed at the bench and without a single verbal command, he hopped up and sat by the bag.

"You're something else," she mumbled, then pulled her shampoo from the bag. She slipped out of her shoes and clothes, working fast to finish before someone reported her. She turned the handles and couldn't help but release a sigh of pleasure when the hot water ran down her neck and back. She would've loved to take her time, even shave her legs if she had a razor, but the bathhouse felt a bit creepy, so she washed her hair and used the runoff lather to clean her body, then rinsed quickly. She peeked through her eyelashes once, checking to be sure Hemi was still there, and she smiled to see he was watching her with a stern expression, as though someone had placed him on guard and he was taking it seriously.

In what had to be less than four minutes, she reached over and turned the faucet off, then wrung the water from her hair. Using the one towel Miss Kim had slipped into her stuff, she dried her body, then wrapped it around her wet hair. Faster than anyone would think possible, she dressed in her only clean clothes and slipped her shoes onto her bare feet.

"Come on, Hemi." She tucked the shampoo bottle into her bag, then grabbed it and her dirty clothes, carrying it all to the long row of sinks and mirrors. She felt relief to see all six of the toilet stalls now stood empty.

Putting the bag on the counter, she dropped the dirty socks and other clothes into the sink, added a generous dab of hand soap, then filled it with hot water.

Hemi sat at her feet and, ignoring the rumbling of her stomach and the fatigue that plagued every muscle of her body, she worked hard, first swirling the clothes round and round, then using the legs of the jeans against each other to work out the dirt.

When she felt she'd done all she could to make them wearable, she let the water out, then ran clean water, rinsing each article a few times until no more suds showed. Finally, when she felt her arms would give out, she finished wringing them out and gathered them all up. She reached for her bag and, balancing it all away from her body, signaled Hemi that she was ready, and they left the bathhouse.

Outside the smell of grilled food from every direction assaulted her senses, making her realize once again how alone she was. She tried not to hear the sounds of family around her, keeping her eyes to the ground as they walked. She needed no more reminders of all she'd lost.

"Do your business, Hemi," she said as she worked to arrange her wet clothes over the canopy of the bike trailer. She was tired. All she wanted to do was feed Hemi, then eat enough peanut butter and crackers to appease her hunger and go to sleep.

Finally she was done and she turned, calling Hemi in. He'd gone sniffing around their site, straying just far enough to make her nervous, but he trotted over at her voice.

"Bedtime." She was grateful for the flashlight and she got down and crawled into the tent. Her eyes got big when the first thing she saw was a small white plastic bag, the type groceries were usually packed in.

Hemi wiggled in and around her, going to the bag and sniffing it. His tail wagged and he looked at Cara.

"Is that your sign for it's safe to look?" she asked.

She could still smell grilled food. But this time it was close.

Really close.

Ignoring her cautious side, she grabbed the bag, quickly untying the knot. Inside was not one, not two, but three foil-wrapped hot dogs. She held one to her nose and inhaled, suspicious even as she silently thanked the anonymous donor. She thought of the old fairy tale, the one where hunger enticed the two children to disregard their own safety, then she pushed her morbid thoughts away. This was the new Cara— the one who was learning to trust people, she told herself.

Hemi looked at her, his expression pleading.

"Well, duh," Cara answered him. "Of course I am going to eat it and of course I am going to share."

She unwrapped the first one and found it conveniently void of any condiments. She said a prayer that her good luck would hold and they wouldn't be poisoned, then handed the entire thing, bun and all, to Hemi. He immediately wolfed it down.

"Slow down there, buddy."

Opening the next one and seeing it piled high with a spicy-smelling chili, she fought her instinct to consume it as fast as Hemi did his, and instead took it slow, taking time to experience the delicious charcoal taste and the welcome sting of the spicy chili. She grabbed at her bottle of water, drinking from it to wash everything down.

When neither she nor Hemi began rolling on the ground in agony from being poisoned, she pulled the third and last one from the bag. When the foil was unwrapped, she smiled to see it was laden with mustard and ketchup only, and surmised that they must have played it safe for every taste. What they didn't understand is that she would've probably eaten them even if they'd peppered squirrel doo on top as a condiment.

But she was glad they hadn't.

Hemi whined and Cara laughed at his misery, then tore the hot dog in half. She gave him one piece, then slowly savored her own.

When she was done, she poured Hemi some water and watched him finish it off. Satisfied at the surprise treat of a hot supper, he sighed, then curled up on his pad, immediately closing his eyes.

Cara crawled under her blanket and lay back, crossing her arms over her chest. She planned to get up really early in the morning and be on the road by sunrise. Tomorrow was going to be a big day—one she'd looked forward to for a long time.

She had to admit, she was proud of herself. She was making progress, moving along and even surviving. And if her sister had been here, she knew this would be one of those times that she would have needed to remind Hana that there just might be a few good people left in the world.

Chapter Seven

For the most part, she and Hana saw the same few judges throughout their time in foster care. Every time they were pulled from a home, they also had to go through a series of court proceedings to determine why the placement didn't work out and what the next best option was for them. Their first judge, a stern woman named Judge Freeman, kept their case for eight years. Usually when they arrived for their court appointments they were put into a room with a sitter—some lower-level employee from social services—while their caseworker presented her latest findings or recommendations, because they were deemed too young to have any say in their own lives. But one afternoon the judge asked to speak to them directly in her chambers.

Cara was worried but Hana stomped in there as though she'd been waiting for the chance to speak her mind.

And speak her mind she did.

The judge began the conversation with a long sigh and the phrase "What am I going to do with you two?" but Hana had finished it with a litany of things she insisted they *weren't* going to do anymore.

Cara smiled, remembering how Hana had stood up and put her hands on her skinny hips, then began her demands to the judge: No more placements without electricity and definitely no more with head lice. No foster mothers with mental problems and no foster fathers with roving eyes. She also wanted a contract drawn up with families saying that she and Cara didn't mind doing their share but weren't there to be free labor while everyone else in the house got fat and lazy.

Even the judge had snickered at that one, but Cara had cringed, thinking they were going to be sent to reform school because of Hana's outburst.

By the time her sister was through, the judge was no longer sitting there all smiles and parental. She'd moved her gaze over to the state social worker and was shooting her a glare of accusation. She pointed her finger at her and said only one more thing, slowly and methodically, before excusing them from her chambers.

"You. Do. Better. For. These. Girls."

And the social worker *had* done better.

At least for a while.

Their next placement was decent—maybe even comfortable. And because of that, Cara was proud of her sister for standing up for them, telling her that it was her bravery that had gotten them to a better place. And it could be a good fit, she'd told Hana over and over, trying to get her to open her heart to the possibility that maybe this once, it would work.

Joan and Harry, as the couple told them to call them, weren't young and they weren't old. Joan had never had biological children, and it was one of those things that made you wonder about why the universe could be so cruel. Upstairs, in the bedroom next to the one she and Hana shared, was a nursery that could rival any ever dreamed up. To this day Cara remembered the vivid colors of the animals and jungle scene painted on the wall, the shelves lined with stacks of diapers and other baby things, all untouched. It was obvious that the two wanted children and had tried desperately to have their own before deciding to be foster parents.

Cara remembered that Joan was a kindergarten teacher and Harry a fireman. They had a white dog named Max that was so tiny he looked like a toy. They would've given Cara and Hana a home full of love and nurturing.

But Hana had refused to listen. For her, it could only be temporary. Back then she clung to loyalty for their mother and her mind was closed to everything and anyone else. Cara was loyal, too—at least she thought she was—but wouldn't their mother have wanted them to stop bouncing from place to place? Wouldn't she rather have them placed permanently with people who would care for them, emotionally and physically?

One night Joan and Harry had sat them down and asked the question: "Would you like us to be your forever family?"

Cara remembered that moment vividly. Her heart had soared at the hope of something permanent, of a *forever* home, as those in the system called it. But before she could even form a reply, Hana had answered for them both.

The disappointed look on the faces of the foster mother and father was something Cara would always remember. It wasn't immediately after that bombshell, but eventually, that the placement ended. Cara couldn't remember what the official reason was. Not long after, they'd also been appointed a new state caseworker, a woman who told them in their first meeting that she was inheriting more than her share of caseloads and they'd better not cause her any extra grief because she didn't have the time or patience for it.

Cara just couldn't understand why every placement interruption was always deemed their fault. Nor could she understand why now all these memories were flooding back when she'd buried them years before. She didn't want to give any more of her thoughts to them. Ever.

"Just go away already," she said crossly, causing Hemi to look up at her as though asking what her problem was. "Not you, buddy."

Hemi whined and Cara fed him a bite of tortilla. Miss Kim must have used magical powers or something because she'd pulled off a miracle with the amount of food she'd stuffed in the tight saddlebags. Tonight was peanut butter and jelly on tortillas, a delicacy she'd never thought to try.

She stood up, stretching her back. Amelia Island was far behind them, as she and Hemi had made some good time in the past few days. He was a worthy partner, and the few times her spirits had fallen and she felt like giving up, it took only one look from his dark eyes and she would trudge on, determined to fulfill her promise to him.

They'd stopped for the night in a small town outside of Jacksonville, and her chosen campground was behind what appeared to be a school gym. It was Saturday so she figured she'd be in and out before anyone noticed. Her tent was already up and the yoga mat she'd picked up at a yard sale was arranged next to Hemi's small mat inside. Cara scoped the area out well enough and found no one near. She was eager to get to bed—looking forward to resting her calves.

She went to her bag and pulled out the book that Miss Kim had snuck in there. She cast her eyes down, letting them fall on Maisy's bandanna, which she'd tied around her wrist that morning.

Maisy and Miss Kim. She smiled, lingering over the memory.

"Hemi, if you want to pee, do it now. I'm about to zip us in."

The dog slowly stood, then took his time to stretch first before easing over to a small bush. He lifted his leg so high and whizzed so long that Cara thought he was going to fall over on his head. She laughed and he shot her a grumpy look, then returned to the tent. She let him go in first and he went to his pad and curled up. She pulled the zipper, closing them in for the night, before covering him with his blanket and getting underneath her own.

She opened the cover to *Pride and Prejudice* and read the inscription, feeling a flood of warmth at Miss Kim's flowery handwriting: "Jane Austen said she must learn to be content with being happier than she deserved. I believe the adage might pertain to you, too. Find your peace. Love, Miss Kim."

The book was obviously used, its dog-eared pages flipped so many times that it bragged several yellow fingertip-shaped stains. But Cara wouldn't have wanted a fresh, brand-spanking-new book. To know that Miss Kim had given her something that was probably special to her, and had been in her possession for years—that meant something. And of course, Cara could never love any book as much as she did her Hemingway, but it could come close.

She snuggled closer to Hemi and pointed the flashlight toward the page where she'd left off the night before. She'd give Jane a few hours tonight, but she planned to get back to Hemingway as soon as possible.

Chapter Eight

Cara breathed in, closing her eyes, almost in rapture, as the smell of the sea found its way into her path again. She pedaled harder, losing herself in the rhythm, proud that these days she and the bike were starting to feel like one. She was a bit tired, but not so much so that it was affecting her stride. It had been a long day and she'd packed in a lot of miles, but it wasn't nearly over. She was determined to make it to St. Augustine before nightfall.

It took all she had, but Cara finally crested the top of the bridge, then warned Hemi as they picked up speed going down the bike path on the other side. To his credit, he'd learned to hunker down when she gave the warning. Along their journey, she'd noticed that many of Florida's bridges offered only the narrowest of shoulders for bikes or pedestrians. She'd had more than her share of tense moments, imagining a strong wind lifting them off the bridge and sending them to their deaths below.

She should've been paying closer attention. She'd taken her eyes off the path in front of her only for a millisecond, so she didn't know how, but suddenly there were a mother and two children on it, walking straight toward her.

If she'd had a horn, she would've laid on it. The mother had stopped and was preoccupied with tying the shoe of the smaller child. The other one, a girl of about nine or so, was standing there with her mouth agape, staring at Cara barreling toward them. While not close enough to hear, she could see the girl mouthing the word *mama* over and over, trying to get the woman's attention.

The seconds felt like they were passing in slow motion and Cara said a prayer under her breath that she wouldn't maim a child or hurt Hemi, and just before she twisted the handlebars to the right, she thought to scream.

At the almost animal-like howl, the woman looked up and her shriek joined Cara's. In a superhuman reflex that only a mother could have, her hands shot down to both her children and jerked them off the path. But it was too late for Cara and Hemi. Luckily they'd already cleared the bridge, but unluckily the fast descent and jerky movements had sent the bicycle out of control.

Cara tried to bring the bike back under control, but she couldn't. She pumped the brakes but nothing happened. They skimmed a few bushes, then the bike went airborne when she hit a railroad tie set out as a flower border. The trailer hit next, just as the bike was coming down, and the two separated. Cara was catapulted over the handlebars and she caught the blur of Hemi's colorful fur flying by her peripheral view.

He didn't even have time to yelp.

She didn't get to see Hemi's landing because she was flying through the air. She remembered thinking that she should invest in a helmet. Her next thought was of Hemi, but then everything went black.

⚜

Cara tried to turn over, but the pain in her shoulder stopped her midway. She inhaled sharply, then, eyes still closed and somewhere between awake and dreaming, she relaxed and settled back into the old memory.

"I'll count to one hundred and you girls hide, then I'll come find you," their mother had said one too many times. On one of those nights when Cara and Hana had slipped behind the stack of trash cans in their overgrown yard to wait for Mama to find them, they'd witnessed a man drive up, get out, and go into their house.

Hana had wanted to go in after him, but Cara had held her arm and convinced her to wait until he left, just like Mama had told them. The man wasn't just any one of their mother's friends—their house always had a lot of coming and going. This man—he was the only one that Mama had specifically warned them about. She'd told them if he came through the door, they were to stay out of sight. So that's what they'd done, even though it felt like an eternity before he'd finally emerged and left.

She and Hana had rushed inside, anxious to see if everything was okay with their mother and eager to tell her they'd remembered to stay out of sight.

That was one night that I wished I'd disobeyed.

Cara heard the sound of running water, then dishes being handled. She blinked, trying to clear her eyes. She wasn't a little girl anymore, hiding in the dark. But where was she?

She looked around, her gaze settling on the small kitchen area. At the sink, a woman dropped something metal. A fork, a spoon, or something that rang out, finally startling Cara out of the fog. She focused on the woman's back and the long, dark hair that framed it. She could've easily been her mother.

No wonder I've been thrown back into my childhood memories, Cara thought.

"She's awake, Mama," a voice called out, sending a thunderbolt of pain through Cara's head.

The woman turned and crossed the room. She was not much older than Cara, and the shiny hoop earrings she wore caught a glint of light and Cara cringed again.

"Well, hello there again," the woman said. "You drifted off to sleep after I bandaged your hands. You feeling better?"

Cara stared at her, confused. She struggled to sit up. She remembered the young woman leading her down a sidewalk. Before that, she was on the bike and climbing the bridge, cresting it and feeling the wind in her hair and then—oh yeah, then she'd seen them and had to jump the path, hitting a tree. The woman had helped her up and brought her home to wash her wounds out. Cara had sat down on the couch, intending to lay her head down for just a second.

"Where's my dog?" She looked for Hemi, feeling a terror she hadn't felt since the last time she'd seen Hana.

The woman—now Cara remembered she'd said her name was Lauren—put out a hand, letting it settle on her shoulder. "Calm down, he's outside with Tommy. He's fine, came flipping through the air like some kind of circus dog, almost landed on his feet! The kids are enamored of him. They've always wanted a puppy."

"Tommy's hogging him and won't let me cuddle." The little girl came over to Cara, putting her hands on her hips. "Hi. I'm Lacy. I told Mama a bike was coming but she didn't listen."

Now Cara remembered the bike and her heart sank—it was a wreck, at least what she'd seen of it before the woman insisted they go to her house and clean her cuts. It had hurt, too, but all the dirt and gravel needed to come out. She'd played tough, biting her lip as she'd stayed silent, but inside she'd screamed as the peroxide had washed out the last of it. Now Cara lifted her hands, examining her palms. She could feel the sting under the bandages.

"Thank goodness you broke the brunt of your fall with your hands," Lauren said. "But you did hit your head. I don't think it was hard enough for a concussion, but I'll be glad to take you somewhere. Have it checked out."

Cara shook her head. She didn't have insurance, and even if she did, that meant she'd have to show her identification. And that wasn't an option. She threw her legs over the side of the couch and the sudden movement sent agony streaking through her head. Still, she felt brave. "No, I'm fine. I need to go."

"Listen, I don't know where you are going or why you are in such a hurry, and I won't ask, but you can't go yet; my brother's working on your bike."

"Brother?" Cara didn't remember another adult being in the house.

Lauren nodded. "Yeah, I called in the favor he owes me. He came right over, took a look, and said it wasn't as bad as I thought. He'll have it ready to go by tomorrow. I'm really sorry I was blocking the path like that. Tommy's always making me stop to adjust this or fix that—everything has to be perfect in his world or he can't cope. I was trying to keep him from having a meltdown."

Cara stared at her, not knowing what to say. Her son sounded like a lot of adults she'd known, striving to keep everything in line and freaking out when something went wrong. But she'd never known a kid that way. Then she realized what the woman had said.

The bike wouldn't be ready until tomorrow.

What was she going to do? Camp out in the woman's yard? She wasn't sure but first, she needed to see Hemi, confirm he really was okay. But she didn't want to seem ungrateful. After all, she'd almost run the woman's family over and now they were taking care of her bike?

"Thank you. I'm Cara. Um, can Hemi—I mean, my dog—come in?"

Lacy ran to the door, opening it and putting her head out. "Tommy, bring the dog. The lady wants to see him."

In just a second or two, the dark-haired little boy walked in, with Hemi right behind him.

"Hemi," Cara called out and he came over, his tail wagging as he nuzzled her hands, then sniffed them, a worried expression taking residence between his ears. "I'm okay, boy. What about you?"

She put her head down to his, letting her hands wander up and down his body, then each leg as she checked that all was intact. She inhaled, relishing his familiar smell.

When she looked up, the boy was only a few feet from her, staring, his face expressionless.

"Oh, hi," she said, cringing at the awkwardness in her voice. She never knew how to talk to kids. "Thanks for playing with Hemi."

He didn't answer, but Lacy came over and put her arm around him, leading him closer. They were a friendly-looking pair. The girl was dressed in old clothes but they were clean. Her shiny hair was braided in two plaits hanging down each side. The boy was also kempt, minus the smudge on his nose and his dirty fists. But he'd been playing outside, doing whatever it was that boys did.

"Tommy doesn't talk," she said. "But he wants me to tell you that he wants to keep your dog."

It was sweet how the sister talked for her brother, her arm protectively around his shoulders, but what she'd said took Cara aback. She reached out, pulling Hemi closer until he jumped up and settled on the couch next to her. She looked around the sparse but neat little room.

Maybe it *would* be a good place for Hemi.

The thought made her head start to pound again. "I . . . um . . ."

"Lacy, stop it," Lauren said. "She isn't looking for a home for her dog. If she was, she'd say so. Now both of you go outside and play while I talk to her."

The girl sighed, but she obediently turned her brother toward the door. "Come on, Tommy. We'll play hide-and-seek. I'll count." They disappeared together, the door shutting behind them.

Lauren came over and sat at the other end of the couch, wringing her dishcloth.

Cara scooted as far back as she could, though the woman didn't look dangerous. Still, you could never know. She looked around, trying to get her bearings and see if anyone else was around.

"I'm sorry," Lauren said. "She's at that age where she tries to be the boss. It's my fault—I depend on her a lot to help with her brother. And she really does seem to read his mind. She knows before I do most of the time what he wants. Without her I don't know what I'd do." She looked down at the floor and Cara got the feeling that Lauren was completely overwhelmed.

"Is it just you three?" she asked, wondering about a father but not wanting to just come out and ask. Lauren was pretty, in a comfortable kind of way. Their house was modest, but truly cozy with lots of personal touches like pillows and colorful throws.

Lauren nodded. "Yeah, it's been us three most of their lives. Their dad's in and out, but mostly out because of our situation."

"Situation?"

"Tommy. He has autism and his father thinks that makes him weak. He just doesn't understand that a person with a disability isn't weak—they're actually the strongest people in the world because they have to learn to overcome so much more than everyone else. Tommy has a few more obstacles than the average kid. Other people have worse problems, you know what I mean?"

Cara nodded. "But how do you make it as a single mom?"

"I barely do." Lauren frowned. "I just take it one day at a time. One week. Or one month. We have to move around a lot, but so far I've managed to keep us together, much to the disappointment of the social services case manager who keeps checking on me, thanks to my overbearing would-be mother-in-law who would love to get her claws on my kids."

Lauren's face took on a bitter expression.

The words hit Cara hard. Her own mother had also tried to keep them together as a family. She'd always worked two jobs, sometimes three. People had warned her she was leaving Cara and Hana alone at way too young an age, but it wasn't as though they had a choice.

Someone had to keep a roof over their heads and food in the pantry, and the only someone they had was their mom.

Cara and Hana had grown up fast after the state had swooped in and taken them. Maybe someone should have told her mother that she was doing a good job, encouraged her or helped her before it was too hard and then too late.

But this mom—Lauren—she was managing. Somehow she was doing what Cara's mom hadn't been able to do.

Cara wondered what her life would have been like if her mother had been stronger. If she hadn't started to slip up, letting life beat her down into a depression and low sense of self-worth that led her into one huge mistake after another.

She would never know because she couldn't go back.

Cara smiled. "It's pretty remarkable."

Lauren wrinkled her brow. "What is?"

"This." Cara waved her hand around. "This home. Your kids. You. I just think someone with an objective view needs to tell you that you're doing a good job. Like I said, with all you have on your plate, it's seems amazing to me."

"Well, I don't consider it amazing," she said, blushing. "I brought them into this world and I love them, so it's my job. It's just what moms do."

Not all moms, Cara wanted to say but held her tongue. *Some take the easy way out.*

Lauren gave her a funny look. "Now let's get you up and moving before you get too stiff from that torpedo move you tried to pull off. You can help me with dinner and then we'll make you a bed right there on the couch. If the kids will leave you alone, you can take a bath and soak in some Epsom salts."

Chapter Nine

Cara was starting to think that the mysterious karma Hana always talked about was beginning to work against her and her goal of getting to Key West. She'd been restless during the night, coming awake several times as Lauren walked through on her way to the kitchen. Each time she moved, she was reminded of the launch over the handlebars and the havoc her stunt had wreaked on her body. It was hard to get comfortable. At one point, she'd turned on the light and read from her book for a few chapters before the massive truck driving through her head stopped that, too.

"I'm so sorry," Lauren had said once when Cara sat up. "Tommy has a fever and I'm fighting to get some Tylenol into him. You can go sleep in my bed if you want."

Cara passed on that offer. She wouldn't take anyone's bed.

It was also hard to sleep without Hemi. Lauren had put him on an old quilt on the floor next to her, but the old couch was too narrow for them to sleep side by side and Cara really missed feeling the security of his warmth next to hers.

After tossing and turning for hours, she got up at the first ray of light that came beaming through the window. The clock in the kitchen read 6:33, and by then Lauren and Tommy were asleep again so she moved quietly.

Once she'd washed her face and pulled her hair up into a ponytail, she went outside, taking Hemi for his morning bathroom break.

Hemi had given her a pleading look just before she'd opened the door, then he'd darted around the side of the house in search of the perfect spot to leave his morning gift.

Cara watched him go, then saw a long-bed pickup truck in the driveway. Her bike was parked behind it, with a scruffy-looking guy straddling the front tire as he adjusted the handlebars. She looked for Hemi's trailer and saw it was still in the bed of the truck and appeared intact. She breathed a sigh of relief.

"Is it ready to go?" she asked.

At the sound of her voice the man stood, then turned around. He wasn't half bad looking once he was upright, his hair falling away from his face. Cara could see some of Lauren in him, the resemblance between brother and sister clear in their sharp features. But where she was thin, he was filled out in all the right places.

She looked away.

"How's the kid?" he asked, ignoring her question about the bike.

Cara shrugged, feeling uncomfortable under his scrutiny as he looked her up and down, from top to bottom. "They were awake a lot last night but they're sleeping now. I guess your niece is, too. I didn't see or hear her in there."

He pointed at the cab of the truck. Cara turned and saw Lacy behind the wheel, turning it while her mouth moved along to the radio. The girl held a hand up and waved at them.

"Oh," Cara said. "She must've slipped by me."

"Yeah, she's sneaky, all right." He laughed, then held out a hand. "I'm Mack."

"Cara," she said, putting her hand in his for only a second, then pulling back. Once again, she'd spit out her name without caution. She sighed. She'd sure never make it in a witness protection program.

"Your bike is good as new—or as good as used. Whatever it was before, it is again." He made a grand gesture with a sweep of his arm. "I had to take the front wheel off and take it to the shop. It was bent up pretty bad. And I put a new tube in the tire, adjusted your brakes, and next time someone's in your way you'll have a horn to honk that's so loud they'll be skedaddling in a mile diameter around you."

Cara saw the red bulb and shiny silver horn. "Wow, thank you. I don't have a lot of money but I hope I have enough to cover the expenses." She felt a sweat break out, despite the cool morning temperature. She hadn't expected or asked anyone to spend money to get her bike back on the road.

He shook his head. "Nothing's new but a three-dollar tube. Everything else was from the shop and just took a bit of elbow grease. Consider it a thank-you for not running over my sister and her kids."

"Oh, that's my fault. I should've been paying more attention," Cara said, embarrassed at his words of gratitude.

He gave her a doubting look. "We both know that it wasn't your fault. Tommy was probably about to go into one of his episodes and Lauren was doing everything she could think of to prevent it. She told me that was the fifth time she'd tied his shoe in just as many places, that she wasn't able to get the bow like he wanted."

Cara didn't know what to say. It sounded like he knew all about the troubles his sister kept behind closed doors. He also sounded like he was a good brother—something Cara and Hana had always wished they'd had.

The door slammed behind them and Cara turned to see Lauren coming out. She looked tired, still in her pajamas and socked feet, her hair a tousled mess.

"You getting ready to pull out?" she asked.

Cara wasn't sure if Lauren was talking to her or to her brother, but she nodded just in case. It was probably to her, as the woman most likely wanted her living room back. "If you mean me, then yes, I'm about to go. Your brother was just telling me what he did to get my bike back together."

Lauren laughed. "I didn't mean you. I was talking to him."

"So you aren't making breakfast?" Mack asked, sounding like a pouting little boy before he crossed his arms and put on a more manly stare.

Cara watched as the siblings glared at each other, each waiting on the other to fold. "I'll make breakfast," she finally said, hoping to keep the peace. She turned to Lauren. "Do you have the stuff for blueberry pancakes?"

At that announcement they heard a holler as Lacy opened the door of the truck and hopped out. She'd been eavesdropping through the window and the talk of pancakes had prompted her to come out, and she wasn't wasting any time leading them all back inside.

❧

With only two pancakes and one piece of bacon left on the platter in the center of the table, Cara stood and began stacking plates. Lauren didn't have blueberries, but the pancakes were still a hit, evident by the almost empty platter. Now she hoped to get the kitchen back to its spotlessness and be out of there in half an hour, tops. The road was calling out to her again, reminding her that she wasn't free to just loaf around when someone could be tracking her footsteps.

Keep moving to stay safe—that was her new mantra.

"You don't have to do dishes," Lauren said.

"Damn right. She cooked. She shouldn't do dishes, too," Mack added before shoving one more bite into his mouth, then handing Cara his empty plate. Then he softened his voice and looked at his sister. "But since you were up all night, I'll do them."

Cara hesitated, then glanced at Hemi on the floor at her feet. "Well, we really do need to get on the road. We've got some lost time to make up for, don't we, Hemi?"

His tail thumped on the floor once, then his eyes shut again.

"Lazy dog," Mack said. "But since you said you've lost time, care to share where you're headed?"

Cara looked at her backpack propped up by the back door. She thought fast, wondering what she could say that wouldn't give up her final destination.

"Don't be so nosy," Lauren said to her brother. "You put her on the spot, dummy."

"Oh. Sorry. I didn't mean to intrude," he said, looking down at the place his plate had been only seconds before.

Cara took the stack of plates over to the sink and set them down, then she turned back to the table. "I don't really know. I was just sort of following the coastline until I figured it out."

He shrugged. "That's your business. I understand completely. Sometimes to find yourself you just need to go where the wind blows. But if you want to make up the time you lost, I'm headed into Key Largo for a one-day job. I'd be glad to load your bike up and drop you off inside the town limits. It's a cool town to explore."

Cara wasn't really looking to find herself. It was more like lose herself, though it was nice of him to offer her a ride. But she didn't take rides from strangers. That was one of her oaths. *Unless it was a police officer who insisted*, she thought, thinking of Miss Kim and Maisy.

"Now that's a more courteous way of talking, Mack," Lauren said, winking at Cara.

"Oh shut up, baby sister," Mack said. "I think I know how to talk to women. I haven't done too badly so far."

Lauren scowled back at him and Cara felt like if she weren't there, they might even start scrapping like two kids.

"Don't go yet," Lacy wailed. "Tommy isn't going to like you taking Hemi away and he's going to melt."

"Lacy!" Lauren said. "Stop that. Cara can't stay on just because Tommy wants to pretend Hemi is his dog. She was on her way somewhere when we got in her way. If he has a meltdown, we'll deal with it like we always do." She turned to Cara, wringing the dishcloth in her hands. "I'm so sorry."

At the far side of the table, Tommy was running his finger round and round in circles, tracing something only he could see as everyone around him talked at once. His fever had broken before morning, but he'd refused any suggestion of eating breakfast. He had sat with them at the table, though. For his sake, Cara hoped Lauren and Mack didn't keep sassing each other.

"Oh, it's fine," Cara said when there was finally a lull. She wished she were already on the road and not here in this woman's kitchen in the middle of a family discussion.

Lacy sniffled her dismay, but Tommy didn't appear to catch on that Hemi was about to leave forever.

"Well?" Mack said. "If you're going with me, I leave in ten minutes. And no, Lacy, this time you can't go with your favorite uncle."

The sound of a foot stomping against the floor made Lacy's angst clear, then she took off out the back door. Just before it slammed, she poked her head in.

"Hemi," she called out.

Tommy heard that and slid off the kitchen chair. Hemi waited until the boy was right beside him, then he got up, too, following him into the backyard.

"He really does do well around the dog," Mack said, then went out too.

Cara hoped that didn't mean they were going to try to talk her out of her dog. The road to Key West was still long and lonely, and having Hemi with her was the only thing that made it bearable to be without her sister for the first time in her life. She wasn't letting him go that easy.

"Have you ever thought about getting a dog?" Cara asked Lauren.

"Maybe one day," Lauren said, then began running water into a dishpan. "But dogs cost money. They have to eat, too. And have shots, and even toys. Who's going to pay for all that? I can barely keep food on the table for just us three."

"I understand," Cara said.

Lauren turned around, putting her hands on her hips. "Look, I know you probably don't trust my brother but I promise you, he's good as gold. If you want to make up some time and miles, you should take him up on his offer. Key Largo is gorgeous and you can get there without much effort if you're riding in his truck. It'll give those sore muscles more time to recuperate, too. You do realize it's almost four hundred miles to Key Largo, don't you?"

Cara hadn't really thought it through, but Lauren was right, four hundred miles would take her at least a week at the rate she'd been going. Before, a week wasn't a big deal, it wasn't like she was expected anywhere by a certain time. But now, thinking of getting that much closer to Key West without any effort, it was almost too good to pass up. And Mack wasn't really a stranger any longer, was he?

"You really think he doesn't mind?" Cara said, surprised at herself for considering the offer. She just didn't trust people often—especially men.

A smile lit up Lauren's face. "No, I assure you, he doesn't mind. And while you have him cornered where he can't run away, do me a favor and talk to him about his love life, why don't you? I sure wish he'd find someone else to do some cooking for him but he won't stop taking care of us long enough to scope out the possibilities."

Cara shook her head. She wasn't much on broaching personal subjects, especially ones pertaining to relationships. It wasn't as though she had any positive experiences to draw from or any well-vetted advice to give. "I, uh, I don't know about that."

She must've been wearing a horrified expression because Lauren looked at her, then laughed loudly. "Or not," she said. "How about this? Just enjoy the ride, as my thanks to you for not taking out one of my kids when you had the chance. I'll admit, I'm a bit partial to their sweet faces, even if they do give me a few gray hairs these days."

Cara could do that. Enjoying the ride and getting that much closer to Key West sounded like a good plan. Though admittedly, these days any plan was better than no plan.

Chapter Ten

The first hour on the road was the most awkward, with only a smattering of niceties passed back and forth. Hemi sat between them and Cara used him for something to do with her hands, stroking him and rubbing his ears until he finally curled into a ball of ecstasy against her leg, sighing his gratitude.

Mack looked over and laughed but didn't comment. Cara realized she was riding alone with a man she didn't even know.

"I . . . um, I didn't get your last name," she said.

"McBride," he said, keeping his eyes on the road.

"Mack McBride?"

"Well, no. Not exactly. My first name is so nerdy that when my buddies started calling me Mack in junior high, I kept it."

She nodded. That made more sense. She couldn't think of any more questions that weren't too personal. She wondered if his real name was something like Herman, or Alfred. But since she didn't want to expand on names, for obvious reasons, she stayed quiet.

By the second hour, Cara was starting to feel really weird about the awkward silence. She asked about Tommy, and thankfully that was the perfect subject to bring him out of his shell. Soon they were behaving like normal human beings, interacting and all, much to her relief.

"Did you see the way he was concentrating on your dog's paw? And people think he doesn't know what's going on. I tell you, that boy has a lot going on in his own little world," Mack said, glancing once at her before putting his eyes back on the road.

"I imagine he does." Cara noticed the way his face softened when he talked about Tommy, and even Lacy. She'd never really known any aunts or uncles, but Mack seemed like a good one.

He chuckled and thumped the steering wheel with one hand. "They'd unraveled almost that entire roll of toilet paper, winding it round and round that paw."

She nodded. It had been a sight and Hemi had given her a look that screamed "Please rescue me!" when she'd come out the door. "I thought his paw should be healed by now. I pulled a piece of glass out of it a week or so ago, but then it looked fine so I took the bandages off. I haven't seen him limping since then, either."

Hemi had been doing a lot of riding, she suddenly remembered. And maybe when he was walking, she just wasn't looking. She felt bad, like a neglectful mother.

"Lacy wasn't happy when you took her handiwork off, either. Don't let her fool you, she's the ringleader in almost everything they do. But she's good for Tommy. She treats him like he's just her sometimes-pesky little brother—not like some invalid."

His comment sounded as though someone in Tommy's life treated him like an invalid, but Cara wasn't going to get too personal so she didn't ask. She'd keep the subjects safe.

"I appreciate you bandaging it up for real. I'll keep an eye on it better this time. I need to stop and get some bandages and peroxide when you let me off in Key Largo." She tried not to think about the cost and how she had no idea how she was going to make it to Key West and still eat on the small bit of money she had left.

Mack turned abruptly, jumping off the main highway onto a side road. Cara looked back, worried about her bike. But it was fine.

"This is a shortcut," he said. "I've used it many times to meet my clients at the courthouse in the nick of time before a proceeding."

Cara looked at him, incredulous at his admission. "You're a lawyer?"

He gave her a sideways grin. "Yeah, technically I'm a lawyer. But don't look so surprised. Lawyers can get grease under their fingernails, too. Some of us also like to drive loud, oily pickup trucks. Don't flip out, but we even wear boots when we need to."

She couldn't think of anything to say. She'd pegged him as a mechanic, or a . . . a . . . she didn't know what. But definitely not a lawyer.

He reached over and turned the air conditioner up a notch.

"I was a big-city lawyer before I came back here. I'd hit the clock each morning at first light and didn't get home to my sterile but valuable condo until it was time to crash, just to wake up and do it all again. I didn't even get to work on cases that meant anything to me. It was all bullshit and cons, petty grievances filed by people who had too much time on their hands. And more corruption than I could stomach. I couldn't take it anymore. I finally walked out."

"Out of court?"

"Out of everything," he said, smirking at her. "I walked away from the corporate rat race. I had enough playing politics and casting a blind eye to corruption in the upper ranks. I packed up, sold everything, and came here."

"Don't small towns have corruption?" She didn't know why she bothered asking, as she thought of Hana and her recent trouble and knew that, yes, small towns have more than their share of bad people in high places, which breeds corruption.

He laughed. "I'm sure they do but at least I'm not wading through it anymore. I decided to go back to doing something I loved doing in high school. Something my father didn't support because he said it was a waste of time and effort."

"And that is?"

He lifted his hands from the steering wheel, turning them over and showing his palms. "Working with my hands. I build things and sell what I can to get by. In the tough months when I don't sell, I take from my savings. But I'll tell you this: I haven't regretted my midlife crisis for even one day because, more than running from the high-paced career I had, I realized I was running back to the one person who needed someone the most, though she'd never admit that."

"She's tough isn't she?"

He looked at her briefly. An intense look for a fraction of a second before he turned his gaze back to the road. "She sure is. You see what she's done and all by herself, too. That house, it just feels good. It feels like a real home. It's not worth one red cent but it's full of love and comfort—everything my condo and my parents' house were missing."

"You're proud of her," Cara said softly.

"Damn straight I'm proud of her. She thinks I swooped in and became her hero, but really, she's mine." His voice got shaky and he fiddled with the radio, searching for a channel, then turning it off again. All in a cover-up for the emotion he was trying to swallow back.

"She's worried about your love life," Cara said, unable to stop herself.

He bent his head back and laughed loudly, turning the tense moment into one much lighter. "I know! She won't stop asking me when I'm going to get serious."

"Do you date?"

"Of course I date. But I don't take my dates around Lauren or she'd have me engaged and buying a house in a neat subdivision and adopting a family pet before we've even gotten to know each other. I like my bachelor pad." He looked at her, raising an eyebrow. "Why do you ask? Are you interested?"

Cara felt the heat crawling up her neck. This was why she didn't get personal; it always came back around to her. A subject she didn't like to broach.

"Um—no. I don't date."

"Don't look so scared. I was kidding. But you don't date? Can I ask why? You seem like a nice girl—and you've got the looks. What's stopping you?"

She stared out at the road. What was stopping her? It had been nearly a year since she'd gone on a date, though she'd been asked several times. Usually she said no because she had to work, or Hana wanted her to do something with her. Sometimes she just needed to spend her time off doing housework.

Now that she considered it, she realized she always had an excuse. But if she was being honest with herself, she knew she just didn't want to get hurt. It's not that she hadn't ever dated. She had. But every man she'd ever known in her life had walked away.

If anyone was going to do the walking now, she wanted it to be her. And it wasn't as though she could really build a family with anyone. But she didn't want his sympathy. She didn't need it. Finally she answered. "I guess I just haven't met the right one who'll make me put everything aside."

After a lot more miles and a few stops to let Hemi relieve himself, they drove into a small community.

"Rock Harbor."

"What?" Cara said, jolted by the sound of his voice. She'd been leaning her head against the window, her thoughts moving back and forth making comparisons between Lacy and Tommy, and how their situation was similar but still different from the one Cara had known as a child. How Lauren refused to let the world beat her down and make her give up.

"This is Rock Harbor. I think it'll be a good place to let you out so I can make my appointment."

Cara was relieved to get back out on the road, just her and Hemi with the breeze in their hair. After he stopped and unloaded the bike and trailer, they said their good-byes, another awkward moment, but Cara was glad for her and Hemi to be back on their own.

Chapter Eleven

By the time Cara had biked from Rock Harbor to Tavernier, conquering bridge after bridge, then pulled into the first island of Islamorada, her aches had become more than simple fatigue and she was starting to feel feverish. Down to almost no money, she quickly discarded the idea of finding a cheap hotel room that would allow dogs and headed for the beach instead. She hoped she'd have enough energy to put up her tent and find something for them to eat before crashing.

"Hemi, I think Tommy passed his bug to me," she muttered but didn't have the strength to turn to look and see if he heard her.

Tavernier had been trying. After Mack dropped them off, she'd taken a turn down a wrong street, then a few more as she'd tried to get herself back on track. She'd almost stopped to ask directions, but her pride had blocked that option and she'd soldiered on to Islamorada as their stopping point.

"We're almost done for the day, Hemi," she called out, albeit weakly. She crooned to him some more, not even knowing what she was saying but trying to make him feel less lonely back there. She wondered if dogs were susceptible to flu bugs or viruses, and hoped they weren't, because she was feeling worse by the minute and had a feeling that just taking care of herself was going to be tough.

Hemi had been good all day, barely making a peep. Cara had let him walk for a quarter of a mile before seeing him limp slightly. She'd called him back into the trailer. She didn't understand why his paw wouldn't heal, but it had her worried. It wasn't oozing but it was red and obviously still sore. She really needed to find a veterinarian, and hopefully one that took charity cases. In her gut, she figured Hemi needed some antibiotics. She told him as much as she kept talking to him, turning her head to the side and working to find the energy to keep going.

They were quite a pair—Hemi with his wounded paw while she babbled on like a feverish idiot.

Fifteen minutes later, her legs were like limp noodles as they finally made it to the beach. Cara didn't have the energy to look for the campground, so she found a grove of trees to camouflage them. She could barely hear any waves and would've liked to camp closer to the water, but she felt it was better to stay partially hidden. She didn't know much about the Islamorada islands, and if they were thick with thieves she hoped tonight wasn't on their schedule. She hadn't seen a No Camping sign, but she wasn't too observant at the moment, so she wouldn't be surprised if she'd missed it.

After parking, Hemi hopped out and began scoping the area. Cara let him go, knowing that he wouldn't go far. He obviously took his job to protect her seriously, evident by the way he continued to lope back and check on her before heading out again.

She put up the tent, laying out their pads and blankets before turning back to her bags for something to eat.

"Hemi!" she called out as she ripped open the pouch of dog food.

The smell of turkey and gravy hit her and her stomach almost rumbled. She felt a bit ridiculous that her dog was eating better than her, but seeing how she was broke and not feeling well, the saltines and peanut butter would be just fine.

In two seconds flat, Hemi came racing into camp just as she'd finished pouring the wet food into his bowl. He was almost done eating it before Cara even had her crackers open.

"Hungry, boy? I'm sorry—I really stretched it to dinner time tonight, didn't I?" She'd known that once they'd stopped, she wouldn't feel like getting back on the bike, so she'd kept pedaling longer than normal. She reached up and felt her head, trying to determine the seriousness of her fever. She'd give anything for a few ibuprofen, but since it wasn't as though a drugstore was near and handing them out for free, she sucked it up and nibbled a cracker.

They finished dinner and she cleaned up, putting all their things away and taking the empty containers to the trash can. Hemi escorted her, making her feel safe as she stumbled through the now dim light and headed for the tent. She opened the flap and Hemi went in first. She followed, zipped it, and was asleep before her head even hit the ground.

Hemi's initial growl didn't wake her but his barking did. And by now she knew the difference—a growl was just a warning that he might have heard something, but a bark was a definite alert. Through the fogginess that surrounded her head, Cara sat up.

"What is it, Hemi?" she mumbled. "I'm sick. Please, please stop."

Her head pounded even more as she spoke.

"Who's in there?" a gravelly voice called out from outside the tent.

Cara didn't answer.

"I said who's in there? This is a no-camping area," he called again. "If you could read, you'd see it was posted everywhere. No camping. Ever."

She could tell it was an old man by his voice, and that made her feel somewhat safer, though not much. Sighing in defeat, she held on to Hemi's collar while she unzipped the tent.

"It's me," she said, poking her head out.

"Well, come out and pack up," the old man said. "You need to get on out of here. There's a camping ground up the road a piece."

It was late and the moon had risen high in the sky, the light reflecting off the sand to give her a pretty good look at the man. He was old. And scruffy looking.

"Are you some kind of ranger?" she asked, crawling out. She still kept one hand on Hemi. Somehow, she didn't think the gruff old man would take too kindly to being bit. When she looked up, she noticed he had his own dog—a well-behaved, quiet dog that sat at his heels, showing Hemi up with his disciplined stance. Black and tan, the dog had long wide ears that hung down either side of his head like the flaps on a hat. She couldn't see his expression clearly, but the fawn-colored circles around his eyes gave her the impression he looked sad.

"No, I'm no damn ranger," the man barked back. "But I've lived near this beach for all my years—about ninety or so of 'em—so I guess I'll tell you when you can't be here if I want to. I ain't having this place turn into no hippy camp. Not under my watch."

If Cara wasn't so dizzy and her head didn't hurt so much, she'd laugh. She couldn't be any further from being a hippy. As a matter of fact, she was the only twenty-nine-year-old she knew who hadn't even so much as touched pot. Now Hana, however, she was the one who could easily—and accurately—pass herself off as a hippy.

Cara struggled to right herself but once she was out and had calmed Hemi down enough to let go of him, she stood and the man shined a flashlight right into her eyes. The beam sent a lightning bolt of pain straight to her brain and she flinched, covering her face. She was already swaying a bit from the dizziness, but the assault on her senses almost made her come crashing down.

"What's the matter with you? You high on something?" the old man yelled.

She shook her head. "No, my head hurts. I have a fever and I don't do drugs, thank you very much." She heard the biting tone of her own voice but couldn't help it.

He flicked the light off, not saying anything for a moment. When he spoke again, his voice was softer.

"You do look a bit flushed, young lady. What sort of fever you carrying?"

What did he expect her to say to that? What sort of fever did most carry? Did they have names? Wasn't a fever just a fever? Then she realized in his day and age, they did have names. What were they? Bubonic fever. Scarlet fever. Or were those plagues? Cara couldn't think and she felt dizzy enough to fall, so she sat down on the sand.

Hemi moved in closer, his shoulder touching her leg. He whined.

The old man wasn't happy. "Get up. Are you trying to trick me? I told you, you can't stay here."

Cara felt the rising in her throat before she could answer. Luckily, she had fast reflexes but unluckily for the old man, they weren't working just right. She did hurl far enough not to get it on her own clothes, but unfortunately it landed exactly on the top of the old man's loafers.

When she finished, she was so weak that she lay down, rolling over on her side and letting the side of her face touch the cool sand. He could do what he wanted with her. Arrest her. Bury her. She didn't care. She was beyond caring. She just hoped someone would take care of Hemi.

Right on cue, he whined again and pushed her cheek with his nose.

Suddenly she felt hands prop her up, assist her to stand, then lead her up the hill and away from the dune. He might have been a serial killer or a geriatric rapist, but Cara complied, not really caring anymore what happened to her, as long as she was led somewhere soft where she could sleep.

꩜

She smelled coffee. That meant she wasn't dead. Yet she was so afraid to restart the pounding in her head from the night before that she hesitated to open her eyes. But where was Hemi?

She reached out a hand.

She moved it to the right. Then to the left. But no Hemi.

Then she realized she wasn't feeling the familiar material of her blanket or her tent.

That made her sit straight up, her eyes open wide in fear.

"Well, there you are. Glad you decided to join the living," the old man said from where he sat at a small table, sipping from a mug.

She looked down at her wrists, surprised there were no handcuffs or ropes. Hadn't she just been kidnapped? Where the hell was she? She looked at him, trying to determine if despite his old age, he really was dangerous.

Then she noticed that Hemi sat under his feet. He looked content. Bored even.

Traitor.

"Where am I?"

"You are where none have traveled before," the man said in a robotic voice.

Cara squinted at him, trying to gauge if he was serious. She had to admit, he didn't look dangerous. But neither did Ted Bundy.

The old man didn't smile, but he winked. "You're in my beach house, and yes, I must apologize for my ungentlemanly behavior as I did have to practically drag you off the beach and up to my home. Though if you'll notice, other than your shoes, you're still dressed. Your modesty was left intact. I am harmless."

"You? Carried me?"

"I didn't say I carried you, but don't look so doubting. I might be old but I'm not dead. You walked, though I probably could've carried you if I wanted to, seeing how you can't possibly weigh much more than a popcorn fart." He laughed at his own joke. When he saw Cara didn't join him, he stopped midchuckle.

"Look, you were obviously ill. I didn't take your temperature or anything but I could tell you were burning up. I might be a grouchy old man, but I'm not merciless. I wasn't going to leave you all sick and defenseless down there, what with all the depraved and unfettered vermin running around this world."

Cara felt guilty for her suspicion. "I'm sorry. I mean—thank you."

"Oh, and I got you to swallow a few ibuprofen and sip some water, though you probably don't remember. You were babbling on like a crazed woman down there. Something about your sister and needing to run, run, and run."

That brought Cara awake completely. What else had she said? She felt a sick, heavy feeling in her stomach. And she felt the need to leave. Fast.

Hemi jumped up from his place on the floor and came to the couch that Cara was on. She turned, putting her feet on the floor. He crawled halfway onto her lap. She puckered and he rewarded her with a kiss. Another trick she hadn't taught him. Suddenly she felt a moment of panic that wasn't related to the one already there from waking up in a stranger's home.

"My bike?" She looked at the man.

"In my shed, along with the rest of your gear. I might have to hold it hostage until you replace my shoes, though." He got up and went to the small kitchen. "Now do you want some breakfast or not?"

Shoes? Oh no. She remembered now—she'd hurled on the man's shoes. She felt her cheeks flush, then shook her head. "No food, but I could take something cold to drink. I don't do coffee."

He snorted. "New Age kids. No coffee. What do you think, it's bad for you? Look at me—I've been drinking coffee for nearly a hundred years. Why hasn't it killed me yet?"

But he went to his refrigerator and got out a jug of orange juice. He didn't ask if she drank it. He poured a glass, then brought it to her.

She cradled it, relishing the cold against her palms. She still wasn't used to the mugginess of the Keys. "Thank you."

He grunted in reply and returned to the kitchen area. At the sink he began running some water.

"Is your wife here?" Cara asked, looking around. It appeared that it was a small mobile home and while not fancy, it was kept up and neat. Much too tidy for a bachelor.

"Yes, she's here," he said, not bothering to turn to answer.

No wonder things are neat, thought Cara. She looked toward the small hall, hoping the woman would come out, make it less awkward for her to get up and slip out.

"She's right in front of you."

Cara flipped back around. There was nothing in front of her but a small entertainment center holding a television, books, a few picture frames, and a vase. An empty wooden rocking chair filled the corner, and the lamp and stack of books beside it made it obvious that it was the most used furniture in the room. But nowhere did she see another person.

"Where?"

Even before he answered, she knew. The vase.

She felt a shiver and fought her urge to get up and run. She had never done well with death, and especially not the subject of people's ashes.

"I'm sorry," she said, not knowing what else to say.

"Yeah, you said that earlier."

"But . . . I mean—"

He turned and gave her a sharp look. "I know what you mean. I don't need no sorry words. I'm doing just fine here and it won't be long before me and Clara are back together."

"Clara?" Finally, a way to get out of the hole she'd dug.

Grabbing a towel, he quickly dried his hands. "Yes, Clara. My wife that's been dead for eighteen years now. Oh wait—is that going to make you say you're sorry again? If so, I take it back."

Well, he was a snappy one.

"No, I was going to say that my name is Cara. Spelled the same, just no *L*."

He rolled his eyes toward the ceiling before returning them to look at her. "See? Another thing you kids do these days. Now why did you have to go on and ruin a good name like Clara? Was there something wrong with it that you just felt you had to twist it into something it isn't? Clara is a fine name. I tell you, it was just fine."

The angry lines disappeared from his face and he sighed. Cara could tell he really missed his wife, despite his tough act.

"I didn't choose my own name," she said, watching him return to the table and sit down. "My mother named me Cara Grace and my sister is Hana Marie."

"Is that the sister you were babbling about last night?"

She nodded. Somehow she didn't think the old man was much of a threat. And honestly, all the secrets were starting to make her feel like a criminal.

"I suppose I should tell you my name, since I know yours, *Cara*." He put a touch of sarcasm on her name when it rolled off his tongue. "I'm Henry."

"Nice to meet you, Mr. Henry."

"What's your family name?" he asked, as though he'd know some of her people.

Fat chance. *She* didn't even know her people.

"Butter." It didn't roll off her tongue—that was for sure. Each time she muttered her last name she thought of the constant teasing she and Hana had taken for it. The Butter sisters—Cara and Hana Butter. The old joke—everything looks good *but her* face. It had been years since she'd heard it, but it always lingered in the back of her mind when she exchanged names.

He didn't react except to nod. "I had a sister, too."

"She's passed on?" Cara asked, looking around the room. She hoped there wasn't another vase somewhere.

He came to the rocking chair and took a seat, falling into it clumsily, as though all the strength had suddenly left his body.

"She has. But that was a long time ago. And now they're all gone, but I still have ol' Buster here to keep me company." He nudged his dog with his foot.

Buster turned his attention to Henry and a look passed between them that Cara could describe only as deep affection between two lifelong friends. When she returned her gaze to Hemi, she hoped that one day he'd find someone like that—a master who could love him unconditionally and give him everything he needed.

She wished she could be that someone but Hemi deserved more. For most of her adult life, Cara had lived from paycheck to paycheck, bouncing from one rental to another—which always prohibited pets—the epitome of an unstable life. Hemi needed stability and a permanent place to settle in, not the uncertain existence that she'd have to offer.

Cara was determined that Hemi would have the life she herself had always craved. If it was her last gesture of kindness before everything crumbled around her, she'd make sure he found a home.

Chapter Twelve

Cara pushed the vacuum back and forth, finding comfort in the sound of the old machine and the repetitive motions. She and Hemi were on day three with Henry and Buster now, and she'd told Henry that morning that it was their last day, no more extensions. She needed to get back on the road, back to her goal to give homage to Hemingway. Now that she was less than eighty miles away, the pull to get there was becoming more than she could fight.

At her declaration, Henry had given her a sour grimace and slipped out the door. The last she saw he was leaving his shed with a fishing pole and a tackle box. He'd glanced over his shoulder once, looking like a small boy checking to see if his mother was about to call him back, then he'd disappeared into the grove of trees that separated his place from the beach.

Hemi and Buster got along fine, though it was amusing how Hemi tried to engage the older dog into playing but was met with aloofness at every turn. Buster was tired all the time, only rousing for breakfast and dinner. Still, it worked out for Hemi because Buster didn't mind sharing his supply of toys and bones, sending the younger and much more energetic dog into a squeaky-toy-hunting frenzy.

In the meantime, Cara had worked hard for Henry. He'd admitted to her that he didn't want anyone coming in when he died and finding out he'd done a less than respectable job of keeping his and Clara's house organized. Sure, on the exterior where anyone could see, it looked well-kept. But once he began opening closet doors, drawers, and kitchen cabinets, it was clear that the old man had spent years stuffing things wherever he could. He obviously had an attachment to just about everything, and he had to leave while Cara worked, finding it easier to cope if he wasn't around to see it thrown away. For instance, it had taken her half a morning to clean out his refrigerator and freezer, tossing outdated items and scrubbing the grime and crud that had built up.

She also cooked for him, making modest but nutritious meals with the simplest of ingredients that he had on hand. It was nice to be able to eat hot food again, but the night she'd whipped up her famous pasta and bruschetta chicken, he'd claimed he didn't want "that fancy stuff." Yet he'd cleaned his plate and sheepishly asked for more.

He talked a lot about his wife, so much so that Cara felt she'd almost known Clara herself. Her favorite story was of the day that they'd met. It was at an old-fashioned barn raising after a particularly rough tropical storm had done damage to a neighbor's property.

Cara loved the reminders of how in the old days everyone in the community worked to help each other. Henry described a teenaged Clara showing up in her brother's overalls with her hair pinned back, setting a still-hot apple pie and a basket of fried chicken on the tailgate of the truck before standing at attention, determined to do just as much as everyone else that day. They'd worked side by side, unloading plywood and carrying it to the men who worked to repair the old structure. And they'd discussed everything from their president, to the threat of another storm brewing over the ocean, to Henry's plans to join the navy when he turned eighteen.

"Besides being the prettiest girl I'd ever seen, she was also one of the sharpest tools in the shed. By the end of the day, I was more than impressed with her ability to talk on every subject. I was smitten," Henry said, grinning so that Cara could see the gaps in his teeth. "I caught her behind the barn and declared my intentions. She laughed, sure that I was only teasing, but a year later, we were married on that same property with everyone who'd worked on that barn raising in attendance. And just like I'd known from the first minute I'd laid eyes on her, she made my life one worth living."

Cara had to admit, he was growing on her. If she'd have ever known her grandfather, she could see him being like old Henry. For a man who had only a dog for company day in and day out, it was expected that he'd put on a grouchy face for those who invaded his privacy. But under it, his kindness slipped through more than a few times. Like when he'd taken her bicycle out of the shed and worked on it all day, slowly but methodically, shining it and airing up the tires, then tightening it all before checking out the brakes for safety.

And he was loyal—she found that out when he told her the story of the hurricane of 1935 and how his first dog was lost. He'd been a small boy and everyone had given up searching. Henry held out hope and he said because of that, he was sitting on his porch scanning the horizon as he did every spare moment when his best friend came limping home five days later.

Most amazingly, that dog sired litter after litter, keeping his lineage going for decades all the way through the years and down to the very dog that now lay sleeping right beside Hemi.

"I've been able to keep the first Buster's memory alive with every dog I chose but now it's the last of both of us. It's been a good run and at least we'll go out together," Henry said.

Cara had looked away at his statement, not wanting him to see the tears that gathered at the finality of his words. She had to keep reminding herself not to get too attached to Henry and Buster, that she and Hemi were simply passing through.

Finally done with the vacuuming, she unplugged the machine and opened the closet. A box on the top shelf caught her eye and she grabbed it, then opened the flaps. It was full of photo albums and loose snapshots.

The first one was of a little boy and his dog. One look at the crooked smile and she knew instantly it was Henry. He was dressed in a matching jacket and pants, a small bow tie skewed against his collar. The colors of the photograph were faded, but Cara would bet the dog looked a lot like Buster.

She held the photo, looking closely, and was taken back to one of her own memories. It was Easter and she and Hana were excited to participate in a neighborhood egg hunt later that day. They'd been told about it at church weeks before, and their foster mom at the time had promised them they could go. The morning of the hunt, she and Hana had found brown paper bags and got out their pail of markers. Together they'd decorated the cheap bags, brightening them up with cartoons of bunnies and spring flowers. They worked while the rest of the family had gone to church.

She hadn't minded the time alone, and to be fair, their foster mom had been telling the truth when she'd said they couldn't go to church because they didn't have the proper Easter attire. In their bags of hand-me-downs taken from home to home, an Easter dress wasn't in the mix.

Hana had pouted for a time, but as soon as the family had left she'd gotten her sister out of her mood by ransacking the pantry and finding a hidden box of Fruity Pebbles, which they'd finished off completely before starting their craft project.

"At least we get to go to the egg hunt," Hana had finally said, the last of her bad mood slipping away.

But that wasn't what happened.

After breakfast they'd finished their bags and dressed in their best clothes—nothing fancy but surely nothing embarrassing—and waited on the porch. It was excruciating, and Hana kept running inside to look at the clock, returning to the porch angrier at each passing minute. When the time for the egg hunt came and went and the family still hadn't returned, Cara had known immediately that they'd gone on without them.

Hana had still held out hope.

And it held for several hours until it got dark and they'd still not returned. Only then had Cara talked her into coming inside and her sister, with the stubborn set of her jaw to keep the tears at bay, had taken her anger out on the kitchen.

Cara had begged her to stop but Hana had emptied out all the flour, cereal, sugar, and every other open container she could find.

Then she started on the unopened containers.

When the family finally arrived home, Hana was scrubbed clean and in bed beside Cara. But her body had stiffened when the door opened, and even more so when their foster mother's first shriek rang out through the house. Still, nothing could stop the satisfied grin that had crept across Hana's face, or the utter terror that Cara felt.

She'd shared the blame with her sister and they'd done the punishment together, living off canned pork and beans for a week straight and doing all the chores in the house. Hana had claimed it was worth it to make that foster mother feel at least some of the anguish that they'd felt at being left behind.

And after leaving that placement, neither of them had ever touched pork and beans again. Also Hana refused every future offer to go to an Easter egg hunt, which meant that Cara would never know the exhilaration of racing against other kids in the pursuit of colored eggs and candy. Because of that afternoon, they'd both sworn off Easter.

Cara flipped through a few more photos and felt like she was seeing a montage of a man's life. Weddings, graduations, family reunions, and even snapshots of fish caught, kites flown, and affectionate moments between couples. It looked like he had lived a life that she'd only dreamed of, full of family and celebrations, children and grandchildren.

But where were they all now?

The door slammed and Cara heard Henry's now familiar shuffle across the hard floor and toward the room where she was. She pushed the box back into the closet, standing to face him.

He had a peculiar look on his face at first, one that she couldn't gauge. For a moment, she wondered if he was going to throw her out for her lack of consideration for his privacy.

Then he smiled. "So you've been sorting through my life, eh? How do you like it that I've got decades of memories packed into one little box? See how insignificant we really are?"

Cara felt her face flush with heat.

"I'm so sorry. I wasn't being nosy, but when I saw the first photo, I couldn't stop. I wanted to see what you and Clara looked like when you met. Please . . . I—I'm sorry."

"Get that box and bring it into the kitchen where I can see. I haven't seen those photos for years and these old eyes need all the light they can get. You started this. Now you'll get to listen to an old man reminisce about a life gone by. If you thought I bent your ear before, just know that now you're in for a lot more of the same," he said, then turned and abruptly left the room.

She turned back to the closet and picked up the box. Old Henry thought he was going to torture her with stories, but what he didn't understand was that to her, hearing about the legacy of a family steeped in love and loyalty was something she knew she'd enjoy. And she couldn't wait to hear him tell it. All of it.

Chapter Thirteen

Cara pedaled hard as she looked over the side of the bridge to the first islands of Marathon. The ride was exhilarating and the constant postcard views that assaulted her senses only made her happier every step of the way that she'd made the decision to seek out Hemingway's house. She tried to concentrate on the end goal, but she had to admit, she missed Henry and Buster already.

Saying good-bye to them had been really difficult. After Henry bared his heart to her when going through his memory box, telling stories about each recorded moment in his history, he'd asked her to stay on, telling her she wasn't strong enough to hit the road yet.

Cara could see right through him. He was lonely and wanted company.

In the few days they were there, they'd fallen into somewhat of a routine but when his house began to feel like home, she knew it had to come to an end. She probably wasn't the best human being on the planet, but she wasn't so callous that she'd drag an old man into her problems. And staying on would mean just that.

When she told him she was leaving the next morning, explaining they had to get going, he'd looked defeated.

Cara had looked away, giving him time to put his pride back on, then she'd shown him his newly cleaned and organized freezer with all the casseroles she'd spent her afternoons making for him. On each one she'd pasted a piece of paper atop it, listing directions for thawing and heating. She remembered one of the photos he'd shown her, bragging that the handsome, trim man was him in his glory days. She reminded him of that when she'd told him most of what she'd made him were healthy options, but truth be told, she'd slipped in a few portions of spicy chili beans, a recipe of hers that he'd especially liked, though his indigestion hadn't.

He'd thanked her and handed over fifty dollars for all the work she'd done in his house, telling her he wished he had more to give. Cara knew he didn't have much, and he'd barely made a grumble about the list she'd sent him to the store with so that she had ingredients to cook with. She hadn't wanted to take his money but he'd insisted. She appreciated it, too, as she thought she'd need to stop for more dog food. But that task was scratched off before she'd even left, as Henry had handed her two gallon-sized Ziploc bags full of Buster's kibble.

Cara had smiled when Henry bent down and told Hemi that his playfulness almost—not quite, *but almost*—made him want another puppy. Then he stood and apologized to Buster, saying he was only kidding.

The ride out of Islamorada had been so scenic and peaceful that she'd almost second-guessed her insistence about leaving. She could tell that even Hemi enjoyed the canopied three-mile neighborhood road they took out.

Now as she scanned the scenery below, she thought how good it would feel to peel off her jeans and jump into the teasingly clear water. One glance behind her confirmed that Hemi was also tempted. The slobber ran off his tongue as he panted, his gaze wandering over the expanse of blue.

Cara could envision them—her hand gripping his collar—as they stopped the bike, went to the guardrail, then jumped into the sparkling water below.

It was much too far down though, and they had to keep going.

"Less than fifty miles to go, boy," she said over her shoulder. They were close—and getting closer with every turn of the tires. Already that day they'd conquered bridge after bridge, each one connecting small pieces of land to the other, a jigsaw puzzle as she chased each piece to the final stop.

She felt a rush of excitement, thrilled that she was so close to her destination. Thus far, she'd refused to think about what would happen after she'd made it to Key West. Right now she had two things in mind. First to finally see the Hemingway House, and then, as much as she knew it would hurt, to turn Hemi over and see if a shelter could help reunite him with his family.

Or get him a new one.

That thought dulled her excitement a bit, but she pushed it away, determined to focus only on good things for the rest of the trip. She was exultant, the way she'd almost completely conquered a goal for the first time in her life. She wished she could tell Hana—her sister would be astonished, as she liked to believe that Cara couldn't do anything without her by her side.

Someone blew a car horn and scared Cara out of her deep thought. She turned the bike closer to the side of the bridge she was on, though she was completely out of the line of traffic. The car went around, but then pulled to a stop in front of her, blocking her way. Two guys popped their heads out of either side of the car, waving their hands. To her they looked and sounded as though they'd started their partying early, even before getting to Key West and the famous Duval party street.

"Great," she said under her breath. "What do these clowns want?"

She kept pedaling, wary of letting them know she was nervous. When she got closer and they didn't take off again, she slowed down.

Just a few feet from the back of their car, Cara came to a stop when one of the guys got out and stood in her path. Behind her she heard Hemi growl.

"Stay, Hemi," she said, putting one foot on the pavement.

"Hey," the guy said. "Where you going, pretty girl?"

"That way." Cara pointed in front of him. Couldn't he see she was almost old enough to be his mother? Or at least his older sister. "If you'll move your car. Please."

He laughed. "Want to park your bike and come with us? We'll get you where you're going and have fun getting there."

Cara kept calm. This wasn't the first time she'd been harassed since coming out on the road. On her first day of walking there'd been other cars, other guys. Most of them just flung obscenities or whistles out the window, but one car had even stopped. What she'd learned was to keep her voice cool and friendly—just not too friendly. But the last time it had happened, she didn't have Hemi yet. She just hoped that he didn't make it an even worse situation.

"Thanks, but I can't. I've got my dog back here, and all my stuff." She nodded back toward Hemi. "You guys go on ahead."

"The dog can come," he said, taking another few steps closer. "And your bike will be safe right there."

Now Cara knew he was out of his mind. Her bike wouldn't be safe, not without her on it. She wasn't leaving it to go anywhere, especially not with a car full of drunken fools.

She held a hand up, hoping it would stop him. "No, I'm good. Thanks."

He kept coming and another guy with shocking red hair jumped out of the backseat of the car. He caught up to his buddy and together, they moved closer.

Cara put both feet on the pedals and tried to move out into the traffic. She stopped when an oncoming car blew the horn at her and swerved.

"Whoa, whoa there," the first guy said.

She had to stop. The road was too busy with traffic to get out on it and their car was blocking her from going forward on the bike path. She looked behind her, gauging if she could turn the bike and trailer around in the small space. Before she could try, the two guys were there, one taking hold of her handlebars and the redhead coming in closer to her face.

Hemi barked once, a bark that sounded to Cara like a warning. Then he switched back to growling. She twisted backward and reached out to grab his collar.

"No, Hemi. Stay," Cara said. She didn't know what he'd do to them, or worse, what they'd do to him. He wasn't a big dog, but they were two fairly strong-looking fellows. Usually he obeyed her; she just hoped this wasn't the one time he chose not to.

That was decided when the redhead made the choice to lay a hand on her arm. Cara jerked it back and when she did, Hemi leapt off the bike, snarling and barking as he went for the guy's leg.

"Hemi, no!" Cara went after him, bending and putting her hands out, trying to shield him from the sudden kicks and flailing of the one he'd gone after.

"Call him off! Call him off!" he screamed.

The other guy was bent over at the waist, laughing at his friend's expense.

Cara didn't see anything funny and, before she could tell him so, Hemi's teeth made impact and the redhead gave one more vicious kick, sending Hemi flying into the air about a foot before he landed on his side with a thud.

She cursed and ran to him. He struggled to his feet and then made like he was going to go after the guy again. She grabbed him just before he launched and she held him to her.

"What the hell?" asked Redhead, clutching his leg. He was wearing shorts and Cara could see where Hemi's teeth had gone in, leaving a trail of blood oozing down toward the ankle.

She would not apologize. She'd done nothing wrong.

He looked up and made eye contact with her. Rage filled his face and apprehension burned in her gut, so much so that she quickly changed her mind about apologizing.

"I'm sorry," she blurted out, hugging Hemi closer as he growled and snapped. "Really—I'm sorry."

The driver of the car got out and jogged back to them, stopping once to pick up the Nascar ball cap that had blown from his head. Now there were three of them against her. The one who'd busted a gut laughing finally lost the amusement and together they stood against her, a wall of misplaced male anger pointed directly at her.

And at Hemi.

The one who'd lost flesh over his decision to grab her arm made a step forward and pointed at them. "Your damn dog bit me," Redhead said through gritted teeth. "I might need stitches. Who's going to pay for that? Huh?"

"I . . . I . . ." she stumbled over her words.

Nascar Guy stepped forward. "C'mon guys, leave her alone. You asked for it, Rusty."

The redhead shoved his friend aside and stepped even closer to Cara.

"*You, you* what?" he said. "Are you paying up? Or do we take it out of your dog's hide?"

His words struck fear into Cara's heart and she picked Hemi up, struggling with his weight as she moved back a step. Hemi didn't like his sudden captivity and he wiggled, trying to get free. Cara held tight.

"He didn't mean to," she said. "You scared him."

Redhead tried to mimic her, making his voice high and alarmed. "*He didn't mean to . . . you scared him.* Bullshit. I say we throw the dog over the side. See if he can swim."

Cara looked around them at her bike, wishing there was some way she could get to it. But even if she did, how could she keep Hemi still while she rode away? He was too big for her lap and she needed both arms to steer. The situation was getting grimmer by the second.

She'd have to talk her way out of it.

"Look," she said. "I take full responsibility and okay, I'll pay. You can have all my money. It isn't much, but it's yours. Just let me get to my backpack."

Nascar Guy gave her a sympathetic look but the other two glared at her. Then the one who'd been bitten moved aside and the others followed. Cara walked around them, keeping as wide a distance as she could.

At the trailer, she set Hemi down.

"Stay, Hemi," she said in the firmest voice she'd ever used on him. "I mean it."

Luckily her backpack was within reach and she kept one hand on Hemi and reached for it with the other. Behind her she heard the guys whispering to each other and was sure she heard something about grabbing her and pushing her into the backseat. Another one of them mentioned the money. From the few words she could gather, Nascar Guy was obviously trying to talk them into leaving her alone, but she had little hope he could sway the amount of testosterone that was driving the rage of the other two.

Cars zoomed by them, taking no notice of the predicament she was in. Cara felt herself begin to tremble but pretended she didn't hear their talking. She fumbled with the zipper of the bag, buying time as she tried to think fast of how to get away.

"How much do you have?" Redhead asked.

She was going to have to give it to them. It was her only option. She pulled the wad of cash from the inside pocket and turned. "About eighty bucks or so."

He came forward and snatched it from her hand, triggering Hemi to start barking again. Cara kept hold of him but it wasn't easy.

The one who'd laughed like a maniac began walking over to where she was, or more accurately, swaggered over. The amused smirk was gone now, replaced by a dangerous glint in his eyes. "Eighty bucks ain't shit. I say we teach the dog a lesson," he said.

Cara pushed her arm through the strap of her backpack, rolling it over one shoulder. She stepped in front of Hemi.

The redhead looked at her, a satisfied sneer on his face. "I agree. But if you'll leave the mangy mutt and go with us for a few hours, we can forget the whole thing."

"I can't leave, and I'll have to pass on going anywhere with you," Cara said, slowly, careful to keep her tone from sounding too unfriendly.

At her words, she saw rage flush his face, reminding her of so many men she'd known in her life. He meant it, she could see that. He was going to get back at her in some way, somehow. She looked behind her, thinking of running. She wished Hemi were on a leash. If she ran, what if he didn't follow?

She was stuck. Looking at the one with the ball cap, she searched his face to see if he could offer any help. She could tell he didn't want to hurt her. But did he have the courage to stand up for her?

He locked eyes with her briefly, then turned to his friends. "You're gonna get all of us in trouble, Rusty," Nascar Guy said. "Let's just go."

Redhead turned back to him. "If you don't shut your mouth, you can walk home. You're either with us or against us. Or maybe you'd like to take a swim, too?"

Nascar Guy stepped back, holding his hands up as though he didn't know what to do. The others ignored him and advanced toward her.

She couldn't help it, she hated herself, but she started crying and backing away. Hemi sensed her distress and started growling again. Cara tripped on something behind her, a rock or a low place, and she instinctively let go of Hemi's collar to catch herself. She hit the ground first, her impact softened by the backpack. She turned in a panic, ready to call Hemi down, but he immediately came to her side, sniffing at her in concern.

Behind him the guys were bearing down on them.

Cara waited until Hemi was close to her face and reached out, pulling his muzzle in near her mouth. "Hemi, we've got to run and I need you to follow," she whispered, then jumped to her feet. "Come, Hemi. Come!"

She took off in the opposite direction as her bike, looking to be sure that Hemi was obeying. And that was her only miracle—he was.

The redhead shouted obscenities but Cara kept running. Hemi was right beside her and she said a prayer of thanks that the guys didn't give chase. Her hope was that they'd give up and drive away, and she could eventually turn around and return for her bike.

They ran another twenty yards or so before she turned to see where they were. The scene behind her stopped her in her tracks. Hemi looked up at her as though to ask what was next.

"Oh no, Hemi," she whispered.

The guys hadn't gotten into their car yet. Leaving may have been their next plan, but only after they'd tossed her bike and trailer over the bridge. As Nascar Guy stood watching, his friends struggled but finally, with a few heaves, it was over the side. The loud splash as her only mode of transportation hit the water and immediately began to sink to the bottom of the ocean made her sick to her stomach.

Utter shock held her there for a few more seconds, but when the guys turned to look for her—to see if she'd witnessed their victory— common sense kicked in. She began to jog again, mindful of the agonizing stitch in her side and the ache of despair in her heart.

Chapter Fourteen

When nightfall came, Cara was exhausted. Still, she and Hemi continued on, but only after she'd investigated and then determined there was no way to rescue their things from the water. What hadn't sunk had quickly floated much too far away from any land to reach.

She thought of Miss Kim and Clyde, and regret flooded her that the gifts they'd put so much into were now gone. But like she'd done her entire life, she took a few breaths, then put one foot in front of the other and got back on track.

Though the trio had taken off once they'd dumped the bike and trailer over the side of the bridge, Cara was still wary that they'd come back and try to find her, so she kept a close eye on the road and when similar cars came round, she and Hemi stepped further into the shadows.

While they walked, her stomach rumbled and her tongue felt dry, but she worried more about Hemi. To know he could be hungry or thirsty bothered her. Of course he couldn't understand why she'd suddenly stopped seeing to his needs. He'd put his trust in her many miles ago and now she was letting him down.

"Come on, Hemi," she coaxed.

Kay Bratt

It had started to rain lightly and he didn't like to get wet. She could tell he was slowing down, and the way he looked at her every few minutes, as though gauging if it was time to stop yet, told her he was getting tired. But with no tent or sleeping gear, she didn't see the sense in stopping. She was also still shaken by her experience with the guys and felt that walking in the dark was preferable, so she wanted to get in as many miles as she could, and hopefully make it to Key West by morning.

What they'd do when they got there, she wasn't sure. With no money it was going to be tough, but she'd figure it out.

They walked on for hours and Cara would've kept going, but the cramps in her calves declared mutiny, urging her to change her mind and find a place to hunker down for a bit.

When she spotted an abandoned strip of stores, she led Hemi around to the back. Obviously it was being used as a dumping place and Cara was relieved to see a pile of boxes behind an overflowing dumpster.

"I've seen them do this in movies," she mumbled as she dug down to the ones that weren't wet.

Now that she'd decided to rest, her body felt limp with fatigue. Quickly she broke down two of the biggest boxes and laid them flat, near the brick wall of the building. Then she tore open the side of another huge box and pulled it over the pad she'd created.

Hemi was nearby, drinking from a small puddle.

"Come on, buddy," she called, crawling into the homemade shelter. He followed and after turning a few circles, settled down beside her.

Cara lay down and curled her body around him, thankful for the sense of security he brought. She barely minded the uncomfortable setting or the putrid odor of trash as she stretched her aching legs, letting them stick out of the box.

She thought of Hana and how she would never in a million years agree to sleep behind a dumpster. Or in a box. No, her sister would probably find a motel and somehow talk her way into free lodging.

But that was Hana. Cara on the other hand, she wasn't a hustler. She knew her limits and a few boxes behind a dumpster would have to do.

Within seconds, she was fast asleep.

⚜

When Cara awoke a few hours later, she and Hemi emerged from the cardboard to find the rain had gone. It wasn't light yet but she wanted to get a head start before the sun began to beam down on them.

She stretched, flexing her arms over her head to try to work out the stiffness, then bending at the waist to touch her toes. She knew she must look a wreck, but other than smoothing down her hair and shaking a few wrinkles loose from her blouse, there was nothing she could do.

Finally, she was ready.

Hemi found more standing water and Cara let him drink his fill before they began. From what she could figure, they'd only slept about three or four hours, and though her muscles still ached, she felt a burst of energy to get going.

They walked.

And walked some more.

It was quiet, giving Cara plenty of time to think. Almost no one was out so early and the silence only broken by the occasional chirping of the earliest morning birds was soothing. Even Hemi appeared to be enjoying himself, his tail wagging slowly as they went.

At times, Cara felt like they'd never make it to Key West but still forged on, hungry and thirsty, focused on the final destination.

She only realized just how long they'd been at it when the famous Seven Mile Bridge came into view. It was an amazing sight to take in—it appeared as though the bridge ended somewhere in the deep blue sea. They were a half mile into it just as the sun started to come up, and Cara gazed at the white gaps just becoming visible in the sunlight, thinking how they looked like sparkling gems floating gracefully on the surface.

"Look at that, Hemi," she said, pausing to take it in.

A faint double rainbow was visible in the distance, an unexpected gift that filled her with hope and renewed energy. Rainbows were pretty, but she'd always been more of a sucker for beautiful sunrises, usually witnessed alone, because she and Hana had always been on different cycles for sleep. She was a morning person, rising early with a strong resolution to take on the day and make it worth it. Because of that, she'd always gone to bed at a decent time for her, but an hour when Hana was usually just getting started.

Hana was the night person—feeling her best when it was twilight and then sleeping in until noon most days. She also liked the afternoon shifts at work, so taking the nanny job where she'd been forced to get up early every day had been quite a challenge for her, but one she thought worth it considering the salary she was making. And it did go well for a while.

Cara took a deep breath, forcing herself to push back the negative thoughts and focus on the beauty of the moment. They were walking along the paved shoulder of the bridge and were exposed to the cross-winds, but it was a mild, gentle breeze that caressed her and urged her forward. Beneath them in the water, Cara spotted a colorful sailboat and the couple on board saw her and waved. She wished she were with them, floating along with nothing on her mind but sky, wind, and water.

As they went, she read each of the signs indicating which island they were passing over. She could see the old bridge that ran parallel to them for most of the way, and her mind wandered to the history of it and the interesting details that allowed her to envision the old train that once ran over it. Below, it was mesmerizing to her that she could see both the Atlantic Ocean as well as the Gulf of Mexico.

When she looked down and saw a stingray gliding gracefully in the water below, she felt her breath catch in her throat. First a lovely sunrise, then a rainbow, and now a stingray? It occurred to her that this was probably one of those life moments that she'd always hold dear and never forget.

In a burst of emotion, she stopped and knelt down.

"Hemi, come."

He turned to her, his tail wagging, and Cara gathered him close to her, hugging him tightly. She'd heard before that dogs didn't like to hug, that it was too close to what they did to each other to assert dominance, standing close and putting a paw on the other dog's shoulder, but she could tell by the way he quivered from his nose to his tail that Hemi wasn't one of those case studies. He was a hugger.

She kissed his nose. "I just wanted to thank you for coming this far with me. Now let's finish strong."

Cara wasn't sure what would become of them, or where life's paths would lead next, but she wasn't going to focus on those mysteries just yet. Standing and stretching her arms over her head, she was ready and excited to finally complete the journey.

Chapter Fifteen

Key West was not what Cara expected, and not even close to the vision she'd built up in her mind for so many miles. First of all, there were a lot of people squeezed into every little space her eyes alighted on. Not even just a lot—but more like *way* too many.

Now that she'd lost the bike and was back to walking, she was able to take in more details. So far she'd seen several signs declaring: Key West, the Conch Republic. Among the packed-in small buildings and strips of shops, she'd also already spotted many flags waving in the air. They were pretty, a rich blue material marked with a symbolic sun and the words *Conch Republic* in big letters over it, then underneath: *"we seceded where others failed."* It was as though Key West was declaring itself an entirely different country than the rest of the United States. Cara wouldn't be surprised—to her it felt like another world.

"Want to take a trolley tour?" A thin teenaged boy tried handing her a brochure, a huge smile on his face. He looked at her wrinkled clothes, then leaned in and whispered, "Discounts when the sun starts going down."

"No, thank you," Cara said, moving past him. A tour would have been amazing, but considering she was dead broke, she'd have to find Hemingway's home and all the other historical sites on her own. She spotted another corner vender under a tent, his wares laid out on a table, with vibrant shirts and dresses for sale hanging all around. The display of sunscreen caught her eye and she wished she could buy some. Her face was blistered, most of the sunburn coming from the walk over Seven Mile Bridge. Her skin felt tight and hot, and she figured that considering she hadn't used sunscreen since she'd left Georgia, she'd probably added five or ten years of aging to her sensitive skin.

Aside from the lines of flea market–type stands, the small town bustled with pedestrians on foot, surrounded by bikes, electric scooters, and cars weaving in and around the crowds. A pink taxicab darted from the curb into traffic, then a tourist bus passed by, the words *Old Town Trolley* painted across the vivid orange side. A few of the patrons waved at her, confirming Cara's initial feeling that the island was truly laid-back and friendly. Looking around at the relaxed faces coming at her, she sensed a certain kind of freedom in the air—the island inhabitants seemed younger, even less stressed out than most she'd run into during her life.

It felt wonderful.

As they walked through the main part of town, Cara worried that she and Hemi would get separated, so she tied the rope leash loosely around his neck, threading the other end through her belt loop. The rope was embarrassing, but she didn't have a penny to her name to buy a leash, much less a meal they so desperately needed. And the rope— well, she was lucky she'd stuffed it in her bag, keeping it from hitting the water, likely just on top of all the sunken items that had made her trip more bearable. Sadly, the atlas that Clyde had given her—gone. The yoga mat that had cushioned many nights on the ground—also gone. Their food supplies! She shook it off, trying to put it out of her mind. There was nothing she could do about it now.

First things first, and she knew she needed to get them both some water.

She stepped to the side quickly, pulling Hemi along with her, and narrowly avoided a mother pushing a stroller. The toddler was looking at one of those board picture books and Cara thought about her two paperbacks, relieved that they'd been in her backpack and hadn't joined the other supplies in the water, maybe on their way to Cuba by now.

The mother stopped when Hemi's leash almost made contact against her child's neck.

"Oh, I'm so sorry," Cara said, pulling Hemi out of the way.

The rope was going to be too much hassle. She bent down, untying it.

"Now Hemi, if you don't want to get lost, you'd better stay with me." She took off again, and when she looked down, Hemi was falling behind.

Leaning against a light pole, she waited, letting him catch up to her as he moved lithely in between people, his eyes never leaving her.

When he reached her, she bent down and put both hands on his head, pulling his face near to hers. "You're a good dog," she said. "I'm going to find you something to drink and then eat, I promise." She didn't know how she was going to keep that oath, but even if she had to beg—something she'd sworn she'd never do—she would humble herself to hold a cup out there. Not for herself, but for him. Hemi had done nothing but loyally protect her and keep her company on many lonely days and nights. She owed him everything.

Together they continued down the sidewalk, crossing through the foot traffic, when Cara spotted a small street café. When she approached it, she refrained from making eye contact with any of the people sitting at the outside tables. She was focused on one table that had just vacated.

The dishes and cups were still there.

Cara felt sick with anxiety, but she pushed those feelings back; she was going to grab one of the cups. Among the glass ones, she saw one Styrofoam cup with a straw. If she could get it, she could use it for water for her and for Hemi. Hopefully, it would already have some in it. She was no longer too proud to drink after a stranger.

"We'll just keep walking and I'll reach out and grab it while we go by," she muttered to Hemi, though she knew he couldn't hear her with all the chatter around them. Miraculously, he somehow knew he needed to stay right with her and he walked close to her heels.

She kept her eye on the table, hoping the waiter or waitress wouldn't suddenly emerge with a tray and take away her cup. Cara didn't relish the idea of digging into the trash for it, though she knew she would if she had to.

"Excuse me," a woman said after her large beach bag bumped Cara's arm.

"It's okay," Cara replied, noting the woman was definitely a tourist, evident by the camera hanging around her neck and the fancy resort-looking clothes she wore. It was hot—scorching even—and she felt a pang of sympathy for the woman.

Cara wasn't faring much better in her jeans, T-shirt, and ragged sneakers, but she didn't really have a choice unless she wanted to run around naked.

"This is it, buddy," she said, making Hemi's ears perk up. "It's our chance. Say a prayer."

Moving as gracefully as possible so as to not draw attention to herself, she walked toward the table, at the last minute leaning over to grab the Styrofoam cup. As her fingers curled around it, she saw a barely touched hot dog on one of the plates.

Hemi would love to have that hot dog, she thought to herself. She hesitated, looked down at him by her side, and reached for it.

"Young lady!" she heard a man's voice call out, and she froze. If she'd have just taken the cup and not gotten greedy! Now she was going to have to face the wrath of someone who thought her a bum or a thief—or whatever.

She snatched her hand back and turned toward the voice, ready to plead her case, or run—whichever option would work best.

An older, bearded man sat at a table near the one she'd accosted. He'd obviously witnessed her attempt at hot-dog robbery. At his feet lay a German shepherd with its head propped up on crossed paws, its expression hot and bored.

"I—I'm sorry," she stuttered.

He waved her over, dismissing her apology with a roll of his eyes and a flick of the cigar he held. "Come here, I'd like to talk to you," he said, then used his foot to push a chair out from under the table. "Bring the dog, too."

Cara hesitated, considering what to do. The man might be a customer, or even the café owner. Either way, she was humiliated that she'd been busted, and she could feel her temperature rise even higher than it already was from the heat. She took a deep breath and turned toward his table. She might as well see what he wanted, so she slowly worked around the tables to get to his, then sat on the offered chair.

"Hemi, down," she said, and he dropped to a sit, then a full down position, amazing her once again with his aptitude for obeying.

"Nice dog," the man said, nodding his approval.

"Yours, too," Cara replied. His dog hadn't moved, even at their arrival into his space. His ears had perked and he'd given Hemi a quick look of appraisal, but then the interest had subsided. "Look, that hot dog was going to go to the trash so I was just going to grab it for my dog."

The confession slipped out of her mouth without warning, making Cara want to kick herself. She'd always folded under pressure—even Hana had known to keep her gagged or hidden when they were guilty of something she hadn't wanted Cara to confess to. She couldn't help it, it was just engrained in her to do the right thing or at least to apologize when she didn't.

He took another long drag of his cigar and raised his eyebrows at her. "I'm not one to judge. I just noticed how your dog was sticking to you as though on some invisible leash. That's unusual in an environment as chaotic as this one, so it caught my eye. I'm a dog lover."

Cara felt a wave of apprehension at his words. What he'd said about Hemi and dogs didn't register after his first statement. His stoic expression, the white beard he wore, and the pretentious cigar suddenly made her wonder if he *was* in fact a judge. But the clothes— they fit right in with most every other man on the street. Khaki shorts and a flowered button-down shirt. If he were a judge, she told herself, he was a retired one.

She eyed the pitcher of water on the table and he pushed it closer to her. There was also an additional glass, and Cara picked it up, then looked down at Hemi.

"Sue?" the man called to the waitress who had appeared and was clearing the other table off. "Bring a bowl for the dog."

Cara watched as the hot dog was carelessly thrown into the black bin propped against the table, along with the other leftovers and dirty dishes. She sighed, thinking of how that hot dog would've held Hemi over for a few more hours.

"How long you in Key West for?" he asked, breaking the silence.

"I'm not sure." And that was the truth. She'd meant only to make a pilgrimage to Hemingway, find a place for Hemi, then move on. But now, with no bike or money, no supplies, how could she go anywhere?

"You hungry?" he asked softly.

Cara looked at him, gauging his demeanor. She'd heard of men out and about, looking for unknowing and desperate girls to add to their disgusting prostitution rings, catering to tourists of the worst kind. Offering food and shelter while they really planned to lock them up, even shoot them full of drugs until they were compliant and ready to work. Was he a pimp? An old, laid-back, Key West style of recruiting to the dark trade?

"I see a lot of distrust going through that head of yours," he said. "I was just offering food—nothing more. You're free to walk away. This is a friendly town and I was just being welcoming."

She let out the breath she was holding. He really did look kind, once she got past her usual paranoia and took a good look at him. And after all, they were in a public place with loads of people around. It wasn't as though he would be able to grab her and stick her into the back of a windowless white van.

"I'm sorry. I've had a rough few days." She thought of the guys on the bridge and the fear she'd felt at their assault. The devastation when they'd thrown her stuff in the ocean.

"Understandable," he said. "I'm Wally. My dog is Indiana Bones, but we call him Indie."

The dog raised its head, looking toward his master, then lowered it again.

"I'm Cara. That's Hemi." She pointed at Hemi. After sniffing at the man's dog, Hemi had eased into a sit, switching his attention to the people going by.

Wally raised his eyebrows again. "Hemi? For Hemingway?"

She was saved from answering by the waitress, who returned with a small plastic bowl and set it on the table. Cara thanked her, picked up the bowl, and immediately poured some water into it, then put it on the ground in front of Hemi. Once he was lapping at it, she poured herself some and took a long drink. It was the best water she'd ever tasted, and as it slid down her throat, she said a silent prayer of thanksgiving.

"Hey, Sue—bring out some of that kibble you have in there for this hungry dog. And get the girl a cheeseburger plate. She's way too skinny. Put it on my tab."

The waitress nodded and moved away.

"Thank you," Cara said softly. She didn't know why the man had decided to be kind to them, but it couldn't have come at a better time. They were desperate so she'd take it. But she was still wary, just in case he was tricking her and planning to call the cops. She looked down at his dog. "I guess he's from Germany?"

Wally shook his head. "No, but that's an easy mistake. Most German shepherds bred for training do come from Germany, but Indie here was shipped from Holland. He was part of a program outside of Indianapolis and imprinted when he was just over a year old."

"Imprinted?"

"That means introduced to and then trained to recognize the odor of human remains." Wally spoke casually, as though discussing the weather or the latest blockbuster movie, not a dog trained to seek out murder victims or lost people.

"I don't understand."

"One thing you'll find out here in Key West, besides it being eccentric on top of wildly beautiful, is that everyone has a story. Some are interesting, some not so much. Some people come here to visit and end up staying forever, then some are here to breeze through as a respite from the chaos of their lives."

"And you?" Cara asked, hoping to keep the focus on him and away from her.

"Indie and I are here to stay. We're both retired now, but Indie used to be on the Los Angeles County force, as one of the nation's few cadaver dogs in law enforcement."

"But he's so calm," she said, watching Indie. People walked by, their voices loud, but he acted as though he heard nothing. His demeanor had even rubbed off on Hemi, who had curled up a nose away from the German shepherd and closed his eyes.

"He was trained to be that way. Just like bomb dogs, cadaver dogs sit or lie down and stare to alert a find. That's so they don't disturb a scene or damage evidence. After so many years of doing his duty, his work persona just became his personality."

The waitress returned, carrying a tray with a bowl of kibble for Hemi and a plate piled high with a fat cheeseburger and fries for Cara.

Her mouth watered and she had to hold herself back. She hadn't eaten in almost twenty-four hours and the aroma of the grilled burger was making her dizzy.

"Go ahead, don't be polite. These burgers are the best in Key West. Eat it like you mean it," Wally said.

The waitress set the kibble on the ground and Hemi dug in without a second invitation. Cara did the same with her food, after thanking the man again.

While she and Hemi ate, Wally described meeting Indie when the dog was a new and overwhelmed trainee, forced to follow a strict schedule of urinating and releasing his bowels at specific times every day, twice a day.

Cara thought how different it was from Hemi, who lifted a leg on just about whatever he could, whenever he could. He was always marking bushes, poles, and anything else while he was on the ground. She didn't know if Hemi would ever make it as a trained dog, but she did know he was smart.

"So, when they released Indie they let me take him and together we decided to spend our golden years in Key West. It's a fine place for dogs here—they're accepted along with every other local or tourist."

He was right about that. She'd seen several dogs sitting with their owners outside of bars and restaurants, or walking with them on the sidewalks. To her, it appeared they treated their dogs like family, the way it should be everywhere.

She finished the burger and ate most of the fries that she didn't slip to Hemi, then she wiped her mouth with a napkin. She thought about offering to pay, and remembered she didn't have anything to pay with. Though desperate, she still didn't like accepting a handout.

"Thank you so much," she said, feeling her cheeks burn.

"You're welcome. Do you plan to stay around here long?"

She thought he at least deserved a real answer this time. He'd stepped in just when she'd needed it most.

"I hadn't planned to stay long at all, but I'm in a bit of trouble with resources. Yesterday I had the unfortunate pleasure of being accosted on the road by some immature boys playing as men."

He looked concerned. "Did they hurt you?"

She shook her head. "Not physically. But when one laid a hand on me, Hemi lunged and bit him. They took my money as restitution and when that wasn't enough, they threw my bike, trailer, and all my supplies over the side of the bridge we were on. I've got nothing now." Her eyes felt moist and she looked away for a moment, cleared her throat, and straightened her shoulders. "I need to find a job fast. I can't even pay to feed Hemi and I don't have anywhere to stay now that I don't have a tent."

"I'm sorry to hear those boys acted in such an ungentlemanly way. That's unusual for the Keys, I can promise you that."

Cara looked down at Hemi. "He protected me, don't worry. Hemi's been my travel companion for the last several hundred miles, but I also promised him I'd deliver him to a better place. Now I'm in as desperate a situation as he was."

"There's a mission not far from here," Wally said. "I'm sure they'll take you in."

"Really?" She looked up, hope filling her. If they could just get somewhere to clean up and to sleep for a few days, then maybe she could find a job, pay for her and Hemi to live for a while or until it was time to decide what to do next.

She listened while Wally gave her precise directions, describing a route to take her out of the touristy district and to the mission located in the historical area. Cara felt encouraged. So far, things were looking up. If it could continue, she and Hemi might just be okay.

Close to an hour later, she spotted the elaborate wrought-iron gate that Wally had described and when she looked at the house behind it, she knew they'd found the mission. Relief flooded through her.

"There it is, Hemi. That's gotta be it."

Hard to miss, the house was the most beautiful home she'd seen so far on the island. Much of it was surrounded by tall, lush tropical trees and bushes, but what Cara could see looked less pretentious than some of the houses she'd passed. This one—it could only be described as modestly stunning.

The crisp white shutters framed floor-to-ceiling windows and created a soft backdrop against the buttery-yellow paint on the house itself. And the porch. She sighed. It was a storybook porch complete with rocking chairs and comfortable-looking red-flowered cushions.

It painted such a picture of peace in her mind that Cara could really see her and Hemi taking a few days there to get back on their feet. Maybe they'd let her work to pay for her stay. Or she could find a job on the island. If she just had somewhere that Hemi could hang out, she'd put her best face on and go get a waitressing job. In the span of a few seconds, she had an entire plan laid out, but she couldn't take her eyes off the house long enough to put it into action.

She scanned the porch again. A cozy wooden table and chairs were set up on one corner, and it appeared that someone had recently eaten there. A pitcher of orange juice and a few glasses remained, teasing Cara with the possibility of sampling it. The one other detail that couldn't be missed on the porch was the woodwork that accented each post. Wally had called it gingerbread when he was telling her which house to look for.

Someone had carved elaborate flowers into the corner pieces—the gingerbread—giving the house its own signature look. Cara saw another wooden piece tacked onto the arched porch, this time a sign. She felt a chill when she read what it said: The Hadley House.

Hemingway's first wife was named Hadley, though as far as Cara knew, the woman had never lived in Key West. Hadley and Hemingway were divorced by the time he'd slid into what most called his Key West era, and he'd been married to another woman named Pauline. But the irony of Cara being led to this particular property—with an obvious connection to Hemingway—was beyond the scope of her reasoning. She shook it off, peering over the gate at the half dozen dogs who barked once or twice, then competed to get the closest, their tails wagging and bodies quivering out a welcome.

Hemi stuck his nose through the rungs of the gate, sniffing in curiosity.

"Hey, guys," Cara said, leaning over to make eye contact. She didn't quite dare to drop a hand in, instead flooding them with kind words as she looked around the yard. At least her question about whether the mission accepted dogs was easily answered.

She waited a few more minutes, hoping someone would come out of the house, and when no one did, she picked up her backpack, then put on a brave face and reached over and unlatched the gate. She opened it just a crack, only enough for her to slip through. She'd meant to make Hemi stay out on the sidewalk until she'd made sure he'd be safe around the other dogs, but Hemi had other plans. And they didn't include being left behind. He slipped in right behind her before she could shut the gate. Immediately the other dogs forgot she existed while they surrounded Hemi, sniffing at him to get acquainted.

Cara almost reached down to pluck him out of the mob, but he was holding his own. He kept his head low and body stiff as he patiently waited, then in a few seconds it was over and it appeared that they accepted him. Off they all went, with Hemi smack dab in the middle, around the side of the house.

"Don't go far," she called out.

She went to the porch and noticed a fat black-and-white cat that graced the top step. It stared at her, its expression none too gracious.

Cara climbed the steps and when she dropped her hand to stroke its head, it ducked away and slipped into the bushes.

"Fine, be snobby." She went to the door and knocked once.

When no one answered, she turned the knob. It was a mission, not a residence, she told herself as she fought back her reluctance to intrude.

The front door opened into a large foyer and Cara stepped in. She worked her way down the hall, peering into rooms as she went. She passed a large sitting room on her right, complete with several couches boasting a few more dogs lounging around. One tiny dog—a Yorkie, she thought—sat up and yipped at Cara a few times, then settled back into a velvety-looking pillow. A ball of red fur lay beside the pillow, and it didn't stir but Cara was fairly sure it was one of those tiny Pomeranians, the ones that were painfully loud when they were riled. She hoped it didn't wake.

"Hello?"

No one answered.

She hesitated, then hearing voices coming from the back of the house, she continued down the hall. It led into the largest kitchen Cara had ever seen in a house, and there at the counter were a man and a young woman, their backs to her as they worked to fill at least a dozen bowls with something. She noticed that the honey-colored cabinets looked like shutters and wondered if the design was part of keeping the house historically accurate. But she wasn't there to admire the décor, she told herself.

"Um . . . excuse me?" she said, feeling completely out of place.

Both of them turned.

"Hi," they said at the same time.

Cara was suddenly tongue-tied and even more self-conscious about how bedraggled and dirty she looked. She reached a hand to her hair, as though one touch could tame the tangles and make it sparkle. She wasn't normally so vain and she didn't like it. She wondered suddenly if she smelled and she clamped her arm back down to her side.

The pause as they waited for her to respond gave her plenty of time to study them. The guy, he looked close to thirty—and something about him made her blush all the way to her toes. It must've been his intense blue eyes, or his rugged unshaved look, or . . . She didn't know, but suddenly she was fifteen again and at the high school prom standing there like an idiot when Josh Taylor had asked her to dance. She'd crushed on him all year but when that moment had finally come, she'd frozen, unable to form words.

Hana had sensed her uncertainty and stepped in, swooping Josh away with a wink and a sexy smile, leaving Cara huddling against the wall, mortified and wishing she'd dissolve in a puddle of shame.

But this time, Hana wasn't there.

Then she remembered the girl—the one who stood there with a ladle in one hand and a can of dog food in the other, staring at her with one eyebrow lifted in an amused expression. The one who stood watching as Cara checked out her boyfriend like he was a lollipop in a candy store. The girl was a looker herself, her skin kissed golden from the sun and her hair the kind that Cara and Hana had always been jealous of—long and silky blonde. To set it all off, she was perfectly petite, like a little Barbie standing next to her golden Ken doll.

No wonder they were together; they were perfect for each other.

"I'm so sorry," Cara said, immediately contrite for the way her eyes had roamed shamelessly over someone who was obviously already taken.

The man tilted his head questioningly. "For . . . ?"

"Is this the mission house?" Cara finally got out. She felt the heat continue to rush up her neck and into her cheeks, and prayed neither of them were mind readers.

The guy was about to answer her when suddenly Hemi and the other half dozen dogs came barging through the doggy door at the back of the kitchen from what Cara assumed was the backyard.

"Whoa, there," the guy said as the dogs surrounded him, pushing against him, excited at the smell of the dog food. He laughed at them, scooting some of them back with a gentle prod of his knee. "Calm down there, you'll all get a share. Even you, new guy."

The man looked up at Cara, laughing even more at the sudden ruckus that filled the kitchen. "Now *I'm* sorry. Let me put this away and we'll go talk. I assume this handsome fellow is the one you brought in?"

He gestured at Hemi and Cara nodded. He turned to the girl at the counter.

"Tori, can you finish this and let me see about checking in a new resident? Make sure Vinnie doesn't take over someone else's bowl," he said, then reached behind and untied the strings to his apron. He peeled it off and laid it on the counter, then looked at Cara. "Vinnie there—the wiggly Dachshund with the potbelly—is on a diet and he's a sneaky one."

He pointed at what Cara had always known as a wiener dog. But this one was the fattest she'd ever seen. His belly nearly touched the tiled floor.

"The shelter called me begging for help after he'd been returned three times. He's too fat and it's making him miserable," he continued.

The girl—she assumed Tori—leaned over the counter to watch him and laughed. "Ava has him on a fitness plan and she's determined his new name will be Skinny Vinnie by the time she's through."

He nodded. "I believe it. Then maybe we can really find him a permanent home." Gesturing to Cara, he went to the back door. "Come on, let's go outside. Believe it or not, it's calmer out there."

She followed him out and he led her to two Adirondack chairs on the back porch. Like the front of the property, the back was also lush with greenery and to Cara, it felt like a gentle oasis away from the busy street life of Key West. Scattered around the yard were balls and other dog toys, and tucked away in the back corner, she could see a line of covered metal dog pens. Though she knew other houses were on either side, the groves of trees stationed around the stone fence made it feel like this property was totally private. It was enchanting, to say the least.

Once they were seated, he held out a hand. "Sorry for the chaos. I'm Luke Dalton."

"Cara," she answered automatically. Her brain was barely working, and she longed to shut her eyes and just feel the breeze on her face, and slip into a nap. But first—she had to make a deal.

"So you want to drop off a dog?" he asked.

She sat straight up, suddenly alert. She wasn't ready yet to let go of Hemi. "No. I don't want to drop off my dog. I was hoping we could both stay."

"Stay? Here?"

"Yes. Someone on Duval told me this is a mission." Cara suddenly felt like a huge mistake had been made. She looked around, hoping to see Hemi, but obviously he was still inside, cavorting with the boys.

Luke nodded. "Well, I guess you could call us that. But it's not for people. Tori and I take in stray dogs, and some cats, and work to reunite them with the owners who lost them, or place them with new families. We're sort of a stopover as they're headed to a forever home, if you know what I mean. Sorry, but we can't do the same with wayward humans."

Cara listened, feeling queasy all over again. She knew exactly what a forever home was—especially since it was a goal that she and her sister had never managed to meet. "Well, I did just find Hemi recently and I'd promised to deliver him to a place like this. I just wasn't quite ready to do it today. I need to do some, you know—research. Make sure I do what's best for him. Leave him at the right place, not just the first place."

He smiled and held his arms out wide. "Then this would be the right place. Just this year we've rehomed about twenty-eight dogs and more than two dozen cats. Not just in Key West, either. Some go into the Upper Keys and beyond."

"I—I just think I need to think about it for a day or two. So I'll be going." She made to get up from the chair. "I need to find a place to stay for the night."

Luke stood, and when he spoke, his voice sounded apologetic. "Did you try the hostel over on South Street? They might have an available bunk and it's pretty clean, but they won't take dogs. Maybe I could work out something to let your dog stay a few days here. But there'd be a boarding fee. I mean, nothing too steep but we have to charge something for the food. We can give you some lunch today if you'd like, and there's a soup kitchen over on Flagler if you need them tomorrow."

Now she really did stand. Something about the kindness in his voice, or maybe just the fact that she'd gotten everything so wrong, made her angry. She wasn't leaving Hemi and she didn't have the money for a hostel or any boarding fee. She felt the hope she'd tried to hang on to slipping away and in its place, just under the anger, a familiar sense of desperation.

For some reason, she'd thought arriving in Key West would be the catalyst to a new start—the place she'd receive an epiphany telling her what to do next. But here she was about to be out on the streets again, with no clue where to go this time. It was enough to make her want to crumble to her knees and beg the universe for mercy.

But as she'd learned to do since a young age, she pasted on a fake smile and remembered her manners. "Thank you, but I can't leave Hemi here without me. Let me go round him up and we'll be on our way."

She moved around his long legs and went back into the kitchen.

Hemi was there, his nose a few inches deep into a big red bowl. The girl called Tori knelt beside him, stroking his back as he ate. Cara felt a rush of possessiveness but then her practical side started whispering. The girl was being really kind to him. And eventually, Cara would have to leave Hemi behind anyway. Was it even fair to continue bonding when she had no intention of being his forever person? She didn't even know how she was going to feed him his supper. With her he'd go hungry, but here he could have his meals and even playmates for a while.

Tori looked up at her. "He should be easy to place. Just look at those eyes."

"Oh, she's not leaving him—" Luke started to say.

"Actually," Cara interrupted. This was Hemi's chance and she didn't want to ruin it for him out of selfishness. "It—it would probably be best. He's not really my dog and Hemi needs a real family." The truth was she didn't want Hemi to have to go from place to place like she'd done all her life. He deserved something permanent. And if Tori and Luke could make that happen, then she'd fulfilled her promise to him.

But still, it hurt and Cara felt a lump rising in her throat.

Tori stood and smiled at Cara. "Hemi? Is that short for Hemingway? Why didn't we ever think of that name for any of our crew, Luke? How appropriate for a Key West dog."

"Actually, he found me in Georgia. We've come a long way together," Cara said, then wished she could stuff the words back in her mouth. Why had she just told them where she came from? All she could surmise was that she was totally rattled by Luke, and then by his assumption that she was ditching her dog.

The girl laughed. "So, a Georgia dog, eh? No wonder he's so sweet. He's got those legendary Deep South manners going on."

Hemi finished the last of the food and looked up, his eyes sparkling with the look that Cara had come to know meant he was hoping for more.

"Did you find any identification tags on him? Any clue to where he might've came from?" Luke asked.

Cara shook her head. "No, I just turned around and he was there, right behind me on Interstate 95 coming out of Georgia."

What was wrong with her? Why didn't she just draw them a map? She felt her hands start to shake because of her slip.

"Whew—that's a long way," Luke said. "We can take him down to the clinic and see if he's chipped. If he is, it'll be a lot easier to find his family. If he isn't, don't worry, we'll put his photo out on the Internet and if no one claims him, we'll make sure he lands somewhere safe."

"Somewhere permanent?" Cara asked. Her gut was starting to give her that sick feeling—the one that made her question if what she was doing was the right thing or not. "I don't want him passed from home to home."

"We'll do our best," Tori said. "But I'll be honest, sometimes our best doesn't stick."

Cara knew that was the truth—she'd been hearing people say they'd do their best for too many years to count. Nothing had stuck for her and Hana either. But she had to give Hemi a chance. And that meant she had to say good-bye. It was going to hurt, probably more than she'd ever hurt before, but it was what was best for him.

"Come, Hemi," she said, praying that he'd obey and not make this sudden exit any more awkward than it already was. To her relief, he immediately turned and trotted over, staring up at her and waiting obediently at her fingertips. "Good boy."

She knelt down and buried her face in his fur, rubbing him behind the ears like he loved her to do. "Be good and these people will help you find your family. Thank you for being my friend," she said, barely choking the words out. "You did your job. You took good care of me."

Her eyes burned with unshed tears and she stood, keeping her face down so no one else could see her pain.

Hemi whined. He knew she was in distress and didn't like it. Another reason leaving him was so painful—no one had ever cared so much about how she felt before or been so connected instinctively. To some, he might only be a dog, but to Cara he was the best and most loyal friend she'd ever had.

She wanted to comfort him but it would be a lie. Her path was set and for his well-being, she couldn't take him with her. It took all she had, but she turned away from him.

Without eye contact, she waved at the couple and headed down the original hall they'd come from, out the door, then stumbled down the stairs and off the beautiful porch. Thankfully, Luke and his girlfriend didn't follow.

Hemi and the other dogs caught up and escorted her to the gate, the other dogs saying their good-byes with a few bumps, sniffs, and tail wags. When she opened the gate, Hemi tried to push through with her.

"No, Hemi. You stay," she said, her voice thick with tears as she pushed him back and latched the gate closed between them. She messed up by looking down at his face. He looked confused, then as sad as she'd ever seen him.

"I'm sorry, buddy. This is for your own good," she whispered.

He tilted his head, not breaking her gaze. He didn't make another sound and his silence hurt even more. She started to apologize once more as she backed away, but her voice broke and then she could no longer hold it back.

Tears washed over her face as she gave him one last look, then whispered, hoping her words made it to him as she turned away.

"Don't forget. I love you, Hemi. I really love you."

Chapter Sixteen

Practically holding her breath, she made it all the way to the end of the block and around the corner before she totally broke down again. An old man in flip-flops and Bermuda shorts so long they almost touched his ankles moved out of her way, letting her have the sidewalk as she barreled by him.

"Miss, are you okay?" he asked, his hoarse voice full of concern but his face a blur through her tears.

She nodded, unable to speak. At the next intersection she saw a bench and went to it, sitting down and dropping her backpack at her feet before burying her face in her hands.

She thought about Hemi's face and the confused look he'd given her as she'd walked away. He'd trusted her. And he'd accepted her—every tiny messed up part of who she was. To him, she'd been perfect. And she hadn't even had to leash him. He'd followed her on his own and chosen with his own free will to stay on his trailer as they'd traveled, their friendship cemented with just a can of tuna and a few kind words.

What had she done? Friendships never came that easy for Cara. And what she'd found with Hemi? The way they read each other and reacted without words? With just a touch or a look? What they had was something special and she'd walked away from it.

She took some deep breaths through her fingers, willing herself to get it under control before she made herself sick. When she opened her eyes and lifted her head from her hands, Luke was standing there, leaning against the light pole and looking in the opposite direction.

"What are you doing here?" she asked, completely embarrassed that he'd seen her crying.

"I guess I could ask that of you," he turned to her answering. "And I might've but then you started that bawling stuff and I don't know what to do when girls cry. So I just decided to wait it out. Like—over here to, you know, give you privacy."

He was uncomfortable at what he'd witnessed, that much was obvious. But he still wasn't telling her why he'd followed her.

"So you stood over there listening while I made a fool out of myself?" she asked, rubbing her face dry with her fists.

He shrugged. "I wouldn't call it making a fool out of yourself for crying over losing a friend. I'd call it being human."

She stared at him.

"Well, that's what he is, right? Hemi's your friend. I guess I don't have to tell you that dogs are amazing and it doesn't take long to build a bond that no outside force can break. And this outburst makes me wonder just why you would give something up that means so much to you. Why you'd choose to break that bond yourself?"

She didn't want to explain to him just how desperate her situation was—that she was flat broke, hungry, and homeless. That she'd left Hemi because it was best for him. It was hard enough knowing that she'd been so stupid to just think she could take off, nothing but a few hundred bucks and a lemon for a car, and expect she'd make it. Let him believe she was just another callous human.

The truth was just too humiliating.

"I just need you to do right by him," Cara finally said. "Find him a home. Someone who will never send him back. Can you promise me that?"

Luke didn't answer at first. He looked like he was having an internal struggle with something. Finally he let out a long sigh. "I can't believe I'm doing this, but it was Tori's idea. She practically pushed me out the door to come after you."

"Come after me for what? You can't help Hemi? You won't?"

He came over and sat down on the bench beside her, looking straight ahead at the street as a trio of raucous teenagers crossed over, then walked by them. When they were past and out of earshot, he spoke again.

"Tori said she could tell with one look that you weren't the average Key West drifter in town to party, that you would be a good candidate."

"You still haven't said for what."

He nodded. "I'm getting to it, Miss Impatience. Tori and I have needed some help, and I've been putting it off for months because I really can't afford anyone, not to mention that I'm not much for having another person underfoot full-time. But Tori won't let it go, so if you'd settle for an embarrassingly low salary that I'd make up for by giving you room and board, I'd hire you on for a few weeks. As she said—before she kicked me out the door after you—that'll at least give you some time to get back on your feet and find something else that pays better. And you wouldn't have to leave your dog."

Cara didn't answer. She couldn't—his offer sounded too good to be true, and in her experience, anything that sounded like that usually never panned out. A poker face was imperative. As Hana always said, never let them know how much you want something. She'd had a few offers of a temporary home along the way to Key West, both with Miss Kim and with Henry, but this was the first one that she felt was far enough from home—and all she'd left behind—that she could possibly accept it.

"You'd have your own room but it ain't nothing special," he added. "I do most of the cooking, though I'd appreciate a hand now and then.

Tori can barely even boil water, but since this was her idea, she might find herself peeling a few potatoes this week."

"I can cook," Cara said carefully. "And I'm a really hard worker. I'll do anything—clean out dog pens, mow the yard, whatever you want."

She blushed when she realized she'd just promised a tall, handsome man—possibly even a married one at that—that she'd do anything he wanted. She'd also just shown him her hand, her words showing how much she wanted what he had to give.

His face turned really serious. "Have you ever committed a crime?"

She hesitated, wishing she could ask him to define *crime*. But she couldn't chance it. "No," she said, unable to keep the guilt from her voice.

But he obviously only heard what he wanted to because he slapped his hands on his thighs and jumped up like he had a spring coiled under his butt. "Great. Then you're hired. Can we go back now before you start crying again?"

He looked so hopeful and afraid of another outburst that Cara decided to ignore the doubt she carried everywhere with her and just this once, take a chance. Just long enough to get on her feet.

She laughed. Then she laughed again, suddenly feeling euphoric that she was going back to Hemi. *And* she had a place for them to stay. *And* they'd eat!

He shot her a puzzled look. "First you're sobbing and now you're laughing. See what I mean? I can't believe I just agreed to add another unpredictable female to my home."

Cara muffled the urge to laugh again. Instead she stood and struggled into her backpack, straightening her shoulders and lifting her chin. When it was all set, she looked at Luke, suddenly back in control of herself. "I doubt you'll ever see that much emotion from me again, but what you will see is some real good Southern cooking. And I can promise you this—I'll earn my keep for as long as I'm there. But right now, I just want to get back to my dog."

Luke muttered under his breath, although all Cara caught was something about being too sassy for her own britches. She didn't give him time to repeat himself. She took off, her feet barely hitting the sidewalk in her hurry to rush to Hemi and tell him she was sorry for almost making the biggest mistake of her life.

❧

When they turned the corner, Luke was right on her heels and Cara's breath caught in her throat. She could see Hemi sitting stoically on the other side of the gate, calmly staring out at the street and waiting. The other dogs moved around him, a few wrestling on the grass while others ran back and forth, checking to see what Hemi was looking at, finding nothing, and going back to their antics.

"He hasn't moved since you walked away. I think he'd probably sit there all day and night if he had to, waiting for you," Luke said.

Cara couldn't reply through the tears in her throat. She moved around Luke and jogged the rest of the way. When Hemi saw her coming, he jumped up, his tail wagging along to the quivering of his entire body.

"Hemi, I'm back. I'm so sorry," she said, letting herself through the gate and squatting down in front of him. He licked her face, flipped around in a joyous circle, then licked her again and jumped against her with his front two feet, knocking her over. She laughed, hugging him to her as she tried to stop her tears.

Luke slipped in and Cara stood, letting Hemi rub against her legs to continue his exuberant welcome. "Okay, little buddy, we're going to stay here for a while," she said to Hemi.

His expression told her he didn't care where they stayed, as long as they were together, and Cara felt another surge of guilt for what she'd almost done.

Behind her Luke cleared his throat loudly. "Now that we got that love fest over, let's get started. I have to make rounds," he said as he led her around the back of the house to a small building. It was the size of a gardening shed, but along the side of it were the half dozen metal pens she had noticed earlier, a dog in each one. All the pens had small doors in them, giving them access to the interior of the shed.

Hemi followed but when a shepherd mix bumped him in an invitation to play, he gave Cara another look and took off with the other dogs.

"We'll catch back up with Hemi in a minute. Mark my words, he'll end up inside getting a sympathy treatment from Tori—which means a full-on snuggling session. When she finds out I got you back, she'll gloat all day, so let's at least get in a little training."

Cara felt a bit nervous. She hoped she could measure up to the expectations. He turned to her and held up a finger.

"First, if you're going to work here you need to know our mission statement and that's this: 'to work to place abandoned and unwanted dogs in safe and permanent homes.'"

She nodded. That was simple enough. Wasn't it?

Luke gestured toward the pens. "These are some of our newest residents. They start in here until we can assess them for illness or behavioral issues. Tori trained as a vet tech before she came here so she can assess them and do basic first aid when they arrive. Then we have a vet on the island who works with us to spay or neuter and vaccinate all the dogs as soon as we can. Once they're cleared of any issues and they've recovered from their medical needs, they can come out and explore the yard, and eventually have access to the house like those others you met earlier."

"But how do you get them? People just drop them off?"

He went to one of the pens and put his palm against it, letting the dog inside sniff him. "Several ways. Sometimes we get a call from someone who sees a dog somewhere on the streets, abandoned. So we go after it. Or we rescue some of them from abusive environments. Then there are those who come from the shelters."

"Why wouldn't the shelter keep them until they find homes?" Cara asked.

"Besides running out of room, the dogs have only a certain amount of time before they're deemed unadoptable. If we can take them when that date comes, we're their last chance before euthanasia."

Cara shook her head, unable to fathom any of the dogs being put to sleep. The one that Luke was kneeling in front of was a large golden-colored dog with a marking that made it appear he was wearing a mask. His eyes were sad, telling her that he had a story to tell, if one could pry it out of him.

Luke put a hand through the chain links, patting the dog. "This is Benedict. He's a mastiff mix and is from the final category. He's pretty depressed right now—aren't you buddy?" He put his face down to the dog and scratched him behind the ears. "His owner of five years called and said he couldn't keep him anymore. He got a new job across the country—with a house rental that doesn't allow pets. So yeah, we have our fair share of those like Benedict where the owner calls or comes in, ready to relinquish the dog because of some new life event. Those are the ones that get me every time because their dogs just don't understand what they've done to be discarded like a piece of trash or unwanted furniture."

Her face reddened. He was talking about her.

"No, not like you." Luke saw her expression and stood quickly. "I swear, I wasn't referring to you. I had no doubt that you'd be back for Hemi. Either today, or tomorrow, but I could see that walking away wasn't what you wanted to do. I get people like you, too."

"People like me?"

He nodded. "Yeah. People in desperate situations who really feel the best thing for the dog is to leave it with us. Sometimes that's the best option, but most of the time what people don't understand is that dogs have feelings, too. They grieve for their owners. They get depressed. Sometimes what seems the best option to the owner isn't the best option for the dog. But I knew you'd be back."

Something told Cara that Luke was right.

"Follow me," Luke said, then led her to the door of the building. When they went in, they were in the middle aisle of two rows of kennels, six on each side. But unlike any shelter Cara had seen, this one was bright and cheerful. Across the top of the building were windows with sunlight streaming in. The kennels were more like rooms, complete with a window and a real door. The kennels were each separated by short walls of white picket fences instead of the expected bars or mesh wire. Three stand fans rotated, blasting air toward the dogs.

If a dog kennel could be cozy, this one was.

"This is really pleasant," she said. "I wasn't expecting it to be so . . . so nice."

Luke pointed to a framed photograph on the wall. It was a really old picture of a woman with several dogs at her feet and one on her lap. "We wouldn't have this at all if it weren't for Ernest Hemingway's first wife, Hadley. It was in her honor that her son set this foundation up. Donations and the occasional volunteer help us keep it going. But volunteers sign up, stay on a few weeks, then they move on. That's why Tori said we need to try to pay someone."

"I hope I can do what needs to be done," Cara said. She was already feeling inadequate and she hadn't even started.

"You'll do fine." He moved on down the walkway.

Cara smiled when she saw a small chalkboard above each door with a dog name printed on it. One read Rags, another Dusty. Then she spotted the one that read Benedict just before he popped through the small hatch from outside, then slowly padded over to put his nose through the pickets, silently watching her and Luke.

"He knows it's time for dinner," Luke said. "They all have an internal clock and get to know the routine fairly fast. If I'm not on time, they give me the signal. I feed them early because having their stomachs full helps them to settle down."

At the end of the shed was an area with a long countertop, an industrial-sized sink, and a metal table that looked like one of those that groomers used. Above and below the counter and sink were wall-to-wall cabinets.

"You bathe them, too?" she asked.

Luke nodded. "We bathe them and trim their hair if needed, though it's not our specialty and, in my opinion, we do a whack job. But volunteer groomers aren't always available and sometimes the dogs are brought in with fleas or even mange, so we have to take them down to skin." He pointed at one dog that looked like he was cringing in the corner of his kennel. With the scalp job done on him, he was obviously one of those Luke talked about. His pink skin shone through everywhere except where he wore a ratty red T-shirt. It read Partying It Up Doggy Style In Key West across his back.

Cara didn't comment, but she couldn't help but feel sorry for the little fellow and his obvious embarrassment. If it were her, she'd ditch the tacky shirt.

Luke pointed at the cabinets. "We keep some supplies in there but also in a storage room off the kitchen in the house. Out here is mostly dog food but also other donations."

"What kinds of donations?" Cara wasn't sure besides food what people could be giving.

"Oh, stuff that we need to keep this place running properly. Paper towels, bleach to clean the kennels, soap for the dogs and the laundry, and we go through a lot of garbage bags. What we're short of right now are collars and dog beds. The dogs like a bit of luxury—something besides sleeping on the concrete floor. The beds don't last long before they're worn out, torn up, or infested by the newcomers. We always need beds."

Cara looked and noticed that some of the kennels didn't have dog beds, instead old blankets were wadded up in the corners of their enclosures. But everything looked clean—much cleaner than she expected it to be, considering how many animals obviously came and went.

The dogs all started coming through their doors from outside, anxiously watching and whining. Cara reached her hand out to one, letting him lick her palm through the fencing. One dog barked and another joined in. Luke let out a loud whistle and they stopped.

He glanced back at her.

"Be careful. You may lose a digit. The new dogs are unpredictable." He lifted an eyebrow, casting a doubtful look. "You're going to need some shelter training stat."

"Oh, sorry. What do I need to know?" She stood, suddenly wary of the dog that seconds before looked like a gentle soul.

"A lot if you want to stay safe. Most of the dogs are friendly, but some have only known humans to hurt them, so they're the ones who are distrustful and scared. Always remember that a scared dog can be a dangerous dog."

Cara looked wistfully at a dog that reminded her of her first dog, Reno. The sign above his head read Digger. "I've never been around dogs much, though I always wanted one when I was little."

She didn't mention that her role as a foster child had made it clear that puppies, ponies, or rainbows weren't to be on any childhood wish list. She and Hana had stayed practical, asking for jeans and socks—simple items that might not be stolen from them in the next placement.

Luke reached through and patted the one under the sign that read Dusty. It was a shepherd mix with beautiful charcoal coloring. "We have a lot of abused dogs come through here. They're wary enough to not want anything to do with us. But most of them come out of it with a bit of nurturing. That's where Tori comes in—she's some sort of dog whisperer when it comes to caring for the worst cases."

Cara heard the appreciation in his voice and caught the lift of half a smile on his face. Tori must really be something, and it was always bittersweet when she came in contact with couples who really liked each other after the initial romance had worn off.

"Let's get 'em fed and watered, then I'll show you around inside," Luke said.

They worked together bringing dogs' bowls over and her filling them with kibble and handing them back. Hose in hand, he went from kennel to kennel, refilling water bowls. Only one or two dogs soiled their inside dwellings, but for those who did, Luke patiently cleaned it up.

"We'll hose down in here tomorrow," he said. "But now we go feed the dogs who stay inside."

She followed him through the kitchen and back down the main hall. Gesturing as they passed, he commented on the living room, telling her that only small dogs were allowed on the couches. Several big dog pillows were scattered around for the large breeds.

"I'm still shocked you let them stay in the home," she said, looking at an old Basset Hound curled up on his pillow.

"Stabilize, assess, treat, and socialize. That's the order, and socializing in a real home is a big part of how we are so successful with our placements. We teach them not to lift a leg indoors, or how the only thing they are allowed to chew on is toys or bones given to them. We try to do the work so when they go to their forever homes, they have more of a chance of staying there."

He moved toward another door that led off the hall while Cara thought about the concept of socializing before placement. She remembered many times their current social worker telling them they needed to be better, to do better—not talk back and help more around the house. Usually no one bothered to find out from them if they knew why they were being put back in the system; instead, they just assumed she and Hana had done something wrong.

At least these dogs were given a chance.

Luke opened the door and stood aside, letting Cara enter.

"This is the original study, with many of the same pieces that Hadley's son used when he first opened this place."

Cara looked around, taking in the bleached white pieces of furniture and the scenes of beach life on the walls. "Are there any hidden manuscripts in here?"

Her question made Luke laugh. He looked at her closer. "So you know the story of the lost manuscripts, huh? You must be a serious Hemingway fan."

Not knowing about the manuscripts would be impossible for anyone who was at all interested in Hemingway's life. Cara had found the story completely fascinating and had devoured all she could about it. There wasn't much to it, just that when Hadley and Hemingway were married, she decided to take some of his manuscripts along with her to Switzerland, where she was meeting him for a visit during one of his journalism assignments. As a surprise, she'd packed the manuscripts in a valise to take along. Her biggest mistake was leaving them in the baggage compartment over her seat on the train. When she went to the restroom and returned, the valise was gone along with the manuscripts, never to be seen again.

"Some say that the loss of his work was the beginning of the end for them," Cara said.

Luke nodded. "He was especially devastated because she also packed the only carbon copies of the manuscripts along in the same valise. All that he'd spent months creating was stolen in one swoop."

Cara shook her head, feeling sorry for the ghost of Hadley and her short-lived marriage to a legend of literature.

"We don't have the lost manuscripts, but we've got copies of all Hemingway's published books, if you want to borrow any of them," Luke said. He pointed at a tall bookshelf along the wall. It was packed full of books, every shape, size, and color. Just scanning the titles gave Cara a shiver of anticipation.

"I just might." Cara didn't tell him that she had one of the same titles in her backpack, dog-eared and a little worse for wear. And that she'd read everything she knew of that he'd ever written, at least once. Some of them multiple times.

But she didn't want to look like some kind of Hemingway fanatic.

Luke took her to the side of the room and showed her the computer. "You can use this any time you need. And I'm sure Tori will be taking advantage of having a helper to post pet pics on our social networking sites. You'd be surprised at how many dogs are placed because of us posting their pictures and stories. It's all about reaching the right people. It's a time killer to keep up, but it's not off-bounds if you want to update your own social networks while you're on there, too."

Cara froze.

She stared at the computer as though it were a snake about to strike. Why had Luke brought her in there? For a second, she wondered if she'd let on to him that people were looking for her. True, she never had been one to play on the Internet. She avoided online games and all social platforms, mostly because with juggling a full-time job along with part-time work in between, she never had time. But she and Hana did have email addresses, and she wondered if she might have some new emails sitting in her account, just waiting for her to open so she could be found.

"Cara?" Luke gave her arm a nudge and she jumped. "If you're not comfortable helping Tori with that part of the job, it's fine. You look like I just asked you to commit murder."

At those words, Cara felt the blood drain from her face.

"Are you okay?" he asked, his words trailing off into thin air as she turned and practically ran from the room.

Chapter Seventeen

Over the years, Cara could count dozens of bedrooms that she and Hana had shared. Some were barely able to be called rooms, others were nice in a humble way. Many of their foster parents tried to give them a decent place of their own, no matter how modest. But none had ever compared to the room they had together before they were dumped into the system.

Their mother, before she got sick, always used her sewing machine to make things. Stuff like aprons, doll clothes, dresses—she was talented with the needle. She'd even taught them, or at least tried to, how to do a few things with a machine. Cara had enjoyed the lessons, relishing every minute spent with her mother, their bodies so close she could feel her breath on her neck. But Hana hadn't wanted to learn, her attention span much too short to be able to handle the lessons for more than minutes at a time.

The year before they'd been pulled from home, their mother let Cara and Hana pick their own material for curtains.

That had resulted in a mismatched room but one that they still loved. On Hana's side, she'd picked a deep purple material. If she remembered right, it was something like velvet, a heavy material that relentlessly held out against the light that longed to pour through Hana's window. But on Cara's side, the sun shone brightly through, illuminating their room because she'd picked a beautiful, feminine white cotton with lace around the edges. When she pictured that room where their mother for many years had tucked them into bed with a soft kiss and a warm touch, she always saw it in her mind with the window open and the white curtains gently floating with the breeze.

And that memory was the first thing that popped up when Tori led her into the guest room. Cara had gone straight to the restroom after fleeing from the study, and when she'd come out, she'd apologized for her unexplained awkward reaction. Luke had shrugged, accepted her excuse, and passed her off to Tori for the rest of the tour.

"We haven't had anyone here for a while, so it might be a little dusty. I don't get much time to clean." Tori went to the window and pulled it down a bit. "It can get breezy here on the island, but we love the fresh air."

Cara didn't want her to close off the breeze. The movement of the curtains had triggered that memory of the bedroom she and Hana shared and it made her feel warm inside. Even if just for a moment, she wanted to hang on to it. The good memories were so few and far between and, as the years had gone by, were getting harder to remember.

"What do you think?" Tori said. "The sheets are at least clean."

"It's perfect," Cara whispered. Slowly she looked around the room, taking in the old-fashioned charm of the huge four-poster bed, the mahogany vanity dressing table, and the antique chest of drawers. The room was painted a peachy sort of pink with crisp white trim, and on the walls hung colorful paintings of what she could only assume were other vintage homes from around the island. All around were touches of lime green, especially in the vibrant coverlet that lay across the white bedspread. When her eyes fell on a small bookshelf packed full of books, she knew that if she'd have had a dozen rooms to choose from, this would still be the one she'd pick.

"You really think so?" Tori asked. "Luke said this room has too much going on for anyone to be able to relax and sleep in here. But it's been kept close to its original décor and I think it's charming."

"Luke's wrong. You're right," she said softly, still taking in the beauty of the room.

Tori laughed. "Oh, keep saying that and we'll be best friends." She went to the chest of drawers and slid a hand over the top, dislodging motes of dust toward the floor. "You can put your stuff in here."

Cara remembered the backpack hanging from her shoulder. She didn't have much, probably not even enough to fill one drawer. She looked at Tori and noted her cute summer dress and flip-flops. She felt her face redden, realizing that nothing she had with her—or even what she'd left behind—came close to appropriate Key West attire. Two pairs of jeans and a few shirts were about it, and certainly wouldn't need much closet room.

"These old houses didn't believe in a bathroom per bedroom, so you and I will share the one at the end of the hall. Luke has a small one outside his room, and believe me, you'll want to stay out of it. He's not the neatest person."

They didn't share a room. Cara thought that was interesting, but she refrained from saying anything. Every couple was different, and maybe Tori truly couldn't accept close quarters with someone who wasn't the neatest person.

"Thank you," Cara said, turning to Tori. "I can't thank you enough for sending Luke after me to offer me a job and a place to stay for a while."

"Oh, you'll earn it," Tori said, letting out a small laugh. "We've needed some help for longer than Luke could admit. I can't believe I talked him into offering you a position. Finally, a sprinkling of common sense made it into his thick head at just the right time. And you, my friend, I'm convinced are going to be a godsend."

Cara hoped she was right and that she'd be able to sufficiently earn her keep, for as long as she could stay. She'd work as hard as she could, but she had no idea when she'd have to run again. In coming to Key West, she'd come to the farthest point she could think of, and if she had to run, where she'd go from there was anyone's guess. Backtracking was the only way out and that didn't feel right either.

She just hoped it wouldn't come to that.

Then she realized, Tori had called her *friend*. Cara turned away, looking out the window over the lush green backyard so that Tori couldn't see the small smile that suddenly emerged.

"Also—I hope you aren't offended, but . . ." Tori said.

Those words never ended well, Cara thought, waiting for Tori to finish what she was saying. She watched her go to the closet.

"I noticed you only have a few lumps in that bag and I take that to mean that you didn't bring many clothes with you. And probably nothing fitting for this heat." She looked at Cara's jeans, her eyebrows lifting.

Cara shifted the bag uneasily. "Yeah, most of my stuff got stolen."

Not quite the truth, but she didn't want Tori thinking she'd taken off in such a hurry that she hadn't packed sufficiently.

"Well, that's okay because I have enough sundresses for everyone I'll ever meet. Most of them look like they'll fit you, even though you're a lot taller than me. And actually . . ." She trailed off as she went to the closet and opened the door, showing a row of colorful dresses of every length. "These are some that I moved in here because I don't wear them anymore. There are new styles all over the street shops every season and I just can't resist."

"They look really nice," Cara said. "But I couldn't."

Tori shrugged. "I get 'em cheap because I know where to go and how to bargain. Please—you can't wear jeans in Key West. It's sacrilegious. And I want you to be comfortable. Plus, it would make me feel less wasteful if someone else was getting some use out of these. These particular dresses haven't seen the light of day in two seasons. Maybe

Luke would stop harassing me about the closet space they take up." She winked at Cara. "But he doesn't know about this stash, so he'll probably just think you magically had them all stuffed in that one bag."

Cara heard a vehicle outside, a big one from the sound of the brakes on the road. Tori heard it, too, tilting her head before moving toward the door again.

"It's about to get crazy in here."

Before Cara could ask why, she heard a door slam and footsteps pound up the stairs and down the hall toward them. She jumped, frightened at the sound.

"What—" She started to ask what or who was coming but was interrupted by a whirlwind of a girl busting through the door. She looked about eight or nine years old and from one look, Cara could tell she was Luke's. Similar eyes and same stubborn thrust of the chin. Her hair was darker than Tori's, though, and a wide blue streak of color added just the right amount of sass.

"Ava Marie, slow down," Tori said. "We've got a guest."

The second the name was out of Tori's mouth, it was like a sucker punch to Cara's gut. Hana's middle name was Marie. Actually, Ernest Hemingway's mother was also named Marie, but that was just one more coincidence that drove Cara's obsession of her invisible ties to the Hemingways. However, Ava Marie and Hana Marie sounded so close, it gave her chills.

The girl looked Cara up and down, locking her big brown eyes on her for only a moment before she looked to Tori with a disapproving scowl. "Where's my snack? It wasn't on the kitchen table and I need to hurry and help Daddy with the dogs."

"Remember what we talked about," Tori said. "After your snack you need to finish your homework before you play with the dogs. They'll still be there when you get done. I'm going down to make you a sandwich right now. I'm running a bit behind today."

Cara was amused when Ava Marie put her hands on her hips and glared at Tori. "It's not *playing* with the dogs. I'm training them," she said, then looked at Cara, finally taking the time to really notice her. "Why are you here? Did you bring a dog? What . . . d'you decide it's too much for you? I suppose you loved having a sweet, fat puppy but now that your dog is grown and a lot of work, you don't want it anymore."

"Ava Marie!" Tori yelled out. "Go to your room. Now. Half an hour of time-out and don't even try to skip out that back door. You need to harness that sharp tongue! I've told you that too many times."

The little girl put her nose in the air, gave a grunt, then disappeared in a flurry of indignation. When she was gone, Tori turned to Cara. "I am so sorry. She's really a sweet girl—most of the time. But she's passionate about advocating for the dogs."

Cara laughed. "Don't be sorry. Yes, I can tell she's just as devoted to your animals as you and Luke are. I think that's great."

Tori shook her head. "Yeah, it's great. Except when she stands up and lectures almost every person who dares to bring a dog in, whether it's theirs or some stray they found and are turning in to us. You'll soon find out that at only eight years old, Ava has quite the reputation around town. But give me a minute to make her a sandwich before she goes all 'your highness' on me, too."

"Can I help? You seem really busy," Cara said. Thus far she'd seen Tori handing out dog biscuits, taking away far-gone chew toys, refereeing canine spats, and even taking the time to comb out one dog's coat that was full of briars. Truthfully, Tori moved around like a cyclone and was making Cara tired just from watching her. But Ava Marie—she was adorable. Her fiery spirit made Cara think of Hana. And dealing with Hana was something she'd been an expert at.

"I don't, uh, think you're up to handling her on your first afternoon. How about you take it easy today? Get washed up, maybe unpack. Comfort your dog and explain to him that you guys are staying for a while. Tomorrow you can step up to the plate and help me juggle some of this craziness."

Cara didn't feel right doing nothing and she tried to change Tori's mind. "If you're sure. I mean, I can handle it. I don't really need to rest up."

"You look absolutely exhausted. Anyone can see that. Clean up and then as my first order to you, I say you get a lengthy nap before dinner. I'll see you when you come down. I've got some emails to tend to and a few new dog postings to get up online. It'll be at least an hour before I'm out of the office. We'll start you out slow so you don't run out of here too fast."

"Okay," Cara said. "But can I get Hemi? Is he allowed up here?"

"You got it," Tori said, laughing as she skirted out the door. "But change clothes first so you'll be more comfortable. I'll be downstairs in the office if you need me. You'll know which room it is by all the furniture I'm going to barricade in front of the door. Maybe—just maybe—I can snatch some peace and quiet and actually accomplish something. Ava will probably be too loud for you to nap long but you can try. Oh—one more thing. If you want to get on her good side, don't call her Ava Marie. Just use Ava."

Chapter Eighteen

Cara sat up and looked at the sunlight pouring in through the window. The clock on the wall told her the short nap had turned into an all-night marathon of almost coma-like sleep and now Saturday morning was staring her right in the face. What would they think of her? That she was lazy? And where had Hemi gone? The last thing she'd remembered, she had gotten him to curl up beside her on the bed, but now he was gone.

The little traitor.

She threw the covers off and jumped out of bed. At the closet, she swiped the sundresses back and forth on the rod, hesitating with each dress before picking one with a softer muted pattern of blue swirls. There was also a basket of cheap—and used—plastic flip-flops in the bottom of the closet, and she doubted that Tori would mind, so she chose a pair of black ones and slid them on. They were at least a size smaller than she actually wore, but her toes were still on board so she went with it.

Normally putting on someone else's clothes and shoes would make her feel weird, but for some reason Tori's things only made her feel more comfortable. She wouldn't deny that it was nice to get out of the heavy jeans and shirt she'd alternated every day for the past couple of weeks. Honestly, she'd have loved to burn them, but since she'd need them when she left Key West, she simply folded them up and put them on the dresser.

After running her fingers through her hair quickly to try to tame a few of the snarls, she pulled it back into a ponytail, then looked in the mirror. Her image was almost unrecognizable. She looked, well, like a girl. A different girl—not the one who'd arrived.

Shrugging at the silly thought, she left the room and took the stairs, relishing the swish of soft material around her legs as she moved down the hall toward the kitchen.

Ava was already there, humming to herself as she gathered ingredients to make a sandwich. On the counter next to a stack of folders and a backpack was a well-worn paperback. *The Hobbit.*

"Nice outfit," Cara said, especially amused when she spotted what appeared to be a toy sword tucked into the wide belt the girl wore around a large black poncho over a white pair of shorts. Around her forehead she'd tied some sort of braided headband and it made her look older. Cara was surprised that Ava was up bright and early, considering it was Saturday—didn't most kids sleep in on weekends?

Ava looked up, appraised her from head to toe, then raised an eyebrow at her. "You, too, but I liked you better in the jeans. Now you just look like Tori."

"Tori? You mean your mom?"

"She's not my mom—she's my aunt." Ava shot her a disturbed look, then returned her attention to squeezing grape jelly from a plastic jar onto the peanut butter.

"Oh," Cara said, feeling embarrassed. She wasn't sure why, but she'd just assumed that Tori and Luke were a couple, and the realization that they were siblings made her feel like an idiot. Though she *was* relieved that it was Ava who had set her straight about it, and not Luke.

"My mom died," Ava said matter-of-factly, her attention never wavering from her sandwich as she plopped the two pieces of bread together, then slapped them onto a small plate.

Ava might not have been affected by her words, but Cara was. Her breath caught in her throat and she suddenly thought of Hana at that age, saying that exact thing to whoever asked, even as Cara fled from the room every single time. Hana had always said it was unhealthy that Cara wouldn't speak of it, but she just wasn't wired like her sister. Some things needed to be kept inside.

Or did they?

Taking a deep breath, she put both hands on the counter to support her weight and the sudden feeling of light-headedness that surrounded her.

"Mine did, too," she said, her voice coming out in a whisper.

There. She'd said it.

Ava looked at her, suddenly interested in what she had to say. "Really?"

Cara nodded, feeling better now that the words were out. "Really."

She didn't know if it was some unspoken code between survivors, or just pure luck, but thankfully, Ava didn't ask how Cara's mother had died. So as curious as she was, she gave the girl the same respect. She grabbed a banana from a wire basket over the sink and peeled it, then took a bite. To change the tone in the room, she changed the subject. "You're doing homework on the weekend?"

"I didn't finish it yesterday," Ava said, pulling one of the folders from the pile with the hand that wasn't holding the sandwich. She flipped it open and pointed at a sheet of paper. "I just have to proof it."

Cara finished the banana and tossed the peel in the trash, then walked around the bar and looked down at the paper. She could tell by the size of the penmanship that it was written by Ava.

"What is it?" she asked.

"I had to do a report about something significant in my life," Ava said. "I chose the importance of spaying and neutering dogs."

The big words she used were impressive and Cara began reading the essay. She could tell that unless someone else had helped her to write it, Ava knew her stuff. It took only a few sentences before Cara got to a fact that even she hadn't known.

"Is this true?" she asked Ava.

Ava peeked to see what Cara was pointing at, then nodded. "Yes. If a dog isn't spayed or neutered, that dog and its mate can be responsible for a line of more than sixty thousand dogs within only six years."

Cara raised her eyebrows. "Hmm. I did not know that."

"If you didn't know that, I bet you also didn't know that when a puppy is born, he's blind and deaf."

"I actually did know that," Cara said, hiding her amusement at the tone of competitiveness creeping into Ava's voice.

Ava slapped the folder shut and crossed her arms. "Then did you know dogs express their emotions with their ears? Their ears have more than a dozen muscles that control movement and they're in a different position for each emotion."

Cara held her hands up in submission. "Okay, you got me. I didn't know that, though I might've guessed it because my dog has some pretty funny expressions that he gives me for different reasons. I didn't know about the ear muscles, though."

Appeased that she had the upper hand, Ava picked up her sandwich again and took a big bite.

"So, you like to read?" Cara asked, hoping to keep things on a less competitive subject.

Ava nodded and spoke with her mouth full. "Daddy calls me Worm."

"Short for *bookworm*?" Cara asked. She'd been called that several times too, when she was a kid. It was a nickname easily earned, as she'd found that burying herself in her books prevented her from thinking too much about what was going on in real life.

"Yeah, and he thinks I hate it. But really, I like it better than Ava *Marie*."

Cara couldn't help it and laughed. "Okay, then. What more do you need to do for the report?"

"Nothing really, just check it for spelling. And I have a half a sheet of math to finish." She pulled another sheet out and Cara had to refrain from showing her revulsion at the line of math word problems. She hadn't thought about the repercussions of offering to help Ava with her homework. Actually, since high school, she'd conveniently forgotten math even existed.

"Do you need my help with that?" she asked, hoping that her reluctance didn't show in her voice.

"Nah—I got this," Ava said, finishing the last bite of her sandwich and using the back of her hand to wipe her mouth. She pulled a pencil from the bag and began working, her head low and her lips moving as she counted in her head. She stopped for a second, looking at Cara before pushing the report toward her. "Here, you want to see if I spelled anything wrong?"

It only took a minute or two. Other than a few random doodles along the edge, the report was spotless, and Cara set it back on the counter before going to the sink. Getting a clean glass from the dish drainer, she poured herself some water from the spigot.

She took a deep drink, watching Ava over the rim.

Observing her while she worked was not boring, to say the least. Cara was captivated by her—not just the total look of concentration she wore, but also the uniqueness that she carried. How many little girls dressed like warriors from an old book, forgoing pigtails and pinkness to look like they were ready to take on any battle that came their way? Maybe what really struck her was that she'd never known any other girl—except Hana—who could so bravely and matter-of-factly state that their mother was dead, yet still feel so passionate about something in the next breath.

Strength.

That was it. Ava, in only minutes, had shown her that packed in that little rebellious body was a lot of fun stuff, but also a well of strength.

Cara jumped when Ava slapped her pencil down on the table and headed for the door. "Come on, if you're coming!"

Cara carefully rinsed her glass and put it in the sink, then followed Ava. She wasn't sure if she could keep up with her, but she'd try.

By the time she'd gotten outside, Ava had somehow gotten four dogs to sit in a row in front of her. Hemi was one of them and sat shoulder to shoulder with a gray terrier.

Hemi looked at Cara, then turned his attention back to Ava as she held her hand palm out, repeating for them to stay while she slowly and carefully stepped back a few paces.

Hemi obeyed. He had *stay* down pat—most of the time.

The largest dog, some sort of shaggy sheep-looking fellow, also stayed. But the smallest dog, a tiny white fur ball, leapt up and ran to Ava.

"No, Sash, I told you to stay," Ava said, then led the dog back to the line, told her to sit, and started it all over again. When they all sat for a minute straight, Ava reached into her pocket and brought out a tiny treat for each of them.

Cara watched, her arms crossed over her chest. She was proud that Hemi was listening and obeying, and she was so captivated by Ava and her attention to the dogs that she didn't see Luke come out of the kennels.

"So I see you've met my little fireball," he said, making Cara jump.

Why was she so jittery? She hated that her distrust of everyone showed in all her movements. And she needed to apologize for crashing on her first day of work.

"Yes, I offered to help her with her homework, but she didn't need me," Cara said as Luke moved up until they were standing side by side. Ava ignored them, instead concentrating on her students.

"She's the most self-sufficient—and stubborn—kid I've ever seen," he said. "But she's great to have around here. I don't let her interact with any of the new dogs, but once they're assessed and allowed yard privileges, she works with them. Sometimes she's successful in teaching them a few tricks, but most of all she's showing them what human interaction should be like."

"They look like they adore her. Even my dog has fallen in with them and he just met her." Cara watched Hemi, noticing the slight wag of his tail whenever Ava directed her words at him.

Luke shook his head. "I know. I don't understand it. It's like she was born with a gift—or some kind of connection that only she and the dogs understand. Once, when she was four years old, I went to check on her while she was sleeping. I about lost my mind when I found her bed empty. Tori thought to check the kennels and we found her in there curled up with one of the new dogs—a scraggly mutt who'd been really distressed since his owner had surrendered him."

"That's amazing," Cara said. "Whatever happened to the dog?"

"He's sitting right over there." Luke pointed to a dog who sat on the porch, watching the dog-training class from the comfort of a padded chair. "She named him Mike and promptly fell head over heels with that mutt and he with her. I just couldn't rehome him."

With those words, Cara knew two things. The first was that Ava had her daddy wrapped snugly around her little finger. And the second was that Luke was a lot more tenderhearted than he'd let on with her.

"Look," Cara said. "I'm really sorry that I fell asleep yesterday and didn't get up. I never sleep that long. I guess I was just so . . . so . . ."

"Exhausted?" Luke finished for her. "Don't apologize for being human, Cara." He cleared his throat. "I hope you grabbed some breakfast in there because this is officially your first day and I need you in the kennels. We've got a lot of grunt work to do while the girls get to do the fun stuff."

She felt a little burst of electricity at the sound of her name on his lips, then felt disgust at herself for being such a girl. Quickly, she followed him into the small building. She didn't mind grunt work—or any kind of work that would help feed her and give her shelter. But wasn't she a girl, too? Either way, she didn't mind. He could call her whatever he wanted. She was just thankful for whatever she could get until she could figure out her next move.

Chapter Nineteen

Cara reached for the bottle of aspirin and popped a few into her palm. She hoped taking them would work fast on the headache that was gathering behind her eyes. She usually avoided any type of medication, but Luke had sent her to bed the night before with a few dog-behavior books. After only a week learning the ropes, she'd picked up so much that he'd piled on even more, urging her to read up when she had time. Most likely, he'd expected her to read only a chapter or two, but after finishing a backbreaking marathon of washing dogs, feeding them, and cleaning the kennels, Cara had cooked dinner, then stayed up half the night reading until she'd finished one entire book.

It felt like she'd just closed her eyes when six o'clock came sneaking up on her.

That meant a blinding headache would be her shadow for the day, and she'd already agreed to accompany Luke and Ava to scout for a missing dog. The dog was last seen when he fell off a boat a few miles from shore, and there was a lot of water to cover, so it could prove to be a long afternoon. She didn't want to show any weakness, either. She felt that so far Luke wasn't regretting his decision to hire her. He'd even thanked her for dinner—a simple spaghetti and garlic bread that at least Ava had gushed over. Cara hadn't known she'd picked the girl's favorite meal for her first attempt to please their palates, but she was sure glad it had ended up that way.

She put the bottle of aspirin back into the medicine cabinet and shut the door. Looking down at the pills in her hand, she felt a wave of sadness, then looked back in the mirror and saw Hana staring back at her. It was inevitable; there was always some of her sister evident in her own face.

She swallowed the pills, then took a drink before bending over the sink to splash water on her face. She couldn't help but remember her first experience with an overdose. They were in their early twenties and Hana had made an attempt—a lame one but one that still required her stomach to be pumped. It had scared the living daylights out of Cara, and the thought that she would have to move through life without her sister was an almost paralyzing one.

It wasn't as though Cara even actually needed Hana to survive. Most of the time it was Hana who needed the help. It was more the idea that the person who knew her better than anyone in the world—all her weaknesses, secrets, and biggest dreams—would no longer be there. And Cara would be alone.

Hana always claimed she hadn't wanted to kill herself, that she only wanted to sleep for a long time, or until things got better. But what Cara tried to explain to her was that if she was sleeping, that was being passive. And being passive would never improve any situation. What she really wanted to do was to yell and scream at Hana until she jumped up and came back to herself, taking on the world in her usual kick-ass way.

When Cara told her how she felt, Hana looked at her and gave her a sympathetic smile. She'd told her: "Cara, depression is hard to describe, but think of it like this; sometimes, I am a gnat curled up in the palm of a huge monster, begging for mercy. And sometimes I am the monster."

Cara knew then that when Hana was thinking about taking a breather from life by swallowing pills, it was when she was the gnat.

But when she was blazing through her days, taking no prisoners, she was the monster.

But she could depend on one thing. Hana's dark days always came in cycles. They could almost be mapped out with a calendar, although Cara preferred to think optimistically and hope that each time they got her through one of her episodes, it would be the last.

She heard Ava's quick footsteps and hesitated, then breathed a sigh of relief when the girl walked on by. Cara wasn't ready to face the day yet, and as much as she enjoyed Ava, she also wasn't ready for her incessant questions.

She thought back to Hana again and the day she'd come home from her new job, excited and hopeful for the future because she'd finally found a way to make a living that didn't include standing behind a cash register or flipping burgers—or even scrubbing someone else's toilets.

"Guess what I'm gonna be doing starting Monday?" she'd asked, a triumphant grin on her face.

Cara had guessed all the usual things—a waitress, a cashier, and a multitude of other positions they'd both floated in and out of. But Hana had shook her head at each one until Cara had given up. Then she'd laughed and told her.

A nanny.

Of all people, Cara would've never cast Hana in the role of a nanny, but obviously someone else thought she'd do fine. She'd found the listing on some website, interviewed, then somehow got the job, miraculously beating out dozens of other applicants.

It might've gone well, too, if the children's father hadn't taken Hana's aloofness toward him as an invitation to pursue her. After a lengthy chase that went on almost right under his own wife's nose, he'd succeeded in pulling Hana in, teasing and intoxicating her with gifts and things she'd only dreamed about owning. He'd wormed his way into their lives, acting like some sort of magical Prince Charming, not relenting until Hana was putty in his hands.

Then he'd dumped her.

It was an act of such betrayal that it triggered Hana's fourth attempt. She'd sucked down more than three dozen of her high-powered anti-anxiety pills, and that time, Cara felt like a pro, knowing what to do. Sadly, she also knew by then what vomit-inducing meds to get into her, how to keep her awake as much as possible, and the importance of watching her for seizures.

Nothing was worse than becoming an expert on how to keep someone you love alive when she insisted that she wanted to die. Each time was a nightmare, and Cara didn't think her sister had any clue how much it affected her.

Much to Hana's satisfaction, her little stunt got her back in the saddle with the sneaky bastard who'd caused the drama in the first place. It was either the fear of her blood on his hands or the threats she'd made to tell his wife everything, but he'd come running with roses and promises. Cara remembered struggling to decide if Hana was the victim or the aggressor that time. Whichever it was, she'd gotten her way because of her actions.

The footsteps were back and this time Ava knocked on her door. "Cara, are you coming?"

"I'll be down in a minute," she called out, feeling rushed suddenly.

She didn't know why the little girl made her feel so incompetent. Ava was a joy to be around, but looking at her made Cara remember something she'd tried hard to push to the back of her mind and not think about.

She'd never be a mother.

The pain and other physical symptoms, like high blood pressure, had started in junior high, and by the time she'd graduated, the state had sent her to more than a few specialists. After months of appointments and tests, Cara hadn't even cried when a diagnosis was finally made. Polycystic ovary syndrome, they'd called it, along with the news that she'd never bear children.

How could she cry when a stranger who was their newly appointed case manager was the one who'd taken her to the appointment and stood there listening as though it were her own life affected? Her future children taken away from her?

Cara hadn't said a word. She didn't let any of them know what she was feeling. The truth was, even at that young age, she'd been shattered. She also didn't have much opportunity to react, because Hana had absolutely melted down. Cara stood aside as her sister yelled at the doctor, told him to take it back, as though he'd said it only as a practical joke or some sort of mean prank. When they'd lain in bed that night, they'd talked about the irony of it all, how Hana always said she never wanted children yet she could bear them, and Cara wanted a family one day and she couldn't.

Through another bout of crying from her sister, Cara had assured her that when the time came, she'd either let Hana carry her babies or she'd adopt. Only then had her sister finally stopped obsessing over what she said was another kick in the butt from the powers that be.

After brushing her teeth, Cara pulled her hair back again, then quickly dressed. Today her outfit of choice was a pair of khaki shorts and a light T-shirt from the newest pile of secondhand clothes Tori had given her. Sliding her feet into the flip-flops, she switched off the bathroom light and made her way downstairs.

Everyone was in the kitchen, waiting for her it seemed. Hemi looked up from his place beside Ava and wagged his tail, greeting Cara. "Hey boy, how about a kiss?" She squatted and Hemi rose, then crossed the room and hopped up to lick her once on the nose. It was a trick she'd seen Ava do with some of the other dogs, and she was thrilled when Hemi picked it right up.

"How long will we be gone?" Ava asked.

"First let's get you guys fed, then we can worry about the details," Tori said, adding a plate of buttered toast to the bar. "The dogs have all eaten, the kennels are hosed down, and next on the list is breakfast."

"What do you need me to do before we go?" Cara asked.

"Just eat," Tori said. "You'll get evening shift on the kennels tonight so I covered your morning chores."

"We don't have time to eat. This is life or death," Ava said.

"It's not life or death now, Ava. He's been out there a long time. And how are you supposed to conduct a rescue mission if you're too weak to move?" Tori asked. "Here, just eat some fruit then."

She held out a slice of pineapple and Ava grudgingly took it.

"Ava, we're not leaving until you eat something more than that. It might be a really long day," Luke said, then raised his mug at Cara. "Morning. Coffee is ready. I want to leave in the next ten minutes so try to hurry."

"Thanks, but I think I'll just have some tea," Cara said, going to the dish drainer for a clean mug. She looked at the stovetop and saw the teakettle sitting there, still steaming, then gave Tori a thankful smile. Since she'd learned that Cara's weakness was tea, she'd made sure hot water was ready each morning.

"Luke, she's drank tea every morning since she got here. Why do you keep offering her coffee?" Tori said, her voice dripping with impatience. "Don't you listen to anything? And do you always have to act like such a guy?"

Luke shrugged and took another long sip from his mug. Cara could see evidence of a hidden smile behind his big hand. She didn't comment. While she felt completely comfortable joking with Tori, for some reason, she hadn't adopted the same relaxed attitude with Luke yet. Most of the time when they worked together, it was without a lot of talk, except to the dogs or cats they tended. But Cara was fine with that. Talking meant sharing, and sharing could be dangerous. Keeping things businesslike with him was in her best interest.

"Are we all going?" Cara asked.

Her hope was extinguished quickly when Tori shook her head. "I'm staying behind. Someone has to be here with the dogs, and in case any new ones are brought in. I've also got a possible adoption today, if the woman keeps her word. She's interested in Bruno. From what I could tell from the phone interview, it'd be a perfect fit. We might have found his forever home."

Ava smiled broadly. She loved more than anyone when the dogs were placed successfully. "Okay, but please don't let him go without me saying good-bye."

"Make sure she passes all the qualifications and double-check every reference. If she can't supply three, then let her walk," Luke said gruffly.

"Yes, brother, I think I know that by now." Tori rolled her eyes, then winked at Cara.

Cara quickly poured herself some hot water and dipped her green teabag into it. She nibbled at a piece of toast between sips. She was happy to hear Bruno might be going to a new home. He was a Rottweiler mix, and from the little she'd seen when interacting with him, a total sweetheart. He'd been transferred to them from the humane society, overlooked and well past his boarding time. For being such a powerful dog, he was surprisingly meek and well-behaved.

"Ready?" Luke slid off his barstool.

Ava let the door slam behind her as she ran out into the backyard carrying a bag of wrapped sandwiches. Tori passed Luke a storage bowl filled with wet dog food and several bottles of water and waved good-bye.

"Be careful," she said.

Cara followed Luke as he joined Ava.

Outside, a pack of dogs surrounded them, begging for attention. With just a few commands from Luke, they moved back, giving room for them all to slip out of the gate and onto the sidewalk.

"Where're we going?" Cara asked.

"The docks," Ava said, authoritatively, leading the way.

Luke laughed and nodded. "Yeah, we've got a small skiff at the docks. I'm sure we won't find the dog, but I promised Ms. Avery that we'd at least try."

They turned a corner and stepped aside, allowing a small elderly lady to have the sidewalk before continuing. Cara was impressed that no one had to tell Ava to do it, either. At the next corner a squat Hispanic man was holding a sign advertising a diner. He sang out to them in a low but pleasant voice: "Wakey, wakey, rise and shine. Pancake breakfast eight to nine."

"That's Pancake Pete. His breakfast is the best," Luke said, giving the man a high five as they passed.

Cara was still confused about the situation they'd taken on and how it fit with the Hadley House. "Do you usually look for lost dogs?" she asked.

"Not a lot, but if it's a local, they usually call me if they've done all they could do on their own and still come up empty. This is an unusual case, and a long shot."

"What happened? How did he get lost?" she asked, watching Ava ahead of them jump to touch a low-hanging branch, then let out a triumphant holler when she succeeded, before moving on.

"A family from the island went out on their pontoon boat and a big gust of wind came up just when they were crossing over a wake. They all got a big splash and when they looked, the dog had fallen overboard."

"They couldn't see him in the water?" Cara asked.

"Nope—it was dark and the whitecaps were getting tall. They had their headlights and a flashlight and stayed out there for hours, but they gave up around midnight. They went back the next morning, then the next. No dog. This is a tough one because Ms. Avery raised Chaos from a pup. She's devastated."

"How long has it been? Can he swim?"

Luke sighed heavily. "He's a golden retriever. They all swim. Well, all that I've known, though I'm sure there might be some in the world who could drop like a rock when thrown in. Chaos has been out there for three days."

"Three days! Do you really think we'll find him? Alive and not drowned?"

Ahead of them Ava stopped and turned around, pointing her finger. "Say yes, Daddy. We have to put good vibes in the air if Chaos is going to have a chance."

"Sure, there's a chance," Luke said, then as soon as Ava turned back around, he whispered, "but probably not."

Ava led them off the beaten path, scooting between alleys and side streets until they arrived at the marina. Cara looked around, taking it all in, and when her eyes stopped scanning, Ava was gone.

"Where'd she go?" she asked, feeling a moment of panic. Did he just let his daughter run off without him? What about creeps? Kidnappers? Or just bad people in general? A lot of fear ran through her mind, but it wasn't her business so she kept it to herself.

He must have sensed her rising panic because he laughed. "She's fine. She ran ahead to the boat. She thinks she's some sort of captain and right now she's checking things over, no doubt."

Cara could see a line of boats, but no Ava. "Which one is it? I don't see her."

"Well, it's not that two-hundred-seventy-foot Sportcraft, if that's what you're looking at," Luke said, pointing at a really nice boat someone had painted *Conch Too* on the side of. "Mine's the J16 skiff. It's got a twenty-foot transom so it's powerful enough for what I need."

"I don't know one boat from the other," Cara answered, squinting to see where Ava had run to.

"It's a boat mostly used for fly-fishing, but I got it for a steal when my buddy wanted to go bigger. We don't fish much, but Ava loves to just go out and explore the small islands, and since it's not a big boat, it doesn't take too much fuel to run it," Luke said.

When they'd passed at least a dozen boats in their slips, she finally saw Ava. Barely visible, she was thankfully still standing on the dock right beside a small—actually, a *very* small—little boat. While most of the ones they'd seen had consoles or covers, this boat did not.

Cara looked out over the ocean. It was a windy day and the whitecaps were cresting with each wave. "Are you sure that boat's safe enough for choppy water?"

"It doesn't look like much, but she's been good to me. Don't you worry. Mr. Suzuki won't let us down and leave us stranded."

They got near Ava and the boat. "Mr. Suzuki?"

Ava laughed. "The motor, Cara. Most people name their boats but until we get a bigger one, Daddy only named his motor."

Once they'd given her a crash course in boat etiquette, with Ava citing most of it, they all put on life jackets and climbed aboard. Cara looked over the side at the bottomless blue water, feeling her heart speed up.

"Does this boat go fast?" she asked.

Luke laughed. "Oh yeah, it gets up to a whopping twelve knots per hour on a good day, so I don't think you have anything to worry about."

"Most important," Ava said, "never stand up."

She didn't have to worry about that, Cara thought as she prayed the sudden rocking would subside.

Luke untied them and pushed off, and when they were a few feet from the dock, he started the boat and turned it around, then they were off.

Cara held on to the side with a death grip. She'd never been on a boat—much less on the ocean. She looked down into the water, her imagination running wild with what could be under them at that very moment. Sharks maybe, though she tried to push that thought out of her head.

"Where you going first, Daddy?" Ava yelled over the motor. She was at the front of the boat, her hat low over her eyes as she searched the horizon.

"We'll just cruise around a few islands. See what we see," he hollered back.

If not for the heart-wrenching reason they were out there, Cara could've really enjoyed the experience. She and Hana had been on the swim team in high school for a year. They were both good and would've continued except for the fact they couldn't come up with their dues— their part of the cost of trips, uniforms, and all that. She'd always been sad that they'd quit because, except for competitions, swimming was a solo kind of sport, and that was something that appealed to Cara. The way everything around her disappeared when she was underwater—no sound and no pitying glances—that had been heaven for as long as it had lasted.

Cara was jolted out of her daydreaming when a splash of cold water hit her full on in the face.

"Sorry about that," Luke said loud enough for her to hear. "These flat-bottom boats are bad about spraying when we hit choppy water."

Fifteen minutes later, Luke yelled out that they were in the vicinity of where the dog was last on the boat. He turned around, debating which direction to take, then headed east.

"I looked up the current patterns for the day he fell off the boat, and if my hunch is right, he'd have been pulled in this direction," Luke yelled. "I have an idea of some places to search that the bigger boats can't get to."

While scanning the water for the dog, Cara let herself relax for the first time since arriving in Key West. She'd been working so hard, trying to convince Luke and Tori that she was worth the job they'd given to her, she hadn't taken in the moment and celebrated the fact that she'd made it.

She also didn't want to think too hard and remember the reason she was even there, why she had run and that people were probably still looking for her. It didn't sit well with her that by omission, she was being dishonest with Luke. He'd asked her if she'd ever committed a crime and she'd said no, but that didn't mean she wasn't wanted for one. And keeping such a huge secret was making her sick.

Luke pointed into the air at a flock of seagulls in the distance and slowed the motor so that he could talk.

"There're dolphins over that way," he said. "The birds are always an indication."

He got the boat back up to speed and covered a lot of distance. They all scanned the waters carefully, but when they came upon any small island or cropping of rocks, that was where Cara concentrated the hardest. Focusing on something stationary also helped the queasiness she was beginning to feel from the motion of the boat rising up and down with each wave.

When they'd been at it for more than three hours, Luke finally came to a crawl about a hundred feet from the tiniest of islands and cut the motor.

"Let's eat a sandwich and get hydrated, then we'll look for another few hours," Luke said. "But if we don't find him by noon, we need to give it up. We won't be able to stand the midday sun out on this water."

Ava kept scanning the waters around them, but Cara could see she looked like she was about to pout.

Then she sat up, her entire body erect and her attention on something specific.

"Daddy, I see something!" she screamed.

"Where? In the mangroves?" he asked, looking back and forth.

She nodded, pointing at two groups of trees that formed sort of a structure, almost like an island. The roots and branches were intertwined, with water lapping back and forth between them. Cara didn't see a dog though.

Luke started the motor again, then turned the boat and headed over, dropping to barely an idle as he crept closer.

"Right there," Ava called out, pointing again as she bounced up and down on the tiny bench she perched on.

Cara looked harder, following the route of Ava's finger down a watery path that ran between the two clumps of trees. At first what she'd thought she was looking at was another twisted pile of roots, but she peered closer and saw it was indeed a dog, only partially visible as he lay over one root, the glistening of the water reflecting off his eyes.

But was he alive?

"Good eye, Ava. We've found him," Luke said. "Now remember, that doesn't mean he's still breathing, but be still before you make us capsize. I need to try to get closer. I don't think we can fit in there, though."

Cara didn't know what they'd do if they couldn't get to Chaos. If he'd been out there for three days, he surely couldn't swim to them. She took some deep breaths, feeling the anxiety heavy in her chest as she watched Ava squirming impatiently, becoming more agitated with each passing second.

Luke tried a few more ways around to get to the dog, but each time he was blocked by more mangroves. So far the dog hadn't made a single move and the foreboding was making Cara feel nauseated.

Finally Luke whistled, then called out, "Chaos, c'mon, boy!"

The dog barely lifted his head, acknowledging them briefly before resting it again.

"Daddy, he's alive," Ava said, then turned around. "And he's hurt."

Cara could see the tears welling in the girl's eyes and felt almost as sorry for her as she did the dog. It was a miracle that they'd found Chaos, but now they couldn't get to him. She also felt like crying.

"We don't know that, Ava. I think he's just exhausted," Luke said. "If I can just—"

Before he could finish his thought, Ava had wiggled out of her life jacket and plunged overboard.

"Ava—no!" Luke screamed.

Cara felt her heart stop. It was still deep in some places around the mangroves and Ava had emerged and was swimming toward Chaos, but what if she got tired?

She turned to Luke. "Go in after her."

"Do you know how to drive a boat?" he demanded, his eyes dancing a panicked waltz back and forth between her and Ava in the water.

Cara shook her head. "No, I've never been in a boat before today."

"The water's too choppy. If I jump in and you float away, how can I get back to you?" He looked desperate, glaring at her as though she had the answer.

And she did.

She leaned forward, taking her own jacket off, but holding on to it. Then she did just as Ava had done and plunged headfirst over the side of the boat.

Coming up sputtering, she realized the ocean was colder than she'd imagined. She shook the water out of her eyes, tightened her grip on the life vest and turned until Ava was in her sight again, then began swimming.

Ava made it to Chaos first and she crawled onto the same root he was straddling. Cara paused to get her breath and saw the girl wrapping her arms around the dog, pushing her head to his as though they shared a secret.

"Stay right there, Ava. Don't move!" Luke called from the boat, his voice heavy with fear. "Cara's coming to get you both."

Cara took off again. It had been years since she'd swum but it came right back to her. She made up the distance quickly and then had to use her one free arm to maneuver herself, half swimming, half crawling over and around the many roots until she reached Ava and the dog. She pulled herself up onto the big root beside them, getting her breath.

In the distance, Luke stood with his hand shielding his eyes, trying to see exactly what they were doing.

Cara turned back to the dog. He was beyond exhausted. She could see his eyes were glazed looking, which told her he was maybe in shock. "It's okay, boy."

"What are we going to do, Cara?" Ava asked, for the first time looking her age and not years beyond it. She was scared, and depending on Cara for the next move.

Cara wouldn't let Ava know she was scared, too. In her most confident voice, she explained her plan. "This is what we're going to do, Ava. Your dad has gotten the boat a little closer. I'm going to wrap this life vest around Chaos, and then we'll pull him loose and get him to swim alongside us until we get to the boat."

"But he can't, he's too weak," Ava said, and Cara could see she was fighting back tears.

"He can. Just like humans, dogs have an instinct to live, Ava. If we can get him off the roots and into the water, the life vest will help keep him afloat and he'll start moving because he won't want us to leave him behind."

Ava nodded, her eyes suddenly taking up more of her face than usual.

First Cara adjusted the straps on the life vest to stretch them out as big as they could go, then she draped it over and around the dog. He whimpered once but Ava consoled him. When the straps were connected under his belly, Cara took a deep breath and looked at Ava.

"This is going to be a team rescue, Ava. You and me," she said. "Are you ready? We've only got one chance at this."

Ava nodded.

"Luke, we're coming!" Cara called out.

He yelled back for them to be careful.

"Ava, when we start, just stay beside Chaos and encourage him. We'll swim slowly so we don't get tired too quick," Cara said as she slipped back into the water, then grabbed Chaos and began pulling him off the tree root. Ava joined her and together, though the dog tried to hold on, they got him loose and down in the water.

Immediately he began to dog-paddle and Cara turned him around to face the boat. "C'mon, Chaos. Let's get you home."

Swimming on either side of him, she and Ava coached him along, taking it slow and sure. Only once did Cara see Ava appear tired when she draped her arm around the dog and he carried Ava's weight along. It was only for a few feet, then she let go and started swimming again. Cara had been ready to grab her if need be, but she was glad she didn't have to, as she knew it would've broken Ava's pride.

Finally, when they were only about two feet from the boat, Luke reached down and in one strong stroke, pulled Ava out of the water and into his arms. He sat there for a few seconds, cradling her in his lap with his face buried in her wet hair, until she wiggled free.

"Daddy, stop. Get Chaos."

As Cara pushed from below, Luke pulled from above, and together they heaved the big dog over the side. Once in, his legs wavered like a newborn colt and he collapsed, falling into the well of the boat.

"Now you, hero girl," Luke said, looking down at Cara. In his eyes, through the sheen of unshed tears, she could see deep gratitude. He held a hand down and she grabbed it. His touch sent a shiver up her arm and then down to her toes, even as they tread in the cool water. Then he broke the moment when, as clumsily as a person could, he pulled her up. Somehow she flipped over the side, landing in a heap beside the dog.

She scrambled to get up, quickly rearranging herself on her original seat, hiding the fact that she was completely out of breath and the epitome of ungracefulness.

Ava was already pulling out the container of dog food and putting it in front of Chaos. He didn't touch it, but when she opened the bottle of water and poured some into the small bowl they'd brought, the dog lapped at it until it was dry.

"Give him as much water as he can take, Worm," Luke said, then started the boat. "Let's get home. That's enough excitement for one day and I know one doggy mom who is going to be beside herself to see old Chaos."

Chapter Twenty

Cara and Tori worked side by side in front of the counter and deep sink, Cara washing and drying, Tori doing inspections, then trimming the dogs. Cara tried not to think on the fact that it was her fault they'd been working so hard since the crack of dawn. Unfortunately, the afternoon before, Luke had been away getting supplies and Tori had been holed up in her office working, leaving Cara in charge.

It was shocking how much work it took to run Hadley House. Tori had told her over breakfast that they had a small handful of approved foster homes for some of the dogs who needed more one-on-one care. But before someone could take a dog, they had to be scrutinized and vetted carefully. They provided personal references, veterinarian information, and housing details. Did they own a home? Rent? Have a backyard? Other dogs? According to Tori, most who applied didn't make it through the approval process because the Hadley House dogs had already been traumatized once by being either lost, abandoned, abused, or neglected. They'd been through enough, and Tori and Luke weren't taking any chances that the dogs would have to go through it again.

That took a lot of work, and Cara was anxious to do what she could to help carry the burden.

Thinking she was stepping up and taking responsibility, she'd taken in a new dog and though she'd done the paperwork exactly as they'd shown her, she'd forgotten to isolate the little fellow. While she went back over the paperwork a few times to be sure it was right, he'd run off with the others, graciously sharing all he had, meaning a nasty infestation of fleas. The little suckers moved fast, and today they were all working together to rid the kennels of every last skin-crawling, relentless-biting critter.

Tori looked over at Cara. "You're getting pretty good at that. I'm trying to keep up and Luke is going to kill me for the job I'm doing with these trims."

Cara laughed. She had to admit, Tori wasn't a great dog groomer. But what she lacked in technique, she more than made up for in passion. It was amusing watching her as she talked to the dogs about the makeovers they were getting, comparing them to canine movie stars like Lassie and Toto—who Cara learned was played by a girl dog named Terry.

The truth be told, Tori was the kind of girl Cara had always been envious of. The kind who could throw her hair back in a ponytail and slap on some mascara and look cute. The kind who danced to music that was only in her head and didn't look like an idiot. She could just see Tori on the top of a cheerleading pyramid, her legs lean and tan as she pumped her pom-poms and smiled widely, leading the stands in one of those fight songs that Cara never really caught on to. If only she and Hana had inherited their mother's fair looks, how different would their lives have been?

"Ava taught me that piece of doggy trivia," Tori said, winking at Cara and breaking her out of her daydreams.

Not every dog was getting a haircut, but since they had to wash every animal in the place, it was the best time to trim those that needed it. Even Hemi had been clipped and he'd sat there pouting, refusing to take his eyes off of Cara as he silently reproached her for his circumstances. The ones who didn't need a cut were sent away with Ava, the relief of avoiding the electric shears evident with the way their ears lay back cautiously as they crept away on the end of the leash Ava held.

Speaking of, she was back.

Ava slammed through the door, her rubber boots making a racket big enough to sound like a grown man. The inner drill sergeant coming out in her, she'd kept the dogs coming and going, leading or carrying them as needed, then escorting the finished ones to the part of the yard that Luke had treated earlier that morning.

"Sash is last and then we're done," Ava said, breathing a loud sigh. "After that can I finally go see Josh?"

"If you've done everything your dad said to do, then I'm fine with it," Tori said, one hand resting on the dog she worked on as she turned to speak to Ava.

Cara hid a smile. She thought it really cool that Ava's best friend was a boy—and not in the crushing kind of way, either. He'd come over a few days before and she'd watched them from the kitchen window, observing the way they interacted as they moved around the yard, playing with dogs and then racing each other to the top of the tallest tree near the kennels.

The two of them just happened to enjoy the same things. Like climbing trees, sword fights, and reading epic sagas that kids their age didn't normally read. And most amusing was that Ava didn't even have a clue how unusual it was for a girl her age to be best friends with a boy.

Cara noticed that Luke kept a close eye on them, though.

Ava delivered Sash to the large waiting crate beside Cara, then retreated back toward the door. "Daddy said Cara could cook dinner again tonight if she wants," she said, then slammed out.

"That little traitor," Tori hissed, then laughed. "But I can't say I'm sad that you've taken over most of the cooking. I hate it—and you're good at it. So what if they prefer your cuisine over mine?"

"Your cooking is just as good," Cara said, embarrassed at the praise. She wasn't used to anyone telling her she was good at anything.

Tori shot her a sideways look. "Now you and I both know that's not true. All it took was one batch of those fluffy biscuits and you had both Ava and my dork of a brother salivating at your feet. I should've told you before, but those biscuits are the closest we've ever had to what our mama used to make. She was from Georgia and good Southern cooking was something she was known for."

"Is she still living?" Cara asked.

Tori nodded. "No. She's gone now. But my father's still going strong. He lives on St. Simons Island."

"Does he visit?"

Tori shook her head. "Not anymore."

Cara didn't ask why, and Tori didn't elaborate. Anytime they ventured into too-personal territory, it was easier to retreat than chance opening up her own story. Cara felt guilty keeping such a big secret from Tori and Luke when they were being so kind to her, but it was really her only choice.

If they knew the truth, they'd make her leave.

"Anyway, what's on the menu for tonight? I can go to the store for whatever you need when we finish here. I think Luke's already bagged all the dog beds and he and Ava took care of hosing the kennels. It's a miracle, but I think we'll finish before nightfall."

They hadn't heard Luke come in. Unlike his daughter, he moved quietly, barely making a peep as he went through his day, other than to throw out a few orders here and there. And Cara hated to admit it, but her heart did a little flip-flop whenever Luke showed up.

"I'm taking Cara somewhere for an early dinner tonight," he said, his voice cutting through their conversation. "If we leave around four, I can show her a few sites beforehand."

Cara froze, her hands still curled around the dog's ears. Luke was taking her out for dinner? Just her?

"Okay . . ." Tori trailed off. "Ava and I will make do with something quick. I might even let her fix it."

Luke approached them, yet Cara didn't turn around. She started washing again, massaging the lather into the dog's neckline. She knew she should speak, yet she didn't know what to say. He was taking her to dinner? Why? She felt tongue-tied and adolescent, her face flaming as she kept her head down.

He cleared his throat behind her. "It's been so crazy around here that I haven't had a chance to officially thank her for going after Ava in the water," he said. "And as island hosts, we've dropped the ball. She hasn't even seen the Hemingway House yet."

Cara still didn't turn around. She didn't feel she deserved a dinner out, considering she'd caused a major flea apocalypse with her moment of incompetence. But on the other hand, it was true that her goal was to see the Hemingway House, and thus far, she'd been too afraid to ask for time off. All of them worked hard and she didn't want to be running off to explore when it meant leaving more of the load for Tori and Luke.

But after she saw the house, then what? She'd saved only a small amount of money over the past two weeks, surely not enough to send her off on a new journey yet.

She stole a look at Tori, only to find her staring back, her eyebrows raised as though to tell Cara to say something.

Cara was at a loss for words.

"Um . . . that is . . . if you'd like to go, Cara?" Luke finally said, suddenly sounding unsure of himself.

Cara feigned interest in searching for wayward fleas, peering close to the dog's fur as she separated it with her fingers. Without turning, she answered, "I guess that'll be fine. I should finish up here soon."

She breathed a sigh of relief when Luke turned and left.

"Cara, what in the world is up with you? He's not giving you a medal—he just wants to get you out of here for an afternoon," Tori said. She unhooked the dog she was working on and gently put him back on the floor.

Right on cue, Ava came through, ready to escort the newly washed and trimmed pup to the corral. "Daddy said he and Cara are going to Mallory Square tonight. I wanna go."

Mallory Square? Was that the name of the restaurant? Cara hoped it was casual.

"Not happening, kid," Tori said. "You and I are flying solo tonight and if you treat me right, I'll let you make your famous grilled cheese and wiener sandwiches."

Ava fist-bumped the air, her latest way of showing her happiness, and then took off with the dog.

"Grilled cheese and wieners?" Cara asked, her nose instinctively wrinkling.

Tori laughed. "It's actually quite good once you get past the thought. It's also the only thing she knows how to cook and she wants to make them *a lot*. But more important, let's talk about what you're going to wear for your first trek around Key West."

Cara felt her cheeks flush as, once again, she gave the poor dog yet another flea examination. She'd owe it some extra petting later, but for now, it was the perfect way for her to avoid falling into Tori's teasing trap.

The first thing she noticed when they approached the Hemingway House was that it looked exactly like it did in the pictures she'd seen. It was two stories with too many elegant windows to count, all of them bordered by the tall yellow-and-green plantation shutters. The house was rumored to be the largest residential home on the island, and even from the road, Cara could see that it deserved the title.

"It's over a hundred sixty-five years old," Luke said. He opened the gate for Cara to pass through before going in himself.

"And it was built by Asa Tift, a marine architect who later let the grounds go wild and barely attended the house when his wife and two sons died of yellow fever. But he had a daughter, Annie, who survived. It remained a Tift house until Asa died of old age," Cara said softly.

He grinned at her. "And then Hemingway found it and bought it. He and his second wife spent years putting it back to its original beauty. They say she brought the glamour in with her collection of chandeliers and her obsession with art. But she also catered to Hemingway's love of the outdoors, allowing him room to display some of his catches," Luke said, guiding her around the house, down a twisting path of tangled greenery with a few wayward cats napping along the way, until they stood by the pool. "Back when they built this pool, they had to fill it with saltwater dug from deep out of the ground."

Cara stared at the water, mesmerized by the thought of Hemingway and his wife there, holding court among their circle of friends made up of Hollywood actors and starlets.

She turned, seeing the small building that was now a bookstore but once was a carriage house, converted to Hemingway's private studio and the place where he wrote many of his most famous books. "He had that huge house at his disposal and felt most comfortable in that tiny building, isolated with just himself, his cats, and his typewriter."

"All in all, despite his many houses and toys, I think Hemingway was a simple man who was most comfortable being alone," Luke said. "Sort of like I've become in the last few years."

Cara didn't comment. From the little bit that Tori had let slip, she'd surmised that Luke had really had a rough time with his wife dying so young. She'd left him as the sole provider and caretaker of a child barely more than a toddler, and he'd struggled, but from what Cara could see, he had done a good job.

"Want to go inside?" he asked. "It's pretty packed today."

They'd come along just as a trolley full of tourists had pulled up and she didn't relish trying to maneuver the inside among dozens of other curious lookers. "Maybe we should do the inside another day?"

He nodded and led her back to the front yard, past a cat sleeping on a bench, and out through the gate again. It was getting closer to dinner time and her stomach rumbled. She'd worked up quite an appetite, washing so many dogs in one day.

The wet-dog smell was still in her nostrils, and she hoped she didn't reek of it to Luke. In the shower, she'd soaped and rinsed her hair three times, then scrubbed her skin until it was pink. The last thing she wanted was to smell like a dog when she was so close to Luke.

Cara jumped when she heard a sudden rustle in the brush next to the sidewalk, then saw a long, colorful iguana scamper up a tall palm tree.

Luke put his hand on her arm. "It's fine. They won't bother you."

"I've never seen one that close. Especially just out like that and not in a pet store. Are there many of them here?"

He nodded. "It's said that the first iguanas were stowaways on ships that brought fruit here from South America long ago. Or even escapees from those in the pet trade circuit. Now Key West is full of them."

"And they don't cause any trouble?" Cara asked. The iguana sat watching them from the safety of a large palm leaf. He was a big one— at least seven or eight inches just in the body.

"It depends on who you ask. The subject of iguanas being a friend or foe has been debated much around here. Some say the iguanas' appetite for their plants and flowers is too costly, while others say they have a right to be here too and don't really eat that much."

"I guess I could see if I put a lot of money into landscaping and some iguana ate all of it that it could be an issue. Perhaps they should grow separate gardens just for their visiting reptiles."

He laughed.

As they walked, he talked more about Key West, feeding her tiny pieces of history that she didn't know. He obviously loved the small town, it was evident in his voice, even when he talked about the frustration of the nighttime partying that got out of hand at peak times during the year.

"I keep Ava home on the weekends after dark," he said. "But really, during the day, especially if it's within the workweek, Key West is fairly low-key. It's just when the sun goes down that those who come to let loose really let it go."

They turned down a side street, then another before ending up on Thomas Street and in front of a colorful building. Blue Heaven, the large neon sign read, with a smaller inscription underneath toting it as a restaurant and bar.

Luke turned to her. "This is kind of tacky but if you don't eat here, you haven't truly experienced Key West." His eyes appeared to be asking her a question and she nodded.

"Sounds good to me," she said, then heard a rooster crow. It was close—really close—and she looked down to find a chicken at her feet. Behind it was a line of baby chicks, or whatever you called them, and their frantic pace as they staggered back and forth to keep up with the mama hen made Cara laugh.

"I told you, it's kinda tacky," Luke said, then took her arm.

They went under the archway and around the side, where it seemed all the action was going on. A waitress waved at Luke and told him to sit wherever, and they maneuvered into the first empty small table they saw.

"Just to warn you, there're cats here, too," Luke said, his voice taking on a teasing tone she'd not heard from him before.

The dining area was under a grove of shade trees, shielding them from the sun, but Luke ordered water with lemon, telling the waitress he needed to cool down. Cara followed suit, grateful that she wasn't pressured into drinking something stronger. Hana had always given her a hard time when she wouldn't drink with her, and it was a sore spot between them.

"Considering we're here because of your dip into the deep, what did you think about the reunion between Chaos and Ms. Avery?" Luke asked.

Cara smiled. "It was so sweet. I don't think she thought you'd really be able to find him." She could still see the moment that Ms. Avery walked through the gate and saw her dog, and he saw her.

Though still shaky and weak, Chaos had struggled to his feet and made it to the woman, then they'd both dropped to the ground in a flurry of hugs and tail wagging, with tears falling from almost everyone's face. Ms. Avery had been so grateful that once she'd pulled herself together, she wrote a nice check as a donation to the house.

"That really was a miracle, wasn't it?" Luke said, his voice wistful. "The lost-dog calls don't always turn out that way. Some folks never see their pets again and always wonder where they ended up. I'm glad for Ava's sake that it was one more win on our side and everything went well. Everything except her jumping in the ocean without a life vest, I mean."

Cara nodded. That had been scary, but at least Ava was fine and the dog was home. It was shocking that Chaos had lost almost twelve pounds while stranded, but they'd figured out that he had braved some really tough currents and had swum more than three miles to reach the mangrove he'd been found in.

Luke laughed again, and Cara realized she quite liked the sound of it and that he didn't do it often enough. She noticed that the laugh lines around his eyes were much more evident—and disarming. "Ava got quite a kick from seeing the sea sponges stuck to Chaos. She said he'd been on a Poseidon adventure. I'll bet it took Ms. Avery quite a few washings to get all the algae and tangles out."

"I'm surprised Tori didn't offer to do it," Cara joked.

Luke rolled his eyes. "Don't even get me started. I should demote her from being our head groomer, but the truth is, I'm not any better. As sad as it is, she's our best option. Unless you . . ."

"Oh no. I don't even cut my own hair. Believe me, you don't want to hand that job over to me," Cara said, holding her palms up in surrender.

The waitress brought their water and set it down, then took their orders. She didn't have a clue what to have and Luke asked if she wanted him to choose, so he did. While they waited for their barbecue shrimp and yellowtail snapper, they listened to the singer on the deck—a laid-back Jamaican man who did a good job of making everyone else relax with his soulful reggae repertoire.

But Cara couldn't.

All she could think about was the secret she carried and the fact that she really should just leave the Hadley House before she got them into any trouble. She was feeling more and more comfortable with Tori and Ava, and even Luke. She didn't want them to find out about her and then hate her—or worse, put the Hadley House in jeopardy.

But she loved it there so much. So she was torn.

"What's on your mind?" Luke said, breaking her out of the thoughts that were starting to spiral to dark places.

She shrugged.

"So," Luke started, and Cara felt herself tense up. "Tell me something about you that I don't know—which should be easy."

He was teasing but she felt the sweat pop out across her brow.

"I . . . I . . . I have a twin." Now why had she said that? She was such an idiot.

He looked surprised. "Now we're talking. I can't believe you haven't told us that yet. What's her name?"

Cara felt herself squirming internally, but he appeared to be enjoying the conversation and she couldn't lie to him. She just couldn't.

"Hana."

"What's she like? Do you get along as well with her as I do with Tori?"

"It's complicated," Cara said carefully. How could anyone really understand the relationship between twins if they weren't one themselves?

"How so?"

He wasn't going to let her off the hook. She tapped her foot under the table, stalling for time. But he had asked her what Hana was like—surely that couldn't get her in trouble.

"She and I are opposites in personality, yet everyone has always said we are just alike."

He raised his eyebrows, encouraging her to continue.

"Hana tends to say exactly what's on her mind. And that's not always a good thing because she has some strong opinions. To me it's always felt like she is a magnet for drama, while I try to stay as far from it as I can."

"So in what ways are you alike?" he asked.

Cara paused, thinking of how she and Hana could pass as one another on the phone, and how they could somehow pick out the same book at the library, a few hours apart. And she remembered one year when out of the rows and rows of birthday cards, they'd picked out the exact same one for each other.

"Our mannerisms and our voices are very much the same," she said, staying to safe things. But even with that, she felt herself getting emotional.

"Do you both take after your mother? Or your dad?" he asked.

Before Cara could recover from his question, the food came.

She shook off the thoughts of Hana and her mother and concentrated on her plate. A few bites in, she had to make an effort not to eat like a caveman. There was no doubt that she enjoyed all the cooking she'd been doing for them, but having such a grand meal catered to her was also a nice change. She couldn't remember the last time she'd been out for a real meal—much less with a good-looking guy.

"Well, I have a brother," he said.

"You do? Younger or older?" Cara asked.

"Just a few years younger. His name is Logan. My mom said she always wanted twins but didn't get them, so she still used the names she'd planned."

"Luke and Logan. How quaint," she said before taking another bite. She wondered if the brother was as handsome as Luke.

"Um . . . Cara," he said.

She looked up at him. He used his napkin to point at the corner of his mouth, grinning at her.

"Oh—wow. Embarrassing," she said, mortified that despite her efforts, she'd still gotten food on her face. She wiped it clean, then forced herself to push her plate away with a bit of food still on it. She wouldn't cave to her desire to lick it clean.

The waitress came and gave them the bill and after dodging a question from her whether they were a couple or not, they ducked out. It was getting late and Cara was surprised when he turned the opposite direction from the way home.

"Where are we going?" she asked.

"I thought you might want to see the famous sunset from Mallory Square. I walk down there sometimes when I can get away. It's a great place to be swallowed up by the crowd and just think."

She didn't answer and he took that as agreement, leading the way as they walked together. A few times he stepped off the walkway to allow a woman or child to go by and Cara was impressed by his chivalry. None of the guys she'd ever gone out with had known the first thing about manners.

They arrived at the square and Cara feasted her eyes on the many people moving in and out, the crowd surging like a wave to and fro. There were a few musicians, and one in particular caught her eye, strumming and dancing along as the people around him chanted for him to go faster and faster, and he did. Strumming, singing, and dancing faster and faster, he finally stopped and threw his hands up, causing the crowd to roar with laughter and applause, many adding bills to the hat at his feet.

"That's Movin' Melvin," Luke said, laughing and clapping along with everyone else, surprising Cara with his good rhythm.

"He's quite a character," she said.

"Yeah, you'll find a lot of characters here on the islands. Some say that if you picked up the USA by its ear and shook it back and forth, the ones who couldn't hang on would fall down to Key West."

Cara smiled. His words created such an amusing visual in her head, so fitting from what she'd seen in the last few weeks. The tourists were one thing, but the colorful locals she'd seen were the ones who really made Key West the eclectic mix it was. She found she loved it—the locals and tourists alike. They were all intriguing to her.

Luke took her arm and led her to a place near the end of the dock, where they stood looking out over the water. It was a bit quieter where they were and they let the silence settle between them as they watched the beautiful golds and browns of the sun disappearing over what felt like the edge of the world.

"Gorgeous, isn't it?" Luke whispered. "Just think of the lost souls who've been known to stand in this spot and watch the sun go down. Mark Twain, Hemingway, Jimmy Buffett—and even some who are still alive, like Kenny Chesney."

Cara laughed. Hearing Kenny Chesney's name thrown in with real-life legends sounded almost sacrilegious, even if the man was a famous country singer. Then she thought of something else. "Wait—isn't Jimmy Buffett still alive, too?"

He winked at her. "I wondered if you'd catch that."

A crowd arrived next to them and within minutes welcomed another couple, their circle increasing. Cara felt a nudge from one of them and stepped back to give them more room, putting her even closer to Luke. It should've felt awkward, but it didn't.

"Do you come out here a lot?" she asked.

He shook his head. "I did when I first lost my wife."

Cara realized that she'd never heard anyone mention Luke's wife's name and wondered why. She could tell he hadn't gotten over the loss and thought perhaps that would be the first step.

"What was her name?"

He hesitated and his eyes filled with tears before he blinked them away.

"Grace."

Cara felt like she'd been sucker punched. How surreal that Hana had the same middle name as Ava, and her own middle name was the same as Luke's deceased wife.

Now she was glad she'd never had reason to tell him her full name, and she struggled to concentrate on the conversation at hand.

"So you began spending time out here?" she asked, directing him back to a safer subject.

He nodded. "Once she was gone, I could barely stand to be at our little apartment. I felt a huge burden of guilt for my selfishness."

"What do you mean?"

"Coming to Key West was what I wanted to do, not her. We sold everything we had and moved here—rented a studio apartment and lived like beach bums for a long time. When she got pregnant, I saw how crazy my dream was and tried to get her to move back to our hometown. But she refused. By then she'd settled in and embraced the Key West lifestyle." His voice got lower and Cara strained to hear him. "Then the cancer came. I took her back and forth to Miami for her treatments, but she said she felt that I'd been right all along, that this was the place we were meant to be—that it was Ava's home—and if she had to die, she wanted to die here."

His words were so sad, so heavy with grief that Cara didn't know what to say. She put a hand out and set it gingerly on his shoulder.

"My father tried to tell me if I'd have been a responsible adult from the get-go instead of chasing some idea of living in paradise, then maybe I could've kept my family together. He tried to get me to bring her home and come work for him until Grace was well. I told him she wasn't going to get well. But maybe he was right and I should've taken her home whether she wanted to go or not."

Cara covered her mouth, horrified for a moment before she could speak. Even then, she didn't know what to say. How could anyone blame cancer on a person's location or life choices? "I'm so sorry, Luke."

He shrugged. "It's okay. I've come to grips with it, though I'm sure he hasn't. First he was just angry. It was only after he says I lured Tori here that he stopped talking to me altogether. And I was really desperate for a while—living from odd job to odd job and surviving off what I could find at local food banks. But I wasn't desperate enough to ask him for help."

"How did you make it with a sick wife and a toddler?"

"It wasn't until after Grace was gone that I found the job at Hadley House. I was too tired and overwhelmed to think of moving Ava anywhere else, but I knew I needed to step up and be a man—make a better life for my daughter. So when the director retired and asked me to take over, I took his offer and we moved in. I didn't know I was setting myself up for an almost impossible undertaking in keeping the place running."

"Then why do you keep doing it? Can't you find something easier— less stressful?" Cara asked. He'd shown her he was a smart man. She thought he could probably do anything he set his mind to.

He turned and looked at her.

"It was only that morning that I found Ava curled up with that dog in the kennel that I realized what Grace had already known. She'd made me promise to stay in Key West because somehow, with the instinct only a mother could have, she knew it was where I'd find the perfect life for Ava. Knowing that now, I could never take her away from the dogs—from the work we do. It would break her heart. Ava doesn't see this as a job. We'll never be rich and I have no idea how I'll send her to college, or pay for a wedding, but Ava feels we are doing something meaningful for dogs—and that it's something she was born to do. I wouldn't take that from her for all the money in the world."

Cara's eyes filled with tears. He was a man who'd put his daughter before everything—a parent who worked night and day, not for self-gain or profit but because he believed it was the best thing for his child.

She would've done anything to have a parent like that in her life. Finally, she found her voice. "One day Ava will thank you for it."

He shrugged. "I just hope I can keep the place running. It's not easy juggling the bills month to month. On that note, we'd better get back. It's going to be an early morning, as usual."

They walked away from the docks, headed back, and the one thing that Cara's mind kept going back to was the electric feeling of Luke's hand on her arm and the confusing thrill that it brought to her.

Chapter Twenty-One

Cara adjusted the skirt of her dress under the table, taking care to cross her ankles. Her mind wandered, thinking of Hemi and the other dogs she'd left at home. They'd taken in a new little girl, a Shih Tzu named Lola, and Cara hoped Tori remembered to praise her if she built up the courage to walk through the door to the backyard.

The dog had come far in the last weeks, but she still had a long way to go to overcome her fear of everything she'd ever known during her time as a breeding dog, and going through doors was one of those new things. Along with grass. And humans. But she was such a quiet, pensive dog and she'd shown a huge aptitude for affection, at least toward Cara and a little toward Ava, too.

It was rewarding to see the dog slowly coming out of her shell and embracing a new life, and Cara didn't like to be away from her.

"And we spent two weeks sailing around the Windward Islands," a voice dripping with superiority said from behind her. "I thought Martinique and St. Lucia were just lovely, but Winston preferred Grenada."

Yes, Cara felt like an imposter here amid the other moms, who flashed their diamond rings and chatted about exotic vacations, carpools, facials, and tee times scheduled at the Key West Golf Club.

She didn't belong. And it was a familiar feeling—one she'd hoped she'd left far behind her when she was younger.

The fact that Ava had invited her to the mother-daughter tea given by the Girl Scout enrollment committee was the only thing that kept her still sitting, picking at the tiny crumpets—as the mother next to her had called them—and sipping the raspberry tea.

Their initial arrival hadn't been that bad and actually had started an avalanche of thoughts in Cara's mind. As they'd waited for their seating assignment, Cara had struck up a conversation with a woman in the lobby.

Luanne, she'd introduced herself as, was tall and blonde but her daughter was Asian. A smiling ball of energy, the little girl was called Pearl.

Cara would've never brought up the subject, but somehow when Ava and Pearl took off for a moment, the mother had eased into remarking about how well her daughter had adjusted in only one year at home. Pearl was really excited about Girl Scouts, and the adoption journey they described was a captivating one.

"How long does it take for the adoption process?" Cara asked. She thought of her defunct reproductive system—wishing it to hell and back for being so obstinate. Because of it, she'd probably never fulfill her fantasy of having a family.

"It took us two years, but if you're trying for a completely healthy child, it can take a long time," Luanne said. "Are you interested in adoption?" She raised her eyebrows, waiting for Cara to answer.

Was she interested in adopting? The girls picked that moment to run back and Cara looked at the two of them, how comfortable they were with each other. Then she wondered, why wouldn't she consider adoption one day? Even international. If that was where her heart led her to believe her child was, then yes, by all means she could do it, too.

Smiling, she shook her head. She never liked to give too much away.

"I was just curious," she said.

"Because if you are," Luanne said, "I can give you the name of my agency. They are great to work with. Is Ava your only child?"

Cara felt a moment of wishful thinking. "Oh, she's not mine. I'm not married. I'm just standing in tonight."

Luanne rummaged around in her purse and brought out a card, holding it out to Cara. "Well, I just feel like I should give you this. Just in case, you know," she said.

Cara took the card. It was for an adoption agency.

She tucked it into her purse.

"Thank you. I'll keep it, but it will be a long time before I'm ready to take on the mother role full-time."

"Could be sooner than you think." Luanne winked at her.

Cara was saved from answering when a middle school girl came and beckoned for her and Ava to follow. She led them into the room set up for the banquet, taking them to their table.

They shared it with three other mother-daughter duos, but as soon as they sat down, the other three girls had looked at Ava as though she were covered in chicken pox, or worse.

Ava had tried to talk to them, but they'd responded with one-word replies, giggling among themselves until Ava finally said she needed the bathroom and took off.

Now Cara was left to fend for herself. And she'd just spent ten minutes listening to the talk about the new, lower-calorie cookies that were coming out the next season, trying to appear interested when she definitely was not. Hana could've pulled it off better than she was doing. Her sister was always the best one at playing a role.

She looked around the room, trying to see where Luanne and Pearl were seated. As luck would have it, they were at the farthest table away.

Cara would've loved to hear more about their journey and what it took to be approved as an adoptive parent. Just for future reference, of course.

How desperate would I look if I asked to change tables?

That would be unacceptable, she mused. Instead, she took a drink and suppressed a grimace. She hated raspberry tea. And she thought the concept of diet Girl Scout cookies was ridiculous. A cookie should be a cookie—calories and all. But most of all, she wished Ava would come back to the table and save her from the small talk. The women around her had moved on from cookies and were starting to reminisce about their days as sorority girls.

Cara felt her stomach clench uncomfortably with fear that they'd ask her what college she'd gone to or about her background. Did they really want to hear about her background? She doubted they could handle it.

"School of Hard Knocks," Hana would've told them with a sneer.

Cara just prayed it wouldn't come to that. Then she searched her mind for the name of a community college in Georgia, one none of them would have ever heard of and couldn't have possibly gone to.

"So, where did you say you're from?" the woman next to her asked. "Are you and Ava's father engaged?"

"I—uh—" Cara stammered, but then was saved when Ava returned.

"Ava, I was getting worried about you," she said, turning her full attention to the girl, relieved for the interruption.

A woman across from them stared, her expression showing disapproval at the long shorts that Ava had preferred over a new frilly dress that Luke had tried to talk her into. Cara had finally told him that if he really wanted Ava to get involved in something other than the Hadley House and rescuing dogs, he'd better lay off her about dressing like a girl, even if it was a tea party.

Ava dropped her plate on the table, then slouched in the chair and crossed her arms. Cara knew that look.

"What's wrong?" she whispered.

"I want to leave."

Cara did too, but she also didn't want the committee tongues to wag even more about her if they headed out before the keynote speaker. Luke was probably already going to hear some gossip around town that she'd been awkward. She didn't want to embarrass him by also being rude.

"Tell me what's going on," she said, leaning in close to Ava. She had an idea she already knew, as she eyed the three little bratty girls across the table.

"What's going on is I'm bored here, drinking tea and eating this weird stuff. Josh is at Camp Sawyer, probably climbing through the rocks crab hunting or building a fire, or something cool like that."

The mother beside Cara heard Ava's outburst and her nose lifted at least an inch into the air at the same time as she turned her body away, as though the conversation stank or might be contagious.

Josh was Ava's best friend and had been for several years. Of course he'd most likely been so excited about his upcoming camping trip that he'd told Ava everything, probably not knowing how envious she was.

"He's going to learn archery and *sleep* in a *tent*, Cara," Ava added quietly, her eyebrows raising as though challenging Cara to defend the statement.

"Well," Cara started, unsure what to say. Ava was not the usual girl and of course activities like crab hunting, fire building, and even fishing were going to be more enticing than tea parties and whatever it was that Girl Scouts did—which neither of them knew anything about yet. "Let's just get through this and we can talk about it at home. Maybe you can do some of that stuff with the Girl Scouts, too. We should at least listen to what they have to say, right?"

Ava let out a long, frustrated sigh, then relaxed. She took a tentative bite of a miniature cupcake from her plate.

Cara was relieved. Ava wouldn't purposely embarrass her. She had manners and also empathy, much more than most kids her age. She looked at her watch. Five minutes to go before the speaker, and then when that was finished, they could scram. But she was starting to worry that her deodorant wouldn't hold out that long. The conversation had her sweating bullets.

"My daughter was the first in her troop to earn all her badges in the Agent of Change program last year," a woman across the way said loud enough for two tables over to hear.

Others chimed in, cataloging the many achievements of their offspring through the years. Girl Scout awards, tennis lessons, gymnastics matches, musical instruments—the list went on and on. When one mother paused, another would break in, breathlessly trying to hurry and do her bragging before she—or her daughter—was overlooked.

Cara was reminded of one of Hemingway's famous quotes: "Happiness in intelligent people is the rarest thing I know." She wasn't sure if the women were half as intelligent as they thought they were, but she could tell their cheerfulness was painted on like cheap makeup, ready to run off at the first sprinkle of a summer rain.

Still, Cara wanted to participate—she could've told them that Ava was an avid reader who gobbled up books like their daughters consumed cookies. That she could train the most ornery dog in the park to sit and stay, usually within an afternoon of commands and rewards. That she asked the most inquisitive yet thought-provoking questions that could make a person really think about her life.

But in the midst of their judging eyes and turned-up noses, she froze.

And Ava watched her, probably knowing that she was too cowardly to try to keep up with the woman who waited for her to step in and act like a proud mother. But what Ava didn't know was that the competitive conversation had made Cara remember her mother and all the things they never got to do together.

Had her mother ever had a chance to brag about her and Hana? Had they ever done anything to make her proud? And what right did Cara even have to act as though she knew a lot about Ava? About her accomplishments?

She'd sound absurd if she even tried to act like a mother.

"My . . . uh, Ava—" she began.

Everyone at her table stopped talking, looking at her as though she was about to proclaim something hugely important—or ridiculously inappropriate. Cara felt the beads of sweat start in her armpits and dribble down the side of her dress. Why had she ever thought she could step in and pretend to be someone respectable?

She looked at Ava, her eyes begging for help.

Ava's gaze went from Cara, to the women around the table, then back to Cara. She sat up straighter in her chair, as though she weren't just eight years old.

"What she's trying to say, *ladies*," Ava began, "is that I don't like frilly dresses, leotards, or chasing a ball with a tennis racquet. And tea parties ain't my thing. But I bet I can beat any one of your daughters in a sword fight." Then she pointed at the three girls. "As for them, I don't do crafts but I can probably make their little foo-foo dogs dance a jig on this table if I really wanted to, which is more than your giggling marionettes can do."

The three girls watched, mouths agape and their lips all ready for a major pout to erupt.

Ava wasn't done. Her eyes glittered with emotion. "I know I don't belong here and you know what? I don't care."

"Ava," Cara said, her shock suppressing her voice into a whisper. She stood up, wiped her mouth, and gathered her glittery purse that Tori had talked her into bringing but that felt so unfamiliar under her arm.

"Good for you." The woman next to her nodded at Cara. "I'm glad you're going to take her in hand. That child needs discipline and a lesson in manners. You can tell she's grown up without a mother."

That statement sent shock waves through Cara. Didn't they see that their words were like knives? Wounding for years to come? Were they so anxious to make themselves look better that they could overlook a child's feelings?

They waited to see what Cara would say to Ava, most likely hoping the verbal admonishment would be one to gossip over for weeks.

When she looked down, she could see through Ava's bravado that there was still a little girl there, upset over the treatment from her peers, and disappointed that her best friend was doing fun things without her. And those words about not having a mother; they'd found a target. Cara could tell. But even so, Ava's chin was high, her proud stance reminding Cara of Hana.

Cara smiled at Ava, ignoring the stares from around the table.

"I say that you are absolutely right. We don't belong here, and if we hurry, we can get to the store before it closes and buy what we need to make s'mores around a campfire." She fished in her purse and handed her phone over to Ava. "And call your dad and tell him to pull the tent out of storage and get started on it. We're sleeping under the stars tonight. You, me, and Hemi. Maybe your dad if we decide to let him."

A smile spread across Ava's face and she pushed her chair back, hopping out of it and accepting Cara's hand.

"Cara, have I told you that you're the best mom here?" she said, loud enough for the entire table to hear.

Cara didn't speak again. She couldn't—for the tears in her throat were too thick to utter a single word.

She looked at the faces around the table, some surprised and some disapproving. Surely Luke would never fall for someone like them—a woman who put more thought into what she was wearing than how she was treating others? Someone who climbed the social ladder as though her life depended on it?

Cara wouldn't let her thoughts go to what one of them would do to the cozy environment of the Hadley House if given half the chance. She turned away, already dismissing them from taking up space in her head.

They weaved in and out of the tables, then down the hall and out the door. Only after they jumped in Luke's truck, then took off with the windows down and the sweet, humid Key West air blowing through their hair did Cara feel like herself again.

Chapter Twenty-Two

Cara worked efficiently and methodically, scratching off every task that Tori assigned to her. She didn't even stop for lunch, and when Ava told her it was time to come in and eat dinner, she'd sent the girl away, telling her she wasn't hungry. Since the evening that she and Luke had gone out on their own, things had changed. In the weeks since, working with him was easier, felt more natural, even during those times when they didn't speak.

Luke had also taken her on a few more walks around town and, on the nights it wasn't her turn to cook, treated her to more dinners out, insisting she sample all that Key West had to offer in the way of cuisine.

After the Girl Scout meeting, things had shifted even more. Cara no longer felt like a visitor or an outsider in any way. Some evenings, she even joined Luke and Ava on the couch to watch a movie and somehow by the time the credits rolled, his arm was snaked around the back of the couch until it lay close enough for her to feel the heat.

At times she was relieved to leave the house and be in his company without fearing her reaction if his skin touched hers. With Hemi always between them, now adjusted to walking on a leash, they sometimes simply slipped out and stopped for smoothies, mingling with the evening crowd and releasing the tension from their heavy workdays. They sat at the sidewalk tables, listening to singers or bands at different places.

A few nights before, she'd found a favorite, and Luke insisted they would go there again soon. The artist was young and soulful, so full of passion as he sang James Taylor songs—Cara had felt a wave of homesickness for her sister, so strong that it had brought tears to her eyes.

As the words to the famous song "Fire and Rain" had sunk in and she'd grown pensive, Luke sensed her sadness and reached across the table, putting his hand on hers. He didn't say a word, he was just there in the silent but strong way he carried himself. It made Cara feel cared for and protected.

And feminine.

For the first time in her life a man—and a handsome one at that—was treating her as though what she thought and felt mattered. It was true, her feelings for Luke were growing, becoming more intense. And she was sure he felt the same way. She sensed it with the way his eyes locked on hers during a moving song at a restaurant or bar, and in the lingering of his fingers when they dropped hands upon arriving home, still seeking to hide their sudden closeness from Ava.

But she'd been let down before. Could her heart be lying to her?

It wasn't just Luke who was making her life feel perfect for once. She also enjoyed every bit of the work she was doing. She knew what it was, too. For the first time in her life, she felt part of something meaningful. Tackling problems in the kennels, learning to nurture the incoming dogs while interacting with sassy little Ava, and even roaming around town with Luke—it all just felt right.

And that's why she knew it was so wrong.

Even if Cara had tried to talk herself into the lie that it was okay to stay, that she was doing more good than harm, then everything would've changed anyway. It wasn't even her who made the final decision—her decision to leave.

It was Ava.

Feisty but sweet little Ava Marie who the night before, in the wee hours just after midnight, came creeping into her room, crawling between Cara and Hemi, her warm body snuggling up against Cara as she whimpered about a bad dream.

They'd whispered back and forth in the dark, Ava telling her that she'd dreamed of her mother, then asking Cara if she ever dreamed of her own. It was that trusting little soul who'd decided to let a few barriers down and confided to her that she'd always wondered if something she had done had caused her mother's death. Her words echoed those unspoken in Cara's own mind, something she'd agonized about during the darkest nights and lowest moments—those times through her life when she herself had needed her mother, longed for the touch and attention of someone who understood her and loved her despite all her imperfections, as only a mother could. The times when she tried to bring back a memory—any tiny one would do—of her mother's voice or touch.

They talked for over an hour before Ava had fallen asleep in Cara's arms, her cries for a mother she barely remembered reduced to the occasional sob. It was a moment that Cara had always wanted to happen with Hana, but never had because of the impenetrable tough shell her sister always insisted on wearing as armor against feeling anything.

Cara stayed awake the rest of the night, studying Ava's perfect profile in the light of the moon coming through the window. And that was the truth of it—Ava was a perfect child, imperfections and all. But she belonged to someone else and she also didn't deserve the betrayal that Cara could make her feel if circumstances came crashing down.

So yes, she'd finally bonded with Ava, but after it happened, she knew it couldn't go further.

She wouldn't let it, because she was leaving.

Love and let go. She'd thought she was learning how to do it because of the dogs, but now she knew that fate had been preparing her for something much harder.

Now she just needed to get through the day and fulfill all her duties, so she could leave with a clear conscience. She'd finally finished hosing down the indoor kennels when Luke poked his head through the door. He held his cell phone in his hand.

"Get my galoshes off and come with me," he said, then disappeared.

She didn't know where they were going, but Cara complied. She kicked off the mud boots and set them back in the corner, then slipped her feet into her flip-flops. She was out the door and on his trail in less than a minute. She caught up with him as he got to the porch. Hemi, along with a few other dogs, were lying on the wooden planks, blocking the entrance to the kitchen.

"Move," he ordered the dogs, then held the door for Cara to slip through.

Cara made eye contact with Hemi and saw the flash of panic cross his eyes.

"I'll be back," she said, and he visibly relaxed. Ava's trick was working. She'd told Cara to use the three words as a command, and practice for days saying them and leaving for only a few minutes at a time, then longer, to show Hemi that when she said she'd be back, he knew she meant it. Most of the time he was perfectly comfortable in or out of the house, as long as he knew exactly where she was and could get to her.

Tori turned as they came into the kitchen.

"We've got to talk," Luke said. He went to the island and sat on a barstool.

Cara could see something was making him really upset. She felt a prickle of fear climb up her back. Did he know? She went to the table and sat down, feeling slightly nauseated.

"What's up?" Tori said, coming to the other side of the island.

Luke looked at Tori, then turned and looked at Cara. "The board of directors is sending someone to do an audit. They'll be here tomorrow morning."

Tori looked at the ceiling, rolling her eyes. She threw her hands in the air, exasperated. "Luke! You scared me. Why are you acting like it's such a big deal? I've got all our financials in order—they can audit me all day long and won't find any mistakes. Now, if they'd have come a year ago before I got here to straighten you out—well, then you might've had a problem."

Cara felt a sudden rush of relief. It wasn't about her.

Luke looked back at Cara, then Tori. "What about Cara? She's living here and we're going to have to at least report her as a paid volunteer. You know the guidelines and I don't want anything to look fishy. We've got until tomorrow to get her through the system. Then we're going to have to make sure all the dog placement papers are in order."

Tori nodded calmly. "You're right. Cara can organize the dog placement log, and I'll focus on the accounts. I should've done it weeks ago but I've been paying Cara out of petty cash. I intended to get her set up legit as soon as I had more time. I dropped the ball on that, but I swear, I can get it all done in time as long as running her through the system goes smoothly."

Cara's relief evaporated. Running her through the system sounded ominously like doing a background check. And that couldn't happen.

Now was as good a time as any to tell them she was leaving. She stood, taking a deep breath. Before she could speak, the two of them were shooting reminders back and forth, lining up everything that needed to get done. She hated it, but she was going to have to leave it all to them. They'd have to get through the audit without her.

"Cara," Luke said. "If you can give Tori two forms of identification, she can get started on that while we take a look at all our checks and balance sheets. Once we finish that, you can come in and fill out the volunteer paperwork, get that all taken care of. Oh, we also need to check all the dates on pet medications, immunizations, and even make sure all our food supplies are still good."

"Good point, Luke. Some of those big bags of dog food donated last week might be out of date. I haven't checked yet," Tori said. "And when I finish that—"

"Luke, Tori," Cara interrupted, hearing her voice shake as it came out.

They both heard it too because they immediately stopped talking and looked at her.

"I can't stay. Hemi and I are leaving as soon as I get my things together," Cara said, pushing it all out of her mouth at once so that it didn't stick. The only relief she felt once it was said was that Ava had gone to a friend's house after school and she wouldn't have to say goodbye to her.

Luke stared at her, speechless.

"What do you mean, you're leaving?" Tori asked, putting a hand on her hip. "This will all be fine. I told you, I'll get your paperwork done and we'll set you up in our payroll system. I'll boost your pay to cover the taxes. We won't be in any trouble over you, if that's what you're worried about. Is that it?"

Cara really felt sick now. That was exactly what she was worried about. But she couldn't tell them. They'd trusted her—not only with the dogs and incoming donations, but with Ava. If they found out the truth of who she was, they'd never forgive her.

"I just have to go. I'm sorry," she said, keeping her eyes on a small spot of syrup that was left on the counter, the remains of the pancake breakfast she'd made just that morning at Ava's insistence. She'd even helped her mix the batter, laughing as Cara had put a blob of it on her nose. Cara felt tears spring to her eyes.

She swallowed past the lump in her throat.

Luke still hadn't said a word and Cara couldn't look at him. She turned and quickly left the room, leaving Tori's question hanging in the air, unanswered. As she took the stairs to go pack her stuff, her legs felt heavier than they'd ever been before.

In her bedroom she opened drawers, pulling out the clothes she'd come to Key West with. She pushed aside the things that Tori had given her, secondhand clothes that Cara had accepted with gratitude. But she'd not leave with them—that wouldn't be right. They didn't belong to her and she felt she'd taken enough from them by stealing their trust. Staying would only bring them more trouble.

She blinked back the tears and the shame.

Quickly she changed into one of the pairs of jeans and a T-shirt, and she slid her feet into her dreaded sneakers. Just putting on the outfit she'd arrived in made her feel lost again, bringing back memories of the open road and reminding her just what she faced out there, this time without a bike and once again with barely any funds.

She stuffed the remaining clothes into her backpack, added her paperbacks, and then her toiletries. She went to the dresser and opened the top drawer, removing her wallet. It only held the few hundred bucks, but that was more than she'd come with. She'd take it—as she'd earned that pay.

When everything was in order, and she was once again transformed to the Cara who had arrived at the house weeks before—a girl she no longer recognized—she turned and let her eyes wander over the room. She lingered on the curtains, watching the wind from the open window blow them gently, reminding her once again of the curtains she'd made with her own mother. Over the bed she studied the framed print, trying to memorize the details. She went to the bed and straightened the pillows, setting them up just the way she liked them. Then she stepped back and looked at the chair in the corner. Luke had moved it in there after finding out her main hobby was reading. Her reading nook, he'd called it after setting it up.

Cara had devoured more than a dozen books sitting in that chair with her feet up on the tiny flowered ottoman and a cup of tea beside her. So comforting, that's what it was.

But it was just a room.

She could say it all day long but she knew that wasn't true. It had become her safe haven—her sanctuary as her heart healed and she discovered what it felt like to be included in family life, and where she gathered her thoughts and scrutinized her growing attraction for Luke.

She'd miss the room. Not as much as she'd miss all of them, but still, enough.

Sighing, she opened the door.

Luke stood there, leaning against the frame, and the sight of him made her breath catch in her throat.

"What do you think you are doing?" he asked, his voice the same calm and low tenor it always was.

"I—I told you. I'm leaving." She clutched the bag to her chest.

He didn't move but his gaze wandered down to the bag, then back up to her. He searched her eyes, waiting for more from her. But she didn't give it.

"Just like that, huh?" he finally said. "It's that easy for you?"

In his eyes, she saw he was hurt and that cut her like a knife. She swallowed hard. He was right—she couldn't just walk out, leave him hanging, always wondering what had happened. He deserved more.

Cara wasn't naïve. She knew there was something new there, a special kind of friendship that was budding between them, taking on the potential for something more. It moved slow and sweet—a feeling Cara had never known, one of anticipation, yet still a little reluctance as Luke courted her so subtly that sometimes she wondered if she was imagining it or not.

But the way he looked at her now, she knew her suspicions were true.

He had feelings for her.

Just like she had feelings for him.

It wasn't right and she wasn't this person—this Cara—he thought he knew. She made a new decision. She'd tell him. But she couldn't do it standing up. On legs that suddenly felt wobbly, she went to the bed and sat down. Luke didn't move, except for a slight tic in his jaw. He kept his eyes on her, waiting for her to tell him something.

Cara took a deep breath.

"No, it's not easy for me, Luke. But I have to leave before your board comes tomorrow. Believe me; you don't want Tori to process my paperwork."

"Why, Cara? Is there something I should know?" he asked, his voice breaking, finally showing the first signs of confusion.

"Yes," she spoke slowly, not knowing what the words would sound like, spoken aloud for the first time. "You should know . . . that I'm wanted for murder."

Chapter Twenty-Three

The look that came over Luke was one that Cara would never forget, not in a million years. First his confusion deepened, then his face was transformed to an expression of quiet determination as Cara gathered that he was thinking of how close he'd let his daughter get to a self-professed criminal. So many things flashed over his face that Cara had expected him to stomp, scream, and throw her out of the house. Yet Luke did none of those things.

He took a few deep breaths, his eyes never leaving hers, then he came into the room.

Cara was afraid at first, but then he turned and went to the reading chair and sat down. He leaned back and put his feet up, folding his hands over his middle. When he spoke it was calmly but with an underlying tone of pleading. One she'd not heard from him and couldn't turn away from. "Start talking, Cara."

And she did.

She started with the catalyst—the night their mother was taken away and she and Hana landed in foster care. She told him of the bad placements, and even of the few good ones, as she wove the tale of a sisterhood formed at birth and carried through life, of twins emotionally supporting each other through the highs and lows, and especially one supporting the other through deep and tragic bouts of depression.

He didn't ask questions and Cara was glad to just keep talking and let it all out. As she spoke of Hana, letting her sister come alive with words and descriptions, painting the picture of the battle-beaten warrior her sister was, the tears flowed. The truth was that Hana could be a controlling, stubborn, and emotionally crippled maniac. But then she could also be a hilarious, compassionate, generous, and loving sister.

Despite it all, she missed Hana—without her she felt like a boat with no sail, a moon with no stars, an oyster missing its pearl.

She also laughed through her tears a few times, telling stories of their many predicaments they'd survived together, using humor as a weapon against the pain a child feels at being abandoned. She told him of Hana's good qualities—her giving nature and the way she made everyone around her laugh when she was in a happy mood. Of how she could attract any man she set her eye on because she could talk circles around a fence post.

Luke listened to all of it, letting her slowly unravel all the details of their life until she finally got to that terrible night, the one that changed everything.

"Hana was in a toxic relationship. One built on secrets and lies," Cara said softly. "I told her to end it, that it was wrong and nothing good could come of it. And she did. Several times. He did, too. But they kept coming back together, his obsession with her deepening as the months went on."

She paused. It was difficult to tell the story, because it was so dysfunctional and so wrong. She wanted to defend Hana in one breath, then blame her the next. Yes, Hana had really screwed up but if she hadn't, would Cara had ever met Luke? Or little Ava?

She took another deep breath. It was hard spilling the secrets. So hard. But she continued. "The last time she broke up with him, he refused to let her go. Hana got a new job, one where she'd never have to see him again. But he found out where we were staying and started leaving flowers on her car, messages on her phone, and sending long pleading emails. So we moved. But then, he found us again."

"Why didn't she get a restraining order?" Luke asked.

"Because he was a judge. In a small town, too, if that tells you anything. He would've laughed at any attempt to bring legal action against him. Hana knew if she tried it would backfire on her somehow."

He nodded, encouraging her to continue.

"We moved to a new town more than a hundred miles away. I don't know if Hana maybe told him where she was, or if he found us on his own, but when I came home from work that day . . ."

She stopped and took a few breaths. She could still see it in her mind—all the blood and Hana crouched in the corner, her eyes glazed with shock. Cara saw the gun lying there, and her own shock had turned to terror. Fear for what her sister had done and what would happen to Hana because of it.

"He'd broken in on her while I was at work. I don't know what happened exactly but there wasn't time to get all the details. All I know is that he lay sprawled on the bed, blood spreading across his arm and chest, and Hana wasn't speaking. I think she was in shock. I told her to call an ambulance and when the police came, to tell them I did it."

"And she agreed for you to take the blame?" Luke said, breaking in for the first time since she'd started.

Cara shook her head. "She didn't exactly agree, but that is just the way it is. I always fix things for Hana. That's how our relationship works. There was no question about it—it's just the natural answer to everything that goes wrong for her. And I couldn't let them take her away."

Luke bowed his head and Cara wished she could see what he was thinking.

"And you don't know what happened next?" he asked.

"No. I grabbed a few things and threw them in the car, and I was gone. I didn't even know where I was headed. I just drove. When my car broke down a few hundred miles later, I started walking. That's when I found Hemi and decided to go as far south as I could manage. I didn't start out with a destination, but somehow I was drawn to Key West."

"I can't believe this," Luke said, pulling his fingers through his hair.

His words jolted her out of her story. He thought she was lying and that she'd targeted him, decided to use him and the Hadley House as cover, instead of just stumbling upon them?

Suddenly she was thrown back to the many times she and Hana were blamed when things went wrong in placements, when no matter what they said, they were the culprits to every mess or broken toy. Because they were foster kids—*from the system*—their word meant nothing and they couldn't be trusted.

She stood up and gathered her bag again. "If you don't believe me I'm sure you can find out all about it online. But for the sake of your family, and for this place, I'm leaving. I've taken care not to leave my name on anything. No one will ever need to know I was here."

She headed for the door, telling him the judge's name as well as her own.

"Sandy Springs, Georgia," she said, urging him again to look it up and see for himself. When she finished, she paused, drinking in the sight of him one more time.

"Good-bye, Luke. Thank you for everything, especially for giving me a place that felt so—" She couldn't finish. Not without baring even more of her soul.

She slipped out the door.

Cara took the stairs as fast as she could and was relieved when she didn't see Tori. Instead of going through the kitchen, she took the front door.

Hemi was lying on the porch and Cara bent down and, without speaking, hooked his leash, then led him through the yard, then out the gate.

She could tell Hemi sensed her distress by the way he stayed close, a silent message that he was on her side, and one that brought more tears to her eyes. She blinked them away, straightening her shoulders.

This was what was best for all of them. And Luke didn't trust her now, so what choice did she have?

They were all the way around the corner and past the bench where Luke had stopped her that first day when she heard his voice again. "Cara, hold up for a minute."

She turned to find him jogging toward her. It still burned in her gut that he'd acted as though he didn't believe her.

"What I told you is true," she said.

"No, it's not." He caught up and bent over, winded as he clutched his knees and tried to get his breath.

"Why won't you believe me? Do you think being wanted as a criminal is something I'd make up for fun? Don't you think I wish this had never happened? That I wasn't on the run? That I could talk to my sister?"

He stood and reached for her hand. Cara let him have it, but it didn't feel right anymore.

"Listen to me, Cara. I just searched for your name and it didn't come up. Then I searched for Hana's—and that judge. The only thing I found was a small news article about him having a handgun accident."

Cara was flooded with confusion. "They think he killed himself? Accidentally?"

He shook his head. "No. He's not dead—it was just a flesh wound to his shoulder. Your sister isn't mentioned anywhere and neither are you. Since he's a judge and he's married, he probably wanted to cover it up. He'd have to in order not to jeopardize his place on the bench."

She was speechless. Joe wasn't dead? She'd run for nothing? Her legs felt weak and she sat down on the curb. Hemi sat beside her and whined, sensing her distress. When Luke hunkered down on the other side of her, she just shook her head, not sure what to say.

If only she had found the courage to do some research herself—somewhere on the road or even when she'd arrived at the Hadley House and had access to a computer—she could've stopped running long ago. She'd been afraid. Too frightened of seeing her name, even her photo, listed publicly with an accusation of guilt. But Hana, she would've moved heaven and earth to dig up every last detail as soon as humanly possible.

Cara felt like an idiot.

Luke put his arm around her, but even that didn't stop the tremors that quaked through her.

"I caught up to tell you that you can stop running, Cara. And that you can contact your sister."

She stared straight ahead, her thoughts swirling around each other. She was free. No more running and no more hiding who she was. She felt lighter, suddenly less burdened by guilt. But she also felt confused. And worried.

What was Hana doing without her? How was she getting by? She knew from the last year of tumultuous events that the judge wouldn't just let her sister get away with shooting him, and not make her pay somehow. It hit her then—she'd run away from Hana, thinking she was doing what was best, but her sister probably needed her now more than ever. She'd done the wrong thing in her grand gesture of trying to do the right thing.

"But you know what I've gathered from everything you told me?" Luke asked softly.

Cara bowed her head, drained of emotion, or just not knowing how to feel.

Luke pulled her closer. "Did you hear what I said? I think you've spent your entire life living for someone else. I don't usually get in anyone's business, but I have to tell you something."

When Cara didn't look at him, he continued. "You can't keep letting your sister dictate everything you do. I understand you feel responsible for her, but you aren't. I will do anything and everything in my power to help you get her through this, but I don't think you should run away from us—from all that's good for *you*—just to keep cleaning up messes for Hana. It's time to think about yourself for once, Cara."

She stared at Luke, unsure how to answer him. Then a quote came to mind, another of Hemingway's famous. It fit what she was feeling. So she said it: "The first and final thing you have to do in this world is to last it and not be smashed by it."

When he didn't reply, she added, "I'm just doing the best I can to keep both me and Hana from being smashed."

Luke gave a gentle smile and his arm tightened around her. "I know that one, too. But then Hemingway said this: 'The world breaks everyone and afterward many are strong at the broken places.' And I don't know anything about your sister, but you, Cara, are stronger than anyone I've ever met."

She appreciated that he thought that, but her strength hadn't gotten her far in life. "I may be strong, but my life is—or was—so different from anything you have ever lived. You don't know what that does to a person, never knowing a real home or belonging to anyone. It changes them and keeps them from being who they were meant to be." Swallowing past the lump in her throat, she turned to look hard into his eyes. "I just don't think it's what you want for Ava, to be around someone like me."

He shook his head and stood, looking down at her. When he spoke again, she could hear barely concealed anger start to gather in his voice. "Then you don't know me well enough, because having my daughter around someone like you would be an honor like no other. You told me that you always wished you could go home. I'm giving you that chance now, Cara. We still need to see where our relationship goes, but I know this, while we are exploring that possibility, you can find your home with us. No more moving from place to place." He held his arms open wide and softened his tone. "Right here—Key West. The Hadley House. Me and Ava. Tori. The dogs. All of it—*we're* your home. Or at least you can allow yourself to see if this is where your journey ends for you."

She looked away, not really understanding what he was trying to tell her, but thinking about everything that had happened to bring her to him and Ava. All her life, she'd thought the world was full of heartache and that no one really cared for her and Hana. They'd always felt ignored, snubbed, and even invisible to most. But now, when she considered everyone who had helped her along the way, giving a little bit of themselves to help her reach her destination, it became clearer.

The world wasn't out to get her. Good people did exist.

And maybe Luke was right. Could it be time to help Hana from afar, but for once make her stand on her own? And who knew, maybe Hana was doing that now, in Cara's absence. Maybe they were both better because of this forced separation?

At her feet, she studied the shaggy bundle of affection that had been the first to steal her heart. Hemi was her little guardian angel, his name alone linking her to Key West. Through thick and thin, the dog remained by her side, a loyal companion and one she felt was imperative in keeping her going, putting one foot in front of the other when all she'd wanted to do was curl up in the leaves and sleep forever.

Then patrolman Greg and his insistence on delivering her to a place that would offer her a good meal, but in reality he gave her so much more. Maisy and Miss Kim had made her feel capable, needed even. Miss Kim had reminded her that there were angels in the world—those who gave of themselves with no thought of receiving anything in return.

Selfless. It was the first time she'd ever had reason to use that word, but it fit Miss Kim exactly.

And Clyde. Without even meeting her he'd worked for hours to put together the bike and trailer—giving her a way to move faster toward what, he hadn't even known, but he had somehow realized it was somewhere important.

Then she'd met Lauren, Lacy, and Tommy. A family so like her own when she was a child, but one that was beating the odds and staying together. Of course, it was with the help of Mack—a man who through all his own troubles and doubts about life maintained his brotherly sense of responsibility, and who she knew would remain loyal as long as his sister needed him.

With the thought of siblings, Hana's face came to her and she pushed it away. She needed to think this through. On her own. Hana would tell her not to trust anyone, that she was bound to get hurt. A month ago, she might've agreed with her sister. But now, memories pelted her and logic seeped in. Maybe the walls she and Hana had spent years building should finally come down, and perhaps that was the lesson fate had been trying to teach her all along.

Even old Henry had taken her in, offered her shelter—a place to recover. She felt the tears gather when she thought of him and his companion, Buster. Like so many she'd known through life, he'd first thought her a nobody and had treated her gruffly, but he hadn't been able to hide his soft side from her for long. The few days she'd had with him had taught her that being alone wasn't the answer. That every person had a soul mate out there somewhere and one should spend every minute with that person before they were gone forever.

She looked up at Luke.

Could he be to her what Clara was to Henry? Her forever? Could the universe be throwing her a second chance at being happy? She had to admit, she'd never worked anywhere that she enjoyed as much as she did her job at Hadley House, interacting with the dogs that, like her, only wanted to feel accepted on a permanent basis, not thrown away or given up on at every turn.

Luke watched her, waiting patiently as though he knew she was slowly sorting through her thoughts, cataloging and filing through the pros and cons of staying in Key West—of possibly trusting him with her heart. The unending patience he carried for everyone around him was another quality she admired in him.

There were so many things about Luke that she respected. Things that she'd tried to deny or ignore over the past few weeks. Like the way when he moved close to her, he breathed in like he was enjoying a fleeting gift. Or when he looked into her eyes and she felt he really saw her—the real person, the one no one else in her life had ever taken the time to know.

As she sat there, she realized something else. Hemingway had once written in one of his books, "You can't get away from yourself by moving from one place to another." She'd known that quote for what felt like forever, but she'd never realized exactly what it meant before. But she did now. All her life she'd thought she was moving from place to place in search of a home. But in reality, she was running from herself and the person she didn't want to be.

But with Luke and Ava, along with Tori and the Hadley House, she'd found a new self—one she liked and that she could be proud of. One filled with a sense of awe for the wonder of life and a realization of the good things in it. But maybe it wasn't such a new self. Just maybe deep down, she'd always been the person she thought she'd become in Key West.

"Cara," Luke said softly. "Just tell me what you want me to do and I'll do it."

And he would, she knew that. If she asked him to walk away, he'd respect that and do it. But if she wanted to—if she could just make herself fight through the doubt, find the courage to step out of the bubble of self-preservation she'd spent years cultivating—maybe she could change her fate.

She hesitated for a second more, almost frightened to believe it could really work out for her when nothing ever had before. Running was all she'd ever known. But so far, she realized, it had never helped.

Taking a deep breath, she put her hand out.

Luke took it and she felt covered in his warmth. Through the tingles that moved through her, feeling his skin on hers, she felt lighter. He pulled her up and to her feet with no effort at all.

"What do you say we start over?" he said, looking down at her, hope in his eyes. "No promises, we'll just take it one day at a time until you figure some things out."

One day at a time sounded easy enough.

She nodded. "I can do that."

He guided her arm through his, clasping her hand. Then he turned her around and with Hemi on their heels, she let him lead her back to the beacon of hope she knew as the Hadley House.

Chapter Twenty-Four

Cara dusted the chicken thighs with the seasoned flour and laid them in the sizzling skillet to brown. She added the minced garlic. A few minutes later she flipped the pieces, waited a couple more minutes, then plucked them out and lined them in the bottom of the Crock-Pot.

Carefully she covered them with the tomato sauce she'd stayed up late making. The sauce was a special recipe of her own that she'd perfected over the years and she couldn't wait for Ava and Tori to try it.

A bit got on her finger and she popped it into her mouth, closing her eyes in rapture at the taste of the rich herbs and tomatoes. She grabbed the chopped parsley from the small bowl and scattered it across the top of the sauce.

She paused when she realized she was smiling. She'd just had an epiphany. With each chop, stir, and flick of seasoning, she was expressing the love she wanted to share, the emotion long bottled up inside her waiting for the right situation and people to fall in place. It wasn't something she could say with words, but a bit of it was in every dish she created.

Like Hana, she hadn't been raised to know how to show outward affection, but she wanted to learn. In the meantime, she hoped they realized that the effort she put into feeding them was actually an extension of how she felt.

Unfortunately, Luke wouldn't be thrilled with just pasta like the girls would be, so she'd thought up a meal that would appeal to all of them. And it wasn't anything new—in the past she'd made it frequently for herself and Hana because it was a cheap meal that could last for a few days.

Six weeks had gone by since she'd come clean with Luke, and though Cara would've thought things would be awkward between them, that was far from the reality. Somehow, she fit within the family at the Hadley House as if she'd always been there. Slowly, she and Tori had figured out what each one of them was the best at, and they exchanged chores and tasks to fit. And Luke. He was just . . . just . . .

She realized she was smiling again, and felt like an idiot.

Now the outside chores were done, Ava was at school, and Tori'd gone to take a dog to the vet. Luke was outside doing something or other, and that left Cara a few minutes to herself. She grabbed a chocolate-chip cookie from the batch she'd made at midnight the night before, and headed to the office. Hemi padded softly behind her, then settled under the desk.

Cara sat down and powered up the monitor.

She'd phoned Hana when she found out that Joe hadn't been killed. Her sister was at first ecstatic to finally hear from Cara and know she was safe, but as she'd predicted, Hana's elation had turned sour when the answer to her next question about when Cara was coming back wasn't to her liking.

Hana was used to getting her way but this time, even though it was taking more willpower than she knew she had, Cara wasn't budging. At least not until she was ready. Maybe life in Key West *wasn't* for her. It could be that she and Luke were only feeling the sparks that come when people first meet each other. But something told Cara that wasn't the case. That Luke, Ava, and the Hadley House were possibly even her destiny. Until she knew for sure, she was staying.

Hana tried to convince her to return to Georgia each time she called. The night before Hana had asked Cara if Luke might be using her for free labor, so Cara told her they needed a time-out. She'd never hung up on her sister before, but when Hana wouldn't stop, Cara began to feel closed in and cutting her off was the only choice.

Would shutting her down send her into a depression? That was Cara's fear, because it would be all her fault. She'd sat there, the phone still in her shaking hand when Tori had peeked around the door.

"How're you doing?" Tori asked Cara, pulling her from her morose reverie.

Cara tried to smile. "I'm fine. It's Hana that has me worried. She doesn't want me to stay here."

"Does she act like this often?"

"Well, it's hard to say. But I can't stand this tension. And I'm sorry it's affecting me and the house."

Tori patted the table. "Do you want to grab a cup of tea and chat?"

Now was as good a time as any, Cara thought. She followed her into the kitchen but she skipped the tea and poured herself orange juice instead. Her body felt depleted and in need of vitamin C.

She took the glass to the table and sat down. She kept the towel with her, twisting it around her fingers to keep her hands busy.

"First, let me say, I wasn't eavesdropping. But I could hear you trying to talk to Hana," Tori said.

Cara let out a long sigh. "I just can't get through to her. She wants me to come back to Georgia. She says she's going through a lot but doesn't want to say exactly what."

"And what do *you* want to do?"

That threw Cara off. What did she want to do? She thought she wanted to stay at Hadley House, that she didn't want to leave Luke or Ava, or even Tori, but she felt torn.

"I want to help her. We're sisters—we should stick together. But she won't even consider coming here," she finally said.

Tori sipped her coffee.

"Let me ask you this," she said. "Exactly what does she think you will accomplish together in Georgia? You don't even have family there."

She didn't have an answer for Tori, because there wasn't one.

"Cara," Tori began, "I'm not trying to be negative, but don't you think this is another circumstance of your sister trying to control you?"

"What do you mean?"

"I've put together a lot of bits and pieces of your stories, and it seems to me that she's possessive of you," Tori said. "By what I've gathered, it's always been Hana who decides where you live, when you move, and even who your circle of friends is."

"In a way, that's true," Cara admitted.

"I know studies say there is always a stronger twin, but I saw who you were before you reached out to her from here, and after you got used to us, you really flourished. Now, it feels like you are withdrawing into yourself again. Is it because of Hana? And if so, do you really think that's healthy?"

Cara let out a long sigh. She was right. Hana was the dominant twin, and she'd always wanted to keep Cara all to herself. But she loved her sister and a spat could send Hana into a spiraling depression. And if she sunk into one deep enough, it could be really bad.

It was always just simpler to let her have her way.

Until now.

"And I really think she's upset that you have someone special in your life." Tori raised her eyebrows, waiting for a response.

Cara felt torn between logic and loyalty.

"Hana doesn't have any reason to dislike Luke. She just doesn't want me to get hurt," she finally said, though she wasn't so sure.

Tori nodded. "I get that. I really do. But don't you think I'm afraid that my brother is going to get hurt, too? You are the first woman he's shown any real interest in since Ava's mother died. He went through so much pain and sorrow. It killed me to see him that way. But he's opening up to you and allowing himself to feel again. If it falls apart, I'm going to be the one left to pick up the pieces again. And I'm terrified. But I want him to fill the empty place in his heart."

Cara blinked back the tears that threatened. She hadn't thought about it that way, and she knew Hana probably hadn't either. Luke was taking a chance, too.

"I know he is," she finally responded. "And he's allowing me to be part of Ava's life, and that means more to me than you can imagine."

"Yes, Ava's special," Tori said. "Do you really want to walk away before you even know where it could go? Don't you think you deserve a chance to be happy?"

Cara shrugged. She didn't think she'd ever done anything to actually deserve being happy. But she also hadn't done anything not to deserve it. Thus far, she'd simply accepted that her lot in life was to continually struggle. And what about Hana? She was right that all their lives it had been them together, against the world.

Tori sighed, lowering her head into her hands for a moment before raising it up to give Cara the most serious look yet.

"Okay, here goes. Just know I really don't want to say this," she said. "But as Luke's closest family member, I just have to."

Cara's stomach dropped. What now?

"If you think you might not be in this for the long term, I wish you would break it off now," Tori said.

They stared at each other, letting the words sink in. Cara really didn't know what to say. She loved Luke—she'd known it from the first week she'd spent with him. But her life was so complicated right now with Hana. Could she—or should she—really make Luke and Ava a permanent part of the constant turmoil that was her life? Was that even fair to them?

"For God's sake, you look like I just ran over your dog," Tori said. She reached out and covered Cara's hand with her own. "I'm just saying at some point, Cara, you might have to choose between your happiness and your sister's. I just hope my brother and Ava aren't collateral damage of the fallout."

"I would never purposely hurt Luke or Ava," Cara said.

"I know that," Tori said. "Now. Let's move on from this conversation. I don't want to spoil the day. I've said my piece and now you know how I feel. And I need to get to work. I'm way behind on emails and paperwork. But I think Luke wants to talk to you about a little day trip."

She smiled at Cara and the air cleared. Just like that, things were easy again. That was something she really loved about Tori.

"What day trip?"

Tori gave her a slow smile. "Oh, I don't know. He didn't give me the details but maybe he just wants to take you away somewhere and ravish you. Hide his actions from innocent children and canines."

For a split second, Cara felt a wave of sadness. The easy back-and-forth she and Tori shared should be what she and Hana instinctively had, but instead their sisterhood felt so full of strife.

She threw the dish towel straight at Tori. "Don't tease! You know we're taking it slow!"

"There's slow, then there's stupid. Get on with it already!" Tori said, then they both erupted into laughter as Luke chose that moment to walk in through the back door, his face clueless.

Chapter Twenty-Five

The receptionist showed Cara into a plush office and told her to have a seat on one of the soft yellow leather chairs, then disappeared. Cara looked around, expecting to see a long couch with a box of tissues beside it, like she'd seen in the movies when the psychiatrist told someone to lean back and recount how their childhood was so damaging.

"You'll like Doctor Serano, I promise," Luke had said just before the receptionist called her name, and she'd left him behind in the lobby.

Cara didn't know about that, but she did know there wasn't a couch. Besides the cheerful chairs, there was a large mahogany desk, but the corners of the room were taken up with tall potted palms, and the blue-and-white striped beach chairs in the paintings on the wall completed the calming décor.

She took her paperback out of her purse and opened it, trying to take her mind off the impending meeting.

Another ten minutes passed and she put the book away, unable to remember a single word she'd read. Cara couldn't believe that Luke had talked her into the appointment. She and Hana hadn't "talked to someone" since their junior high years, when the state made it mandatory for them to meet with a mental health professional every quarter. They'd made a pact then and had never spilled a word of their troubles to whoever sat behind the desk, knowing that anything and everything said could be—and probably would be—used against them. After so many years of keeping their problems personal, could she now open up and share? With a complete stranger?

She reminded herself they were no longer kids. No one could put them anywhere they didn't want to be. And Luke was just outside the door, waiting in the lobby. That gave her a bit of comfort, but she still felt a quake building inside her, threatening to—

"Hi, I'm Jules Serano."

Cara wasn't expecting the tall, willowy blonde who came through the door behind the desk. She wasn't sure what the name Serano was, but she'd thought the doctor would possibly be Cuban or Italian, or some other ethnicity.

This Serano was anything but what Cara had expected, and in her pencil skirt, sheer white blouse, and high heels, she didn't even look like a shrink.

Where was the old bald *male* doctor with spectacles and a clipboard? The one she'd dreamed up in her imagination? Or pulled from an old childhood memory . . .

The goddess thrust her hand out, leaving it hanging as she waited for Cara to respond. "And you are?" she prompted.

"I'm Cara."

They did a quick, awkward shake made worse by the sweating of Cara's palms.

The doctor ignored the hulking desk and settled into the chair next to Cara, as though they were simply two friends meeting for coffee. She fidgeted until she was comfortable—crossing her legs first one way and then the other—then settled her gaze on Cara.

"What brings you in today?" she asked, smiling broadly.

Suddenly Cara was twelve years old and at the mercy of whatever someone wrote in her file. The bad memories were flooding back so fast she felt she'd drown in them before she could get out of there.

First, all Cara could think about was how dumpy she felt next to her. And those legs—she wondered now how Luke knew her. Had he dated her?

"Cara?"

"I—I, um . . . I really don't know." Now along with physically inferior, Cara felt like a total idiot.

"Luke asked me to see you."

Cara wondered what else they had talked about. Luke knew her well enough to ask for a favor in getting her in right away. That didn't bode well.

"Yes. Um, Doctor—"

"Call me Jules," she said.

Then Cara saw her pick at her nails and she looked down and noticed they looked terrible. She'd expected a perfect manicure but, hey—Jules was human!

She took a deep breath.

"I guess you could say that most of my problems stem from my relationship with my twin sister. Right now I'm being pulled between what I want to do and what she wants me to do."

"And how does that make you feel?" Jules asked.

"Guilty."

"Then why do you let her get away with it?"

Why did she let her get away with it? Cara thought about the answer—really thought about it. Jules sat there. Patiently waiting.

"Hana has fought depression all her life and I've always had a sixth sense of when it's about to grab her again. We've always kept it quiet— just between us. But now I'd like to know how to help her without giving up everything I want."

There, that wasn't as bad as she'd thought. Except that she'd have rather eaten nails than disclose one of her and Hana's many lifelong secrets. But it was done.

Jules put the pencil to her lip, thinking.

"If you could pinpoint one major thing that you think causes your sister to dip in and out of depression, what would it be?"

Before Cara knew it, with only a few well-placed questions and comments from the sharply dressed doctor, she was telling all. She took nearly thirty years of memories and condensed them into one sad, tight package, and she sat there and spat them out at Jules like a jammed machine gun. Their mother's death, the many foster fails, Hana's depression spirals, her twisted tryst with a married man, then as she winded down, she lowered her voice and told Jules of Hana's suicide attempts.

When she finished, she was breathless and felt ashamed of laying her and Hana's life out there for a stranger to judge.

"I'm not sure if you were telling me what causes your anxiety or your sister's," she said. "Do you feel better that you've talked about your mother's death?"

"I feel surprised," Cara said. She never talked about it. That was a twisted little secret she liked to hold to her heart with barbwire, taking all the pain of the pricks instead of sharing it with others.

"Do you think that bottling up your memories and your frustrations over your mother and how you felt left behind to falter in foster care is healthy for you or your sister?"

Cara shrugged. "That's just the way we've learned to deal with it."

"Well, I think we need to teach you some more tools, but first, let's talk more about your sister, since that is what brought you in. Has she seen a professional?" Jules asked.

"Not since we were kids."

"And you are afraid she's going to leave you the same way your mother did, is that right?" Jules asked, her eyes locked on Cara's.

Cara looked away. She wasn't going to answer that.

Jules tapped her pencil. "Do you think she's in danger of harming herself right now?"

Cara paused. That was a tricky question. If she told the truth, that Hana was always just a step away from harming herself, would they send the crazy van to get Hana? Grab her and lock her up?

But if she lied, then she was wasting time. And after all, Cara had tried and failed for years to help Hana. It wasn't easy taking on such a responsibility. It had taken its toll, sending Cara on so many guilt spirals she couldn't even count.

It was time for reinforcements.

"I'm not sure if she's at that point right now, because I haven't seen her in a while. But she's tried before, and my gut tells me she's headed for a big one right now."

"A big one?" Jules asked.

"The cloud. We've always called it the black cloud, because Hana says that's what it feels like when the depression descends upon her. It's like she's suddenly enveloped into a heavy darkness where simply breathing is difficult, moving is a challenge, and basically her body wants to shut down."

"You talk about the black cloud and how it settles on and around her, smothering her," Jules said. "I want you to try to think of it differently from now on."

Cara looked at her blankly.

"Hana is not the cloud," Jules said.

"I know she's not the cloud," Cara said, feeling ridiculous.

"What she is, is the sky," Jules said. "And the clouds—even the heavy, dark ones—will pass over and through her, representing each emotion. Some are happiness, some peace, and yes, others are sadness and distress. But they are all moving. The dark clouds feel heavier and slower than the light ones, but they won't stay forever. We have to make her see that she can get through and still be whole when they've passed."

Cara listened intently. She'd never thought about it that way and knew that when the next dark cloud came, she'd deliver the same description to Hana to help her through.

"I'd like to see her," Jules said. "Do you think you can get her here?"

"No way. She'd kill me if she knew I was here talking to you about her. Anyway, she's in Georgia. At least for now."

"Well, we'll work on that but today, let's go over a few ways you can be there for her to help her out of this particular bout."

Cara nodded and they began a dialogue about the past several years and how Hana's episodes had gotten progressively worse. The longer they talked, the more Cara liked Jules and felt bad for judging her by her good looks. She was actually quite warm and personable, her relaxed manner putting Cara at ease.

"The best thing you can do for your sister is be there for her," Jules said. "Even if it's just to listen while she cries. If she won't talk, you do the talking. Tell her how important she is to you. Try to find ways to reduce her stress. Ask her what you can do to make her feel better."

"I've done just that. I've sat with her every time and promised her that I love her, that she's important, and all those things."

Which is going to be hard to keep doing from a state away.

Jules nodded. "Good. Some people think the tough-love approach is the way to go and I can't tell you how damaging that can be to someone who is already at their lowest point. It's useless and harmful. Can you imagine pushing someone away or giving them tough love when they have cancer? I'm not saying that depression is just like cancer, but it is a disease, not just a voluntary mood or crisis. Never make her feel like she has a choice in whether to be depressed or not."

"I've never done that," Cara said. "I just need to learn as much as I can so when these episodes happen, I'm more use to her. Right now I feel so helpless."

"I don't think you're helpless at all. It sounds like you're a good sister," Jules said. "But once you understand depression, then you can better support her and get her through it."

Cara felt the first beginnings of hope, that perhaps she could one day help Hana get to a healthy, happy place. As she listened to the doctor talk more about small gestures, refraining from being judgmental, and offering advice, she soaked up every word, cataloging it in her mind to think about later.

"I'd like to refocus the conversation a bit," Jules said, uncrossing her legs and leaning forward. She reached out and took Cara's hand, which was blessedly now dry. "Before you leave, I need to tell you that I see a more important issue. I've let you talk about your sister for the most part, because I think you needed to get it off your chest. But the most pressing issue to me is that you think you are your sister's keeper and are responsible to keep her mentally healthy. You cannot take that burden on, Cara. You can be a support system, but ultimately you are not responsible for how she lives her life—or if she chooses not to."

She paused and Cara felt a catch in her throat at the last few words. When she didn't respond, the doctor continued.

"I feel you're holding on to a lot of bitterness about your childhood, and especially your mother. I suggest that instead of bottling up your feelings about that situation, we find a way to talk about it. If you'll come back, I'll help you through it. But that's enough for today."

Cara doubted she'd be back. She'd bared her soul and though in a way, it was freeing, it also made her feel naked and vulnerable.

Jules stood, smiling at Cara.

Cara joined her. "Thank you so much, Doctor—"

"Jules," she said. "Please, just call me Jules. And even if we can't get Hana here, I'd really like to see you again, Cara. As her supporter, you need to remember your own mental health. Take some time for yourself. Don't let her problems become yours."

Wasn't that what twins did? Cara wasn't sure that piece of advice was going to be helpful, but she nodded anyway.

"I'm just trying to get the courage to stand up to her and not fold to what she wants, without making her depression worse," Cara said.

Jules stopped, her hand on the doorknob. "Wait. What is it that you think she wants you to do?"

Cara hesitated. She knew what Hana really wanted.

"She doesn't want me to be with my boyfriend. She wants me to come back to Georgia for good," she whispered, as though giving voice to the words made them so much worse.

"But what do *you* want?" Jules asked.

"I want to be happy. But I also want my sister to find peace," Cara said. And that was the truth. She'd always done whatever she could to try to help Hana find balance in life. But now she was beginning to see that every sacrifice she'd ever made had not been the cure for Hana's issues.

Jules watched her for a moment, then reached out and patted her shoulder.

"Well, I want you to think on this: At what point will you stop trading your happiness for your sister's? And then I also want you to search your mind for some good memories and start replacing the bad ones," she said, then opened the door.

Cara could've told her that she remembered almost nothing of her mother before that tragic night, that her memories—if there were any good ones to be had—were all locked away too tight for her access. That she'd tried many times, and failed, to bring them to the surface.

But Jules didn't allow Cara to answer. Instead she peered into the lobby. "Luke? Is that you, you handsome devil?"

Cara's back stiffened as she watched Luke stand and come forward, then envelope Jules in a heartfelt hug. Once again, she felt like the ugly stepsister next to a shimmery lovely Cinderella. She remembered Hana telling her years before to never fall for a hot guy because every woman would always be after him.

Luke and Jules parted and she reached up and pinched his cheek. "Look how tall you are! What are you, part giant? I still expect to see the awkward pimply faced boy who liked to follow me and my friends around."

Then she looked at Cara and winked. "So did my little cousin tell you that I used to beat him and Tori at fishing every summer? Don't let the fancy clothes fool you. I'm the official grand bass master of this family."

Chapter Twenty-Six

Cara slept better than she had in months, and when she rose, for the first time in a long time, her mind didn't go straight to her sister. It went to Luke—and she wondered if they'd get time alone that day. She rose from the bed and tiptoed into the hall.

It was early and when she peeked into Ava's room, she saw a little bare foot protruding out from a lumpy bundle of covers on the bed. She pulled the door closed, then made her way farther down the hall.

Quietly, she opened Luke's door and stepped in, then shut it behind her. When she crossed the room, he stirred.

He lay sprawled across the bed, his long limbs touching from corner to corner. She crawled in beside him and put her hand over the wide expanse of his back. He didn't move and she inhaled, pulling in his scent and letting it fill her senses.

He smelled like strength. Courage. All man.

Cara knew she'd never felt about someone the way she did Luke and it scared her. She didn't deserve someone like him. She didn't deserve the life she was living.

She moved her hand from his warmth, holding it just above his skin.

He sensed her hesitation and turned, gathering her close then leaning her back on the bed. She let him cover her completely. If it were possible, she'd crawl inside him, using him as a cocoon to protect her from the dysfunction that continued to stalk her, uninvited and unappreciated. But suddenly, his lips were on hers, his skin against her own, and she forgot everything else and heard nothing but the beating of her heart and his, joined together in perfect rhythm.

They wouldn't go further, not until she was ready. She didn't need to tell him that, he just instinctively knew. Part of her wished she could give the signal, but the other part—the piece of her that had been hurt too many times in the past—was still satisfied with just being close to him.

For now she enjoyed touching him, kissing him, and taking it to the edge each time as they learned more about each other. Once again she marveled that she was experiencing a relationship so unique and practically unheard of in this day and age. So different from those she'd had in the past where she'd jumped in too deep too soon and it had fizzled out like a wayward star.

Luke and I are sharing a real romance, she thought, as he nibbled at her earlobe and sent delicious waves of pleasure through her.

A half hour later, they heard little footsteps coming down the hall and they parted. Luke picked up his shirt from the end of the bed and had it over his head and down his body when Ava opened the door.

"What are you guys doing?" she asked.

"Wrestling. What are you doing?" Luke said, his face serious.

Cara bit her lip to keep from giggling.

Ava rolled her eyes. "It's time to get up. The dogs are whining outside."

She closed the door and Cara shrieked when Luke grabbed her, smothering her in a bear hug. He slammed his hand on the mattress beside her.

"One. Two. Three. I win," he said.

Yeah, big guy. You win, Cara thought as she untangled herself and went to her room to dress and meet the day.

A shower, splash of makeup, summer dress, and sandals and she was downstairs, moving quickly to keep everyone on schedule. After she'd fixed a light breakfast of oatmeal and fruit, then called them in, she made her way to the office.

She wanted to not think of her sister, for just one day, but like a moth to flame, Hana's face snuck in. Cara couldn't stop feeling responsible for her twin's well-being.

Maybe once Hana calmed down, they could talk. It most likely wouldn't be easy. But what was easy these days? It made her wonder. Would they ever have a peaceful life? Now that Hana was resentful of Luke, Ava, and the Hadley House, it felt that their communication was worse than ever. Cara didn't want that.

Hana needed her.

They needed each other.

Sighing, she opened her email and scanning through, saw mostly junk mail until one email caught her eye. The subject line read *to Cara and Hana, my CASA girls.* She looked at the sender and felt a moment of confusion. She hadn't heard from the woman in years—so at first she didn't recognize the name in the sender's box.

Cara was shocked. Ms. Melinda had to be really old by now, and why she would be contacting them was a mystery.

She noticed that Hana wasn't copied on the email.

She clicked to open it.

Dearest Cara, I do so hope this note finds you well, or finds you at all. I'd like to meet with you and your sister. I would've copied Hana but I've lost her email address. Please reply quickly, as I am in poor health. Best regards, Ms. Melinda Barnwell

Cara realized she wasn't breathing only when she felt a wave of light-headedness. What could the old woman want?

She picked up her phone and dialed Hana. It rang once then went straight to voicemail. She didn't want to leave a message.

Luke walked in just as she hung up. She told him about the email.

"What do you think she wants?" he asked.

"I just don't know," Cara said, then released a long sigh. "I wouldn't have thought Melinda would still be alive. But it can only be more bad news and I don't need that right now. I want to leave all that behind. I don't need to hear the dirty details of how Mom died and we were taken away."

"But what if there's more?" he said. "Maybe it's not even about your mother."

Cara didn't answer. A part of her had always thought that there was a huge gap in the story told to them, that perhaps if the system hadn't been so overwrought with cases, their caseworker could've found a family member to take them in rather than turning them over to the state.

"I don't know what else it could be. And if it is about our childhood, we've already got that branded into our heads," she finally said. "Our father ditched us before we can even remember him. Our mother fought depression until she couldn't any longer, and then she left us. No one else in her family or his stepped up to claim us. End of story."

The words felt like lead on her tongue and hearing them aloud made her heart pound. It wasn't the fact that they were in foster care, though that was no picnic, but knowing their mother didn't love them enough to stay with them provided the constant ache in her soul. Suicide—the ultimate abandonment.

"Then you're right. Maybe digging it all back up again would just hurt you," he said, coming to sit down on the edge of the desk.

"Maybe it can't hurt me any more than it already has," Cara said.

"Yes, it can. It can send you back to where you don't want to be. And what if this time, you can't come out of it? You've made so much progress. Please, for me, let it go."

Cara hesitated. He might be right. But answering the email couldn't hurt, could it? Just a few questions and they'd put it to rest. Their story was already one full of dysfunction and tragedy, did she really want to open herself up to more pain?

But she had to know.

She'd follow up, but she just wouldn't tell Luke. Or her sister. No sense giving Hana something else to stress out about. Cara could handle it on her own. And she didn't want to remind Luke that she was damaged goods. He needed to see her as she wanted him to—strong and capable—not some pitiful person continually attached to dysfunction.

"You're right," she said, glad he couldn't see right through her empty words. And she would let it go. After just one itty-bitty reply to the email.

Chapter Twenty-Seven

Cara looked around the restaurant and tapped the table, nervousness filling her at leaving Hemi behind with Tori and Ava. They weren't even close if there was an emergency. Anything could happen. What if Hemi got out? The other dogs were all secure in their kennels, the littles in the house. But she'd left Hemi pouting at the gate and she could still see his eyes, begging her not to leave. Her mind was also on Melinda and their conversation. After they'd exchanged emails that told her basically nothing, Cara had called her.

Melinda definitely had something important to talk to her about, but she wanted to tell Cara in person and refused to give any details over the phone.

Luke had said she should probably let it go, but Cara didn't think she could, especially now that Melinda refused to talk about it further until Cara came to Georgia. That made it even more intriguing. How was she just supposed to simply forget about it?

She'd told Melinda to give her a few days to consider, but if all went well, she would be making a road trip. That meant she needed to tell Luke. And soon.

She took a deep breath. Nothing good would come from obsessing over it. For now she needed to be completely present with him. They had so little time alone and Luke was excited about taking her on a real date.

He'd talked her into driving thirty miles up to Big Pine Key so that he could be the first to introduce her to the No Name Pub, a landmark well known in the Keys. It had roots from way back in 1936, and he insisted she'd been in the area long enough without visiting it. The drive was nice and they'd even been lucky enough to see several of the Key deer along the road, little miniature deer only known to the Keys area and protected from hunting.

One had looked Cara straight in the eye as they'd rolled to a stop beside it. Luke said it was full grown, even though it was only half the size of any deer she'd ever seen in Georgia, and it had stared at her as though trying to convey a message. Such deep, dark eyes, full of intelligence—it had for a moment captivated her attention and kept her from worrying.

But now here they were, and conversation had all but stopped.

The waitresses moved about them.

"I've found a recipe for dog treats that will save us some money from buying them," Cara finally said, hoping to fill the awkward silence.

Luke raised his eyebrows at her, an invitation to continue, she hoped.

"It's only four ingredients. Peanut butter, pumpkin puree, eggs, and whole-wheat flour. Roll it out, cut into shapes, and pop it in the oven for twenty-five minutes. We can make it in mass quantities and freeze it, then take out what we need for three or four days at a time."

He smiled and she looked down self-consciously. Why didn't he talk instead of just letting her ramble? Now she wished she would've come up with something more exciting than dog treat recipes. She felt her face going hot. Would she ever get used to just being a girl on a date?

Thankfully, a waitress approached them. She handed them menus, then set down a stapler and a red marker. She smiled at Cara. "A little birdie told me this is your first time here so I brought over what you'll need to mark your visit."

Cara looked at Luke for direction.

"I'll explain," he said, then directed his attention to the waitress. "Please bring us iced tea to start."

She nodded and took off.

"What do you see all around you, Cara?" Luke asked.

"People." So many of them that it made her nervous, especially since she'd walked in with a guy who could turn everyone's head and made her feel self-conscious that she wasn't pretty enough to be his date.

He laughed. "What else?"

Cara took another look, then it hit her. Stapled to every wall and much of the low ceilings were dollar bills, most with signatures or initials scribbled on them in red, blue, or black marker.

"Oh," she said, feeling silly. "But I don't have—"

Luke was already anticipating her excuse because he was digging in his wallet and pulled out two dollar bills. He slid one to her, then took the marker and wrote something on the one in front of him.

When he passed her the marker, Cara quickly wrote her name.

"Where do you want to put them?" he asked.

She shrugged.

He leaned toward the wall that their booth hugged. "I say they go right here to commemorate our first visit to the No Name Pub." He stapled his bill to the wall, then reached for hers. When hers was posted up there next to his, he leaned back, smiling at her.

"What?" Cara said. His smile was weird. Like he knew something she didn't.

Cara scooted closer to the wall and looked at the bill he'd written on.

"Luke & Cara, destined for great things together," it read.

"What great things?" she asked, feeling her face flush.

He reached over and put his hand over hers. "Lots of great things. If you'll only stay in Key West with me, who knows what we can accomplish?"

The waitress returned with the tea and took their order. Cara grimaced when Luke asked for a pizza, half Key shrimp and half Caribbean chicken. He winked at her and promised she'd love it, and the waitress agreed, encouraging her that she had nothing to worry about, the pizza was made from an old, secret recipe brought over from Italy.

The waitress left and Luke took a swig of his tea, then leaned back in his chair. Cara tried not to think of how calm, cool, and just completely masculine he looked. He needed a haircut, but the way his hair curled just over his collar drove her crazy. And the way he turned eyes when he walked through the room was causing her to feel all possessive.

But Luke was hers.

The tingling that started in her toes and worked all the way up her body as she stared at him told her that much was true. She smiled slowly at him.

"What's that for?" he asked.

"I'm just glad to be out with you," Cara said, her voice barely registering over the buzz in the restaurant.

"No, I'm the lucky one. You're the prettiest girl in this place," Luke said, leaning forward, "but excuse me for a second while I hit the restroom."

He stood and went across the room and disappeared down a hall. Cara watched another couple coming in, noting how the young woman clutched the arm of the man she was with. The girl laughed loudly, her mannerisms flamboyant and flirtatious, reminding Cara of Hana.

The waitress later returned with the pizza and two plates. She set it all down in the center of the table just as Luke returned. He thanked her and she smiled back, leaving them alone.

"Let's eat," Luke said, pulling a piece from the platter and letting it slide onto one of the plates, then handing it to her.

He served himself, then nodded, waiting for her to take the first bite.

Cara looked at it, glad he'd given her the chicken side. She hesitantly lifted the plate and nibbled a bite from the end of the slice.

Her eyebrows raised at the same time that her taste buds were tantalized. It was delicious.

Luke put down his slice, then smiled as he shook his head.

"What?" Cara asked.

"I saw Old Mad Billy on my way to the bathroom. He's a character, that one. He said he saw us come in together and wanted to tell me that I'd better put a ring on your finger before someone else does."

Cara's face burned.

Luke reached over and took her hand. He touched her ring finger. "I made him smile when I told him we were just courting for now. He said that it was old-fashioned, just before he punched me in the arm."

He paused, then lowered his voice and leaned in. "But I do want to tell you something."

"What?"

He turned her hand over and began drawing circles on her palm with his finger, the action starting a fire deep down in Cara's belly. She squirmed but he held fast, the pressure from his hand drilling into her own.

"I'm putting a deposit on this hand. Don't be renting out space to anyone else while we see where this goes. I know I shouldn't even have to say it, but you never know what that sister of yours will talk you into." He said it teasingly, but Cara could tell he meant it. He wanted them to be exclusive, and he also didn't want what they were building to be brought down by Hana's long-distance influence.

She decided that she would wait until the next day to tell him she was going to Georgia. This moment was too special to ruin.

He waited on her response but she just nodded, glad they'd taken yet one more step. But was the thing that was budding between her and Luke so obvious for everyone to see? Being the private person that she'd always been, it made her squirm in embarrassment that her feelings— and his, obviously—were on display for the world to witness. She also had to remind herself that she wasn't being an imposter, that Luke was indeed seeing who she really was. The problem was that *Cara* couldn't see who she really was.

Chapter Twenty-Eight

The drive to Sandy Springs took her most of two days, but Cara had taken the eight hundred miles slowly, staying in a hotel one night and stopping frequently so that Hemi could relieve himself. She knew she was procrastinating and found herself slowing down the closer she got.

Luke had urged her to go once she'd explained to him about the hole in her past and how she just felt like if it was filled, she'd be able to move on more easily.

"I was wrong before but now I understand," he'd said. "As Jules has said, if we're ever going to really have a good future together, you'll have to confront your past and put it to rest."

Then, as they'd discussed it with Tori, both she and Luke invited Hana to come stay at the Hadley House, a safe place to sort out her future. Cara was so overwhelmed with their kindness, once reserved for only her but now flowing over to even her wayward sister, that she'd been speechless.

"Hana, they said you could come stay here at the Hadley House," she'd said when she called her sister that evening.

"No thanks," Hana responded.

Cara hadn't replied for a moment. She'd covered the phone to mask the sound of her heavy sighing as she fought to keep her next words civil.

"Just think about it," she'd said finally. But she knew Hana wouldn't. Her sister had the patent on stubbornness. Once she'd made up her mind about something, almost nothing could change it.

Now here Cara was, in the town that had brought her nothing but bad memories.

I don't belong here, she thought as she waited for the light to turn green. *I never belonged here. This town and the people in it were ugly to me. Let's get this over with.*

"We made it buddy," she mumbled to Hemi, who still lay sleeping in the passenger seat, curled up comfortably, always willing to do whatever and go wherever it was she went.

He didn't stir.

Ava had surprised her by being overly emotional when she said she was leaving for a few days, and that weighed heavy on her mind, too. A part of Cara thought maybe since Ava had lost her mother, she was vigilant with everyone in her life, always fearful they'd also go away and never come back.

Cara would call her before bedtime. Reassure her.

Hana had no idea she was coming, and Cara didn't know if she'd even tell her she was there. No doubt her sister would insist she stay for good, and it would only end in a battle between them.

But Cara wasn't making any decisions until she'd talked to Melinda to find out just what the old woman wanted to tell her. On their phone call, Melinda had been guarded and hesitant, as though she weren't sure she even wanted to go through with the meeting at one point.

But it was too late now to back out, because Cara was here, rolling into town in Luke's pickup truck, feeling out of place because it no longer felt familiar to her. It just felt wrong.

Her plan was to go straight to Melinda's house. Find out what it was she was being so secretive about, and then most likely turn around and go back to Key West. She and Hana could argue just as well over the phone, and Cara honestly didn't want to spend one more minute than she had to in the town that held nothing but bad memories.

Melinda lived on the far side of town and Cara headed that way. She finally passed Morgan Falls Dam and the drop-off where for the previous six years, she and Hana had participated with most of the rest of the town in the Chattahoochee River Summer Splash, floating six miles down the river to the finale of an evening of music and food. They'd bought used kayaks and it was one of the better memories Cara had, one of the many traditions they'd started after a talk about how with no family, there were no annual traditions. Hana had insisted that they start that very summer making their own. She was like that—always bent on solidifying their small family of two.

A wave of sadness came over her and Hemi looked up, as though he could feel it.

"Yeah, I really miss her," Cara said. "She's not always a pain in the butt, you know. You might even like her."

Springs Landing was coming up on her right. Hana said she'd rented a duplex there, the rent cheaper than their apartment. Cara wondered what it looked like.

Just before they got to the intersection, she looked over at Hemi. He sat there, his stance erect as he gazed out the window.

Cara was so lucky to have him. He'd been her best friend out there on the road, a solid companion who helped her complete her quest to get to Key West. If she hadn't had him with her, would she have finished the journey? Would she have ever met Luke?

She reached out and put her hand on the scruff of his neck, weaving her fingers through his fur. He was special, Cara knew that without a doubt.

She also knew that Hana didn't have anyone like Hemi to help lead her to a new beginning. She was alone, dodging the punches of life as best she could without the support and loyalty of anyone beside her.

Cara thought of Jules and her advice. But holding on to her own happiness didn't mean she had to completely let go of her sister. Did it?

Somehow, Cara could have both. And that sixth sense she'd always had about Hana—it was telling her to go check on her.

Cara had been feeling it for the past two hours, doubting her choice not to go to her sister first and involve her in whatever it was that Melinda wanted. After all, if it was about *their* past, then Hana had a right to be involved. She'd pushed off the guilt for as long as she could, but now she recognized that her gut was telling her something else. More than guilt, Cara felt like something was wrong.

She pulled over to the side of the road. Maybe she could just call her.

Hemi looked at her, his expression questioning whether he was being treated to a bathroom break.

"No, sit still, Hemi, then we'll be back on our way," she said, then pulled her phone from her purse and dialed Hana's number.

It felt like an eternity as it rang.

No answer.

She hung up then tried again.

Nothing.

She hung up and did an Internet search. It only took her a second to find the number of the latest café Hana had said she was working at, and she dialed it.

"Rumi's Kitchen," a man answered.

"Um, hi. This is Cara Butter and my sister, Hana, works for you. I'm trying to get a hold of her about a family situation. Is she working, by chance?"

He paused. "Nope. She hasn't shown up or called for three days."

Cara barely waited for him to finish before hanging up and pulling back onto the road, her foot firmly on the gas.

"We're making a detour, Hemi. But I'm not going empty-handed. You don't know my sister and how she can scare the crap right out of you. If she's just mad at the world and hiding, she'll tear me up without a peace offering."

He looked at her with a doubtful expression.

Cara laughed. Hemi couldn't know he was about to be taken into the eye of a storm like no other. He was about to meet the tumultuous Hana Butter of the Butter twins.

Chapter Twenty-Nine

Cara held on to the bag of food and Hemi's leash with one hand and with the other pounded on the door. She knew it was the right place—on the steps she saw their pitiful pot of flowers that Hana dragged from place to place, doing her best to keep them alive. They'd bought the plain pot at a flea market and then took an afternoon painting it blue with sunflowers springing up all over it. A project they'd done together—laughing at the ugly but memorable end result. Then they'd planted sunflower seeds in it. They never took root.

Next was live daisies. They'd lived a few weeks.

Then it was petunias.

Every time the flowers in the pot died, Hana put something new in and tried again. Her sister was tenacious, if anything. They joked about their black thumbs and that doomed pot. And it was right there on the porch, overflowing with wilting begonias, a big red flag to Cara that her sister was behind that door.

She pressed her face to the glass, trying to see through the crack in the blinds. Nothing was visible.

Hemi pulled, trying to get back to the untidy bush he'd just watered at the edge of the walkway.

"No, Hemi. Stay."

Pounding again, she said a few colorful words under her breath, as though that would make her sister suddenly appear.

But Hana either wouldn't or couldn't answer. Cara looked back at the truck sitting in the driveway. Did Luke keep any tools in the back? She was going to have to find a crowbar, or else try to kick the door down.

Then it opened.

Whoa.

Her sister looked worse than death, dressed in a rumpled T-shirt and baggy sweatpants, her feet bare and her hair hanging limply around her ashen face.

Cara recognized the look in her eyes. It said her sister had retreated from the world and everyone in it. She glared at Cara, one hand on the doorframe as she leaned on it for support.

"Well, I'm here," Cara said, resisting the urge to hug Hana, instead going around her to set the bag on the counter.

"Why?" Hana said, her voice dry and monotone.

Cara ignored her and she let Hemi in and dropped the leash, letting him race around the room to smell every corner before relaxing his protective stance.

"He better not pee on my floor," Hana said. "I'm not supposed to have pets in here."

Cara was relieved to see her sister up and walking. That meant she hadn't done anything too stupid. Yet.

She began to unpack the food, pushing aside an empty bag of chips and an overturned carton of milk to make room for the new food containers. She peeked into a takeaway container and saw the remains of what appeared to be old jambalaya, wrinkling her nose at the stench that rose up to meet her. She plucked the bowl up and threw it in the plastic trash bag propped against the cupboards. It looked untouched.

"Go away," Hana mumbled, then turned away and headed down the hall. She went into her room and crawled into bed.

That's not happening, sister.

"I brought your favorite spicy chicken soup and some panini. I didn't get tomatoes on yours, don't worry," Cara said, keeping her voice neutral. "The soup's still hot if you want to come eat it now."

Hemi wiggled around her, taking off to explore the rest of the place.

"Why are you here?" Hana moaned, throwing a pillow down the hall. The place was so small, it was as though they were still in the same room. She could hear Hana fine and even see her as she lay back, covered by a rumpled quilt. "You said you weren't coming back."

I can't tell you why I'm here, Cara wanted to say. But she kept it safe. Unthreatening so that Hana couldn't provoke an argument and order her to leave. This time would be different because Cara was determined she'd get Hana to agree to talk to a counselor. She'd tell her about Jules and how light she felt leaving her office.

"Because of a lot of reasons. But let's start with the fact I called your work and your boss said you haven't shown for three shifts and won't answer your phone. He was worried," Cara said, looking around and taking in the cramped room with its cheap orange linoleum in the kitchen and mismatched plaid furniture in the living room.

"He doesn't even know me," Hana said, her voice bitter. "He probably wants something."

"You said he was really good to you giving you a job when you lost the old one," Cara said softly. "Hana, we've got to start allowing people to help us. I found that out on my way to Key West. Not everyone is as bad as you want to think."

No answer.

She felt claustrophobic in the small room. No wonder Hana had fallen into depression again. Who wouldn't be suicidal living in such a dismal and ugly place? Sure, it was all that Hana could afford, and together they'd lived in worse, but it didn't make sense why she wouldn't come to Key West and the Hadley House—where she could stay for free and it was beautiful—to instead suffer all alone in misery.

I'm not going to force my new life down her throat. I will not beg her. Unless, of course, it comes to that.

"Come eat, Hana," she said.

"I don't want it," Hana said from the bed, practically spitting the words out.

Cara would not let Hana's tone get to her. She'd keep her cool, take care of Hemi's needs, then—if luck was on her side—she'd eventually be able to convince Hana to eat. Knowing her sister, it would not be an easy task, so first she'd let the aroma of the soup fill the place, hoping to tantalize and tempt until *no* was no longer the first word on her lips.

Cara filled a bowl with fresh water. Beside her Hemi wagged his tail, waiting to be served. She set it on the floor, then began taking the dishes out of the sink, stacking them neatly beside it as the water ran. When the sink was full of hot, sudsy water, she dumped the plates and glasses in it, letting them soak while she bagged the trash to take it outside. Hopefully then the smell of rotten food would fade so they could eat without it lingering over their heads.

"What are you doing?" Hana said, forcing the words out in between gritted teeth and a long growl.

At least she's still awake.

"First I'm going to clean up your kitchen," Cara said calmly. "Then I'm going to pick you out some fresh clothes and you are going to take a shower."

Hana didn't answer. Cara wanted to go in there and gather her sister close, hold her and tell her that it would be okay, that the dark would fade and she would get through it. But their relationship didn't work that way. Hana wasn't wired for touching, and neither did she appreciate affection or soft words.

Patience.

That's what it would take to get Hana out of bed and back on her feet. Cara knew it from experience, and she also knew that she was the only one in the world who could guide her sister toward the light again.

She remembered some of Jules's advice. But even without that, she knew how Hana was and what she responded to.

First step was to put everything around her in order, then get her to bathe and wash her hair so she could start to feel better. Then they'd talk.

Cara would number off all the things her sister had to live for. A future husband. Future children. With Hana's tenacity and strong personality, Cara didn't doubt her sister could figure out a real career and be a success at it, then hopefully write her own ticket out of the hellhole she was living in.

Slowly and with conviction Cara would trick the dark cloud into receding to leave her sister alone, and when it was gone, she would help her put the pieces of her life back together.

Help her to reduce her stress, Jules had said.

Oh, and together they'd call her boss. And maybe Cara would include Hana in the meeting with Melinda. Or maybe she wouldn't. Whatever the news, Cara would spin it to feel more positive and keep Hana grounded. And hopefully sometime during all of it she could convince her sister that it was time to speak to a professional. That perhaps her life didn't have to be a roller coaster of ups and downs, dark and light. That she shouldn't be ashamed and that depression could be treated.

But this time there would be one more component to Hana's route back to normalcy—Cara would find a way to make her understand that their paths wouldn't always lead the same way. And that it was okay.

Was it all an overwhelming responsibility for Cara to take on yet again? Yes, but it was also an overwhelming relief that she'd arrived in time. Other scenarios that she could've found crowded her mind, making her feel unsettled and panicky.

Like the scenario of living life without Hana. Forever.

But her sister was still there. Emotionally bruised and battered, her body weak and smelling of desperation, but at least in the land of the living.

Another reprieve—the thought crossed Cara's mind as she scrubbed at the dirty bowl, the crusty remainder of ravioli feeling the brunt of her anger at the silent disease that stalked her sister.

⤳❀⤶

Hours later it was dark outside and Cara sat behind Hana on the bed, combing through her wet hair. It had taken longer and was more difficult than she'd hoped to get Hana into the shower, but now her sister was clean and slumped over a pillow, her body too weak to even sit up straight. Cara felt everything that Hana felt, knowing she was sapped of energy, anger, and anything that made her feel human.

The darkness did that to her. It also lied to her. Time and again.

"Hana," she said, keeping her voice low and logical. Never condemning. She'd learned that over the years. One misplaced word could set them back for hours. "You know that when this starts to happen, you have to fight it. Don't let the darkness steal your joy."

For once, Hana was silent. But Cara knew her sister so well, she could almost hear the words in her head. No doubt she was silently screaming, "What joy!?"

Cara felt guilty, remembering what waited for her in Key West, a kind of joy that Hana had never encountered. But she continued.

"I know right now the darkness is whispering that you are worthless and no one loves you." She put down the comb and divided the hair into three sections, then began to braid, using as gentle motions as she could, willing comfort to go through her fingers and into her sister. "But I love you. Hemi probably even loves you already. Or at least he will, when he gets to know you."

Hemi heard his name from where he lay at the end of the bed, his muzzle resting on his paws as he watched them. His ears twitched.

Cara recalled the day a few years ago that she'd come home to find a note on the door of their apartment: "Cara, if you find this note, don't go in. Just call 911. I don't want you to see me like this. Don't cry because I'm not worth it."

But Cara had almost broken the door down in her hurry to get to her sister, and she'd reached her in time. She'd begged her to see that she was worth it—that there was light at the end of the cycle of darkness, if she could just make it through again. But since then there'd been even more years of torment for Hana.

"Are you listening to me?" Cara asked, hardening her voice, filling it with confidence and authority. "You are so strong. We've had years of hard times and stress, and you carry it on your back like a nine-hundred-pound gorilla. Most people would roll over and give up, even become addicted to something to help numb the pain, but you don't. You handle it on your own. You amaze me, Hana, but you don't have to carry that gorilla by yourself. I'm here. Hand that sucker over to me once in a while."

Hana still didn't speak.

"You think I'm planning a life without you. That you're all alone. But that's not true. I want you to be a part of it."

She could feel the shake of silent sobs beginning in her sister. But she knew that Hana wasn't yet ready to accept an embrace. She possibly never would be. But Cara could accept that. She just had to get Hana to listen to her.

"I would never want a life without you in it. And I'd be mad at you forever if you took that away from me. Don't leave me here without you, Hana."

They both knew she was talking about death. About suicide. But neither would say the word. She finished the braid and twisted the hair tie on the bottom strands.

"Remember what we found out last year on that website? Depression doesn't mean you are crazy. It just means you are sick. It's a disease. Like a virus in your brain. Please—let's get some help. You can get treatment for this. You are not our mother. You're stronger."

Hana bolted from the bed like a jack-in-the-box, stomping into the bathroom and slamming the door behind her.

Hemi jerked to an upright position, looking around to see what was going on. Cara let her sister go. She wasn't surprised. The only surprise was that she'd gotten to say as much as she had before the eruption. Hana never saw herself acting like their mother when the dark cloud enveloped her. And perhaps Cara shouldn't compare them, but she wanted her sister to remember the pain her mother caused with her ultimate decision.

Cara unfolded her legs, standing and going to the door. She pressed her hands against it, then against her cheeks.

"Hana, don't listen to the voice of depression. Listen to the voice of someone who loves you. Listen to me. Things will get better. Please come out."

When there was no answer, she went to the bed and lay down, feeling spent and exhausted. She'd already cleared the bathroom and there was nothing in there Hana could hurt herself with. Cara wasn't entirely sure, but she thought maybe her sister was through the worst of it.

Now it was only time to wait. And pray.

If luck was on her side—or even something more than luck—Hana would emerge from that room and be ready to face the world again. Ready to give it another chance. And hopefully, ready to look depression eye to eye and kick it in the shins, then spit in its face. And then it would be time to talk to her about Luke, and the finality of her decision to live her life in Key West.

"Hana, I'm staying here tonight," she said, surprised at the sudden decision. Melinda could wait. Her sister could not.

She wanted to get out of the clothes she'd traveled in but she didn't want to leave long enough to go out to the car for her duffle bag, so she rummaged through the stack of clothes on the shelf in Hana's closet and found a man's white shirt. She undressed, then pulled it on and buttoned it up.

Quickly she remade the bed, straightened the pillows, then climbed in to wait for Hana.

Finally, she emerged, her face pale and pinched. She stared at Cara for a few seconds, her eyes narrowing.

"That shirt—" she started, then stared again.

"What about the shirt?" Cara asked, looking down at it.

Hana crawled back into bed. "It was Joe's," she said.

"What? Eww, gross," Cara said, pulling it over her head and throwing it on the floor. She grabbed her own shirt from her discarded clothes on the dresser and pulled it on, then climbed back into bed. "I can't believe you kept that. It's not healthy, Hana. Tell me, what else of his do you have?"

Her sister hesitated, then let out a long breath before speaking, as though the air she expended was a heavy secret being released from her body. "His baby."

❧

Two words. That was all it took to change everything about their present and their future, but Cara was proud of herself that she'd taken it so calmly. Hana was still too delicate coming out of the latest cloud. She didn't need accusation and judgment. She needed help. She needed her sister.

Her physical reaction was another story. Cara had jumped out of the bed and begun to pace the room, searching for the right thing to say.

"How far along are you?" Cara's legs finally felt weak and she sat down on the end of the bed, her fingers automatically looking for comfort in the softness of Hemi's fur.

Hana shrugged.

Cara could see the sheen of tears in her eyes and she didn't push. What did it matter now anyway? It was so ironic that it hurt. Cara wanted a huge family, but she'd never give birth to a child. And her sister—the one who always said she never wanted to be a mother—was pregnant. She would soon have a real live breathing, crying . . . *baby*.

"Oh, Hana," she said, unable to come up with anything better. Her sister was in a lot of trouble.

"I know. I know, Cara." Hana dropped her face into her hands.

"Are you too far to get a—" Cara couldn't even finish her question. She and Hana had both agreed long ago that they respected every woman's choice when it came to their bodies and they'd never judge, but they personally could never terminate a pregnancy. That's why they'd always been careful.

Hana nodded, answering anyway.

"What happened?" Cara asked.

Hana looked up and sneered at her. "Well, there's this thing, dear sister. It's called the birds and the bees and when the—"

"That's not funny. You know what I mean. Weren't you taking birth control? And what the hell were you doing sleeping with Joe? I thought it was over a long time ago?"

She remembered suddenly that Jules said to come across as nonjudgmental. But—too late. She needed answers.

"Which question do you want me to answer first?" Hana said, her sarcasm coming back full force. "Yes, I was on birth control. It failed. And yes, we were broken up but I'm human, okay? I got lonely. Really, really lonely, Cara. If you remember right, you left me and went skipping to the wonderful world of Oz in Key West."

Cara breathed deeply. It wouldn't help to point out that Hana—and Joe—was the reason she'd gone to Key West in the first place. But somehow, it always ended up being her fault.

"He's sick, Hana. You shot him! And he still came sniffing around you again? Playing his little mind games? What is wrong with that man?"

Hana shrugged. "He came by one day and offered to take me out to dinner, just to cheer me up. Please—don't say it. I know, I'm the biggest idiot on the planet. But I never saw him again after that night. I swear. I finally saw him for what he is."

A lot of good that did. The damage was done.

"What are we going to do?" Cara finally said. "You can't raise a baby on your own."

Hana shrugged. "What are my options? I suppose I'm stuck in a corner, aren't I?"

"You're not going to tell Joe?" Cara asked, afraid of the answer.

Hana looked taken aback.

"Have you lost your mind, Cara? Hell no, I'm not telling Joe. He'd take this baby from me so fast my head would spin. Or he'd find a way to make me get rid of it so it wouldn't hurt his career. And who knows what kind of tricks he'd pull on me?"

"So you want the baby?"

"I don't know. I really can't even think of that right now."

"There's always adoption," Cara said softly. "If you aren't ready, you can give it to someone else who is. I have a friend, Mack, who is a lawyer. He could possibly make some quiet arrangements or at least knows someone who could help."

Hana nodded. "I know. I've thought of that, too. It's an option. But don't worry, I'm not going to mess up the gig you got going on. That's why I took the waitress job. I'm going to work until I save up some money, and I'll figure it all out on my own. I have no plans to embarrass you in front of Luke and Tori, or be a pimple on the ass of the propriety the Hadley House stands for."

"Stop it, Hana. I want to help. And it's not a gig. It's my life."

But Cara didn't know what would happen to the baby. She thought of all the fellow foster children she'd known—boys and girls who landed in the system for various reasons, but some simply because their parents hadn't wanted children and therefore did a horrible job of parenting.

For a minute, she wondered what it would be like if Hana let *her* adopt the baby. She thought of her and Luke, holding a fresh-faced infant between them, naming it, bringing it home. Giving Ava a sibling.

In her next breath, the fantasy crumbled. That would mean she and Hana would have to stay away from one another because Hana couldn't have her child within her view and not be its mother. Her sister might try to look tough but Cara knew underneath it all, Hana was sensitive.

But Cara didn't even want to think about how hard it would be if Hana took the easy route and decided to turn her child over to the state. It was too much to even fathom.

So she didn't. In this moment, her sister needed her. She would not be like their mother and abandon Hana just because things got rough. They would have to work through each decision slowly and methodically.

She stood and went around to the side that Hana was at, then sat down. She then leaned forward, putting her arms around her sister. At first, as predicted, Hana was stiff and unyielding, but at least she didn't pull away.

"You won't embarrass me, Hana. We'll get through this together, just like we've done everything else. It's okay to be scared, but don't even think I'm going to let you face this alone," she whispered.

She thought of what Tori had said about Luke. Telling him about Hana's latest problem wouldn't be easy, and what if Hana kept the baby? Would they still let her come to Key West?

She had another thought. Maybe she should just stay in Georgia instead of bringing him more bad news. Was it really fair to deliver Hana *and* a baby to Luke's doorstep and upset the solid home he'd built for Ava?

But the thought of never seeing him again, of never feeling his skin on hers, made her feel weak with regret. Could she go back to living without him, to being a constant crutch for Hana? To feeling overwhelmed and lonely?

"It will be okay," she continued, speaking to herself as much as to Hana. She had to find a way to be there for Hana without giving up her own happiness.

A few seconds went by and she felt her sister start to soften, then one of her arms encircled Cara's back. It was a small gesture of acceptance. It wouldn't be counted as much to most, but coming from Hana it was epic.

Chapter Thirty

Melinda had aged gracefully. That was Cara's first thought when she and Hana slid into the chairs at the dining room table, urged there by a nervous woman with fluttering hands who now stood at the stove. At least in her late sixties or even early seventies, Melinda was as pretty as Cara remembered, just with more wrinkles and now a headful of gray hair.

"You girls haven't changed a bit," she'd said when she opened the door and ushered them in. "I can't believe you're really here."

The kitchen was small, but neat and clean. Little handmade doilies, embroidered towels, and crafty magnets on the fridge marked it with grandmother's touches.

Cara had always wondered what Melinda's house looked like. Did she have children? Grandchildren? The system rules stated that as a volunteer in the social welfare system, Melinda couldn't bring the children who were her cases to her home or even put them in her car. Therefore, their meetings were always somewhere else and never broached details about Melinda's personal life.

"I'll have tea ready in a minute," she said, looking over her shoulder.

"This feels so weird," Hana whispered.

"I know," Cara said, keeping her voice low. It felt as though she and Hana were eleven again. Or twelve. Sitting and waiting for Melinda to tell them what their immediate future held. A foster disruption. A new home placement. More hearings.

But now they were grown women and the state no longer held control of their lives. They could get up at any time and walk out. And Cara was tempted. Melinda had always been good to them, but she still represented the memories that were better left in the past. The loss of their family. The system. The rejections. The heartbreak.

"I feel sick," Cara said. Her head spun wildly, her anxiety building out of control. "Maybe we should go back. I don't like leaving Hemi there alone and he doesn't really know Dixie yet."

"Shhh. I want to hear what she has to say," Hana said, her voice strong. "The dogs are fine."

Cara was glad for her then, relieved that she'd brought her sister. Now she knew she couldn't have come alone. Thinking of her past—of her mother—was excruciating to her. Talking about it would be like accepting torture voluntarily. She pictured Jules, sitting in her office. Cara had done all right there.

"Okay, I can do this," she whispered, more to herself than to Hana.

Hana looked better than she had the night before. With Cara's news that Melinda had contacted her and requested a meeting, her sister had snapped out of her depression, or at least pushed it to the back burner in her interest to find out what the woman had to say.

The pot sang and Melinda poured the water over the three cups, then set them on a tray with a bowl of sugar and brought it to the table.

"You girls always did like hot tea," she said, smiling kindly. "Go ahead and fix it up while I go get something."

She left them and disappeared through to a hallway.

Cara slid a cup over and spooned some sugar in it, grateful for something to ease the ache building in her gut. Hana did the same.

Melinda returned, a huge binder in her arms. She set it on the table and took a seat. Then she crossed her arms over the binder, sighing loudly.

"What is that?" Hana said.

"Your records," said Melinda.

"Our records?" Cara stared, barely able to believe that the almost five inches of paperwork, tinged yellow at the edges, was all about her and Hana.

Melinda nodded. "Just my own—nothing from the state," she said. "As a CASA, I had to submit reports for every little thing. Detailed notes on our meetings, copies of the findings from hearings, your school records and teacher observations. It's all here. I kept duplicates of everything."

For most people, their childhood was chronicled in photo books or on computer drives full of images, but Cara marveled at the injustice that theirs was entailed in one fat, dusty binder of official paperwork.

Melinda tapped the cover. "But first let me start by telling you girls that I've always thought the system treated you unfairly. What they did to your family was unconscionable. Especially your poor mother."

Cara felt a wave of dizziness. She couldn't find words.

"Our mother?" Hana asked.

"Yes, your mother. I'm retired now and after my latest checkup, I know I've not got long on this earth. Stage three breast cancer," she said, waving her hand in the air as though brushing off condolences. "I've decided that at my age, I'm not going to take chemo, so it's time for me to tell you the things that have weighed on me all these years. You girls deserve the truth."

Cara felt guilty that she couldn't feel any sympathy for Melinda's diagnosis because her mind was filled with too many questions. Their entire childhood was one big mystery. Could it finally be the time when some of the gaps would be filled?

She took a deep breath, trying to still her nerves.

"Damn right we deserve the truth," Hana said, her voice turning bitter. "We've deserved it all along and now you're going to tell us that we didn't have it?"

Melinda looked frightened then. "I was bound by the courts. Please understand that I could've been in a lot of trouble if—"

"It doesn't matter now," Cara interrupted. She felt drained and couldn't take any more discord. She wanted it to be over. "Please, just tell us what you think we need to know. Please."

Now that they were at this moment, at the precipice of knowledge, she couldn't wait another minute.

"I hope you're ready to hear it," Melinda said, speaking slowly. She looked first at Hana, then at Cara. "To begin with, your last name isn't Butter."

⊷✦⊶

Cara's first thought was, *Thank God*. She'd always hated the name Butter and ironically, it had never flowed off her tongue. It felt stilted. Wrong. Always had. But her next thought was, *How?*

"When you were pulled into the system, we didn't have anyone who would take sisters, so you were transferred out of South Carolina and into Georgia, to a foster home that could keep you together."

We're not from Georgia! No wonder I never felt like I belonged in Sandy Springs.

Melinda continued. "The first foster couple—Charles and Nancy Butter—adopted you both, but you were so young, you didn't understand. Because I was allowed to be your advocate for one year after you were adopted, I came to your home and found out it was not what the courts thought it to be. I considered them unfit and I made my reports. Under fire, the parents asked for a dissolution. It was allowed, and you both were put right back into the system, except instead of sending you back to South Carolina, they kept you here. And that's how I stayed in your lives."

Silence fell between them.

Adopted.

Cara had always secretly hoped they would be adopted, even though Hana was vehemently against it. Cara had always wanted a family. She'd wanted permanence. Hana couldn't let go of the dream that somehow their mother would return for them. Cara tried to remember their first foster home, the people who'd adopted them. But mostly she just remembered their dog, Reno, and what did it matter anyway? They'd ultimately abandoned them, too.

"No wonder I could never find any family online," Hana said, her voice steely. "So what is our name?"

Hana had searched for family? Cara was struck by the thought that maybe she didn't really know everything about her sister.

"Morgan. Hana and Cara Morgan," Melinda said, her eyes tearing up. "I'm so sorry, girls. I know that's shocking news but even more important, I want to tell you that you should've never been in the system at all. Your mother—bless her heart—she did everything they told her to and more. But the state was determined you two would never go back. It was a travesty of justice and I'm ashamed that I was not able to stop it."

Cara listened but she was confused. How could her mother have done everything they told her to? Her death was their catalyst into foster care.

"What do you mean?" she finally said.

"Our mother died," Hana said. "How could she do anything? We saw her that night, taken away in an ambulance."

Melinda shook her head.

"But she didn't die that night. Your father had come visiting and they fought, and she took some medication to calm her nerves. But she confused the dosage. I believe her on that."

Cara remembered the night the man had gone in while they waited outside—the man her mother had warned her about. That was their father?

Melinda dabbed a paper towel at her eyes. "When she woke in the hospital and they told her that state children's services had taken her girls, she might've wished she'd have died. But she didn't. She fought for you. She fought like a madwoman, jumping through every hoop they threw at her, going through the parenting classes they ordered, the therapy sessions, submitting to home assessments. She even underwent medical and emotional examinations to prove she was fit. She swore your father was out of the picture for good, that she'd protect you both from him. It was a lost cause, though, because she had no idea where you were."

"How is that possible?" Cara said, finally finding her voice.

"Because at that time, the focus was on the state taking timely action. They wanted files to be open and shut, and that meant cutting off any possible reunification plans without even seeing where it could go. You have to understand, in the system, if a mother doesn't have the means to hire a fancy attorney, there's really no one to be on her side. The fate of the child—at least in these circumstances—is usually sealed by a judge or a handful of magistrates who decide the result on a balance of probabilities, that because your mother overdosed one time, she would be unfit to raise her children," Melinda said.

"Was she on drugs?" Hana asked.

Melinda shook her head vehemently. "No. I interviewed her several times myself and I was there at every mock hearing she attended. She passed every drug test. She was clean. And she was not a bad mother—she just had a bad moment."

Cara saw a tear form in Hana's eyes. Bad moments were what made up most of her sister's life. They weren't unfamiliar with that term.

Melinda reached her hand across the table, but it stopped just short of reaching them and Cara was glad. "You must believe me, she never wanted to lose either of you. That poor girl didn't mean to overdose! It was all a mistake. But it was too late. Giving you back would admit they'd done something wrong and they weren't about to do that. You were lost in the system and I tried to be your voice. I really did. I told them you needed to be with your mother. But they wouldn't listen. Every appeal was declined."

By now Melinda was crying. Her guilt spilled over with every tear, the tracks making slippery little trails through the powder on her face, coming to rest on her lips, so neatly lined in pink.

"I don't want you girls to ever doubt for a moment that you were loved," Melinda whispered.

Cara was speechless. Their mother didn't die that night? She hadn't tried to kill herself? And most of all, she hadn't abandoned them?

All these years, all the lonely nights she went to sleep thinking of her mother. Longing for her touch. Her voice. She'd known her mother loved her! She'd known it. She'd felt it somewhere deep in her bones. She'd *known*.

"Wait a minute," Hana said. "You said our mother didn't die *that night*. Do you know if she is alive now?" Hana said.

There it was. The big question. After more than two decades of thinking her mother was dead, Cara wasn't ready to hear anything different. She wasn't ready to grieve her mother yet again. She felt her heart pound and a wave of dizziness that was her signal for stress overload. Suddenly it felt like everything was happening in slow motion.

Melinda was hesitating, and what did that mean? Cara looked from Melinda to Hana—her sister for once struck silent as she also waited for the answer to a question that would change their futures. Hell, it would change their past, too, and Cara didn't know if she could go back there and rewrite history. It was all too painful to fathom and she couldn't take another second.

"Wait," Cara said, pushing back from the table and standing up. "I have to get out of here."

Through so many tears she could barely make it to the door, she stumbled, gasping for air, reaching for something—anything to make it all go away, to take her back to the last night her mother put her to bed. Touching her forehead with her lips, telling her she loved her, the smell of fresh lilacs coming from her hair. To the afternoon they worked together on curtains, her hands on Cara's to guide her stitch. To the day she was standing with her in the snow, grasping her warmth, reveling in her smile. To her kindergarten graduation, looking out over the crowd, nervous at first but then comforted by her mother's smile.

There it was! Finally the vault was open and it all came flooding back as she ran down the steps and started walking. She couldn't face Melinda anymore in that moment. Or Hana. She wanted to absorb every thought, every recollection—take them out and examine them on her own. She wanted to revel in the good memories that had been locked away and inaccessible for so long, and bask in the knowledge that she hadn't been abandoned.

Finally, she knew the truth and her chains of anguish were broken. She felt light. She felt free. All because of three little words. Whether her mother was still alive or long dead, Cara now knew something of monumental importance. Something that she could hold close to her heart and use to help heal her years of hurt.

She'd been loved.

Epilogue

Cara sat in the back of the room, surrounded by the people who meant the most to her, quietly observing and feeling so full of pride in Hana that she could barely contain the urge to break out in applause. Mingled with her pride was something completely new for her—she felt at peace.

Complete and utter peace.

At her feet, Hemi lay quiet, his ear perked and ready for her next move. In her lap, her nephew slept, a look of content across his face as, in slumber, he reveled in the comfort of his mother's voice ringing out over the room. His chubby fist wrapped around a piece of Cara's shirt, as though to tell her he wasn't letting go.

No worries, little buddy. You aren't going anywhere. It amazed her how much love she felt for the little guy, and she knew she'd go to the ends of the earth to protect him. But she wouldn't have to, his mother was like a protective mama bear watching over her cub. Despite her fears, Hana had turned out to be an amazing mother.

And there she stood. The indomitable Hana, at the front, leading the meeting. Finally in Key West. Calm and collected. Strong and commanding. People from their past would never recognize her today, but Cara always knew that Hana had it in her to be a leader.

On the table beside Hana was their homely decorated pot, but this time it was filled to the brim with lush, blooming heather, a vibrant lavender-colored flower they'd discovered symbolized protection and was a sign for wishes to come true.

What a difference a year made.

A year of healing, of them coming together to really examine the wrongs done to them and find ways to overcome it. With Melinda's records in hand, they'd appealed for a legal name change and finally could drop the stigma and bad memories that the name Butter evoked. They were now Cara and Hana Morgan and in time, after at least another few months of sessions with Jules, they would begin the search for their birth family. But not now—this time was for them. They needed a respite from pain, a time to welcome in the joy of Brody's birth, to find new beginnings, and to revel in their new and improved sister relationship.

"Who wants to tell me what one of their first experiences with depression was like?" Hana asked, looking around the room.

One of the biggest surprises was that after months of therapy, Hana had started her own support group. She was in charge and she was good at it, making sure that all she'd gone through counted for something as she helped others going through the same things.

A woman raised her hand and Hana nodded at her to continue.

"I couldn't stop crying and I didn't really know why. I just know I felt alone, even when I wasn't."

The seven or eight heads around the room bobbed in agreement.

"I just wanted to sleep my life away," a man said. "Still do sometimes."

Cara was familiar with that one. So many memories from trying to help Hana through her storms, and the heavy fatigue and lack of energy her sister suffered. Sometimes it was all she could do to get Hana to brush her teeth, or even bathe after three days in the same clothes.

"We all have our memories of those first episodes when we didn't understand what was happening," Hana said. "And statistics say that if you have had more than three or four episodes, the chance of a relapse for you rises to almost eighty percent. Therefore, when we are not depressed, it is imperative that we take that time to learn as much as we can about treatment and ways to avoid the dark. We can develop new skills to cope and pursue better lifestyle options."

Murmurs of agreement went through the room.

"We have to take responsibility for our own recovery," she said, looking directly into Cara's eyes and smiling, "and we have to be committed and learn to depend on ourselves instead of others to get us there. But let's break here and grab something from my sister's refreshment table, then divide into discussion groups."

They gave her a smattering of applause and everyone stood, going to gather around the refreshment table. Cara had stayed up until midnight putting together a variety of healthy treats. Hana had reminded her that eating habits could be a contributing factor to depression, so they worked together to come up with easy options that the members could possibly take note of and create at home for themselves.

Hana came to the back and plopped into the chair beside her. Gone was the bravado, and she looked spent. She bent down and tangled her fingers through Hemi's fur, making Cara smile at the gesture. Her sister had finally accepted Hemi and was a little in love with him too now. She'd figured out what Cara already knew, and that was that Hemi was a huge source of comfort.

"You okay?" she asked Hana.

"Yeah, I'm fine. I get all worked up before each meeting, but once I'm up there, I feel good. It really takes it out of me, though."

"I'm so proud of you, Hana," Cara said. Jules had emphasized to them that they needed to articulate their feelings for each other more, to verbalize what they felt.

At first she thought Hana wasn't going to respond. But then she reached over and put her hand over Cara's.

"I couldn't have done it without you, Cara. Why else do I ask you to come to each meeting? I look out and see your face, and remember all the times you told me not to listen to the voice of depression. *That I was loved*. You saved me so many times. You just don't know it. But I do. I won't forget it, either."

Cara felt the tears come. Hana had never so openly given her credit for being there during her darkest times. Her sister had really matured, and their relationship was on the road to recovery. They'd come a long way and finally, best of all, Cara was getting the sisterhood she'd always dreamed of with Hana.

Someone gave her shoulder a nudge and Cara turned to see who was behind her.

"Hey—what's with the tears? You're going to be looking all sad tomorrow and who shows up to their first dress fitting looking all red-eyed and weepy?" Luke said. "Jeesh, why must the Morgan girls be so emotional all the time?"

Hana laughed and pulled her hand from Cara's. "So that's what's poking my hand. That huge rock! Wow, Luke, way to be humble," she teased. "It's not like you're going anyway. You can't see her in the dress!"

"Hey, lay off my big brother," Cara heard from the doorway, and she looked to see Tori standing there with Ava at her side. Her soon-to-be sister-in-law crossed the room quickly, her arms out. "Ava's talking my ear off out there waiting for you guys. Are you done?" she asked, taking the baby and nuzzling him, her words lost in the tsunami of affection.

Everyone wanted their share of Brody love.

"Come on, Cara," Ava called out, then ran to throw her arms around Cara's waist. She hugged her, squeezing Cara extra hard. "Daddy's taking us on a date. Key lime pie and it's outdoor movie night at the park. But first we have to go check on the dogs."

Cara felt the warmth spread all through her. It all felt so right. This was what it was all about. This was her family. *Her life.*

Fairy tales did come true.

"Or . . . you could stay here and help me clean up," Hana said, raising her eyebrows at Cara.

"Whatever works," Luke said, shrugging.

His eyes said something different, a message just between him and Cara. But Hana caught the look.

"Where do you want to go?" she said, leaning over and whispering in Cara's ear. "Go ahead. Say it. You know you want to."

And she did want to.

"Wish me home," Cara said back, but this time when she thought of home, she thought of the Hadley House and the protective family there who loved her.

Author's Note

Sibling relationships are complicated, and none more so than that of twins. Being a twin myself, as well as having a mother who is a twin, I've been captivated by other twins most of my life. I've found myself wondering if they, as my sister and I do, feel a need to remain attached to each other even if only by the faintest of invisible threads as they trudge through life. Or do they want to convince the world that each is his or her own person as they try to remain loyal to the one they shared a womb with? While I pulled from my own emotions to write about the twins and their complicated relationship, they are not my sister and me, and their story is not ours. However, like them, we strive to keep our twinship strong while traversing life's many obstacles.

I would like to remind all my readers that depression is a real medical illness that interferes with a person's normal functioning abilities and is not something they can snap out of at will. Most people who experience depression need treatment to learn to cope. Caregivers for those who suffer a mental illness are valuable and many times under acknowledged, so I'm recognizing them now.

If you or someone you know is experiencing debilitating depression, please keep this number handy: the twenty-four-hour, confidential, toll-free National Suicide Prevention Lifeline: 1-800-273-TALK (8255).

A big call out to foster parents everywhere, and a reminder that though Cara and Hana experienced a lot of unhappiness in their placements, it is not always that way and there are many generous and loving foster mothers and fathers who nurture those in their care. To CASA and Guardian ad Litem volunteers, as a previous CASA volunteer, I sympathize with how hard your role can be, and I also know the rewards are too great to number. Thank you for doing what you do, and may more volunteers surface!

To those who have survived the foster-care circuit, I hope there will continue to be books that tell your stories, giving voice to situations that can harm a child's psyche for all time. You are the real heroes in life, refusing to give up as you work through tragedy to reach for something better and to find a place to call home.

Acknowledgments

Writing can be a solitary experience, but I am so grateful to acknowledge that over the years, I've met many like-minded friends and colleagues to help me through the process and emphasize that I'm not alone. Kate Danley and Karen McQuestion, thank you for cheering me on and keeping me accountable for productivity each week. To the other Ladies of the Lake, I'm thrilled to have you as a sounding board and a group I can commiserate with when needed. To Joan and Harry, I love that you are such faithful friends as well as supporters of my work.

Once the story is born, it's like a chalky lump of coal, and thankfully I have an amazing publishing team who makes it shine like a new diamond. Danielle Marshall, thank you for taking a chance on this novel, one that strays from my usual genre. Your excitement for it spurred me on to make the difficult edits needed to fulfill both of our visions for the story. To Charlotte Herscher, to know you are waiting in the background to guide me toward logic and sensibility in each book gives me the confidence to really stretch my imagination. To everyone else at Lake Union, I am grateful you took this book under your wings to get it in front of readers. I couldn't ask for a better publishing team.

To my readers, if it weren't for your support, I would've stopped after publishing my first book, *Silent Tears*. I can't even express my gratitude for your loyalty and the constant encouragement you give through messages and by writing honest and mostly favorable reviews.

And of course, I couldn't write a book about siblings without mentioning mine. Lisa, as twins we'll always be connected. I wouldn't trade it for the world. Misty, I still see you as the pigtailed little sister who followed me everywhere. You always make me smile, and now that you've kicked cancer's butt, you make me proud. John, no matter the distance, you'll always be my big brother and I'll never stop worrying about you.

To my daughters, Heather and Amanda, I hope I've been an example that no matter what obstacles fate throws at you, it's possible to overcome who you were, to be who you are meant to be. Being your mother has given me so many experiences to pull from, and you may not always appreciate my parenting style, but just remember you are loved dearly. If you read this book carefully, you will have found snippets of me within the pages and you will know that above all, I wish for you to go through your lives scattering kindness.

Lastly, I couldn't write a single word if I hadn't been granted such a miracle as the life I've found with you, Ben. When we met you didn't see the broken person I was. Just like with Luke and Cara, you saw the real me—the possibility of a happier and settled soul—that was hiding beneath the pain. The last twenty-three years with you have been the biggest blessing of my existence and together, we've accomplished much and chronicled many adventures. I can't wait to see what the next decade brings. May it be our best yet.

About the Author

Photo © 2012 Eclipse Photography Studio

Kay Bratt is the author of eleven full-length novels and two children's books. Her writing became her solace and support while she navigated a tumultuous childhood, followed by a decade of abuse as an adult. After working her way through the hard years, Kay came out a survivor and a pursuer of peace—and finally found the courage to share her stories. A wise man once told her to "write what you know," which resulted in Kay's pet project and her bestselling series, The Tales of the Scavenger's Daughters. Learn more about Kay and her writing at www.kaybratt.com.